# BY MAT JOHNSON

### NONFICTION

*The Great Negro Plot: A Tale of Conspiracy
and Murder in Eighteenth-Century New York*

### FICTION

*Invisible Things*

*Loving Day*

*Pym*

*Hunting in Harlem*

*Drop*

### GRAPHIC NOVELS

*Incognegro*

*Dark Rain: A New Orleans Story*

# INVISIBLE THINGS

# INVISIBLE THINGS

A NOVEL

## MAT JOHNSON

ONE WORLD
NEW YORK

Published in the United States by One World, an imprint of Random House, a division of Penguin Random House LLC, New York.

ONE WORLD and colophon are registered trademarks of Penguin Random House LLC.

LIBRARY OF CONGRESS CATALOGING-IN-PUBLICATION DATA
Names: Johnson, Mat, author.
Title: Invisible things : a novel / by Mat Johnson.
Description: New York : One World, [2022]
Identifiers: LCCN 2022003915 (print) | LCCN 2022003916 (ebook) |
ISBN 9780593229255 (hardback ; acid-free paper) | ISBN 9780593229262 (ebook)
Subjects: LCGFT: Novels.
Classification: LCC PS3560.O38167 I58 2022 (print) | LCC PS3560.O38167 (ebook) |
DDC 813/.54—dc23/eng/20220128
LC record available at https://lccn.loc.gov/2022003915
LC ebook record available at https://lccn.loc.gov/2022003916

Printed in Canada on acid-free paper

oneworldlit.com
randomhousebooks.com

2 4 6 8 9 7 5 3 1

First Edition

*Book design by Elizabeth A. D. Eno*

For Gloria

# PART ONE

# CHAPTER 1

After months in deep space conducting an intensive field study of social dynamics aboard the cryoship SS *Delany*, Nalini Jackson, NASAx Post-Doctorate Fellow of Applied Sociology, D.A.Sc., came to an uncomfortable conclusion: She didn't really like people, on the whole. It was an embarrassing realization, given that her life's work was studying them. Sort of like a dentist who hates teeth, she feared. It was incredibly isolating as well, as the universe lacked any other intelligent life to talk to.

There were several human beings, among the (likely) millions she'd encountered, whom Nalini appreciated on an individual basis, which is why she didn't consider herself a *true* misanthrope. She even loved some of them, sometimes. *Individually,* people could be great. Studies showed that even the most antisocial primates made similar exceptions; all the data were clear on this. When feeling particularly optimistic, Nalini would advocate for the theory that, if limited to very small bands, people could even be enjoyable. In limited doses. But the unavoidable truth was that, when people were given the chance to form groups of significant size, tribalism erupted among them like recurring blisters, and thus *Homo sapiens*'s true nature was revealed. Because with the tribes came the bickering, the rancor, the fighting among polar opposites, the infighting among ideological twins, the rejection of empirical evidence in favor of the soothing myths and partisan lies. Nalini could list the faults of humanity all day; it was all rather predictable, but still fascinating. Sometimes, Nalini wished she could simply enjoy the study of her own species solely for the comedic exercise it was, without the haunting knowledge that these same traits would likely result in their extinction. For, though humanity had faced a myriad of existential questions over the course of its enlightenment, Nalini had the misfortune of coming of age during an era when there was really only one: Would we destroy our planet before we figured out how to escape it?

If humanity achieved interstellar migration, it could pollinate the universe with sentient life for millennia, avoiding extinction via diversification of location. If humans didn't accomplish this goal, the only unanswered question would be which combo of consequences for humanity's collective sins would deliver the fatal blow. Climate devastation, nuclear Armageddon, systemic xenophobia, virulent partisanship, pandemics man-made or man-fault—they were all strong contenders. The range of cataclysms was dazzling, but as an academic, Nalini was most impressed with humanity's ability to embrace the delusion that everything was fine.

In her application for NASAx's advertised "Open Social Science Astronautic Research Position," Nalini proposed examining whether the *Delany*'s crew, consisting, as it was, of society's most capable, intelligent individuals, could overcome humankind's known social limitations. "Effects of Prolonged Interstellar Expedition Isolation on Group Dynamics," she'd titled her proposal, then submitted it on a lark, inspired by hubris, free time, and a depressed job market. But someone must have agreed with the argument she made in her cover letter: that, as a sociologist with an undergraduate degree in planetary science, she was uniquely qualified to study humans beyond their Earthly habitat. This undergraduate focus was a mere vestigial tail of a long-abandoned dream that lived solely on her résumé, but it was enough to give her an advantage. Within a year, she was bidding farewell to her life on Earth—her great-aunt; her studio apartment; her younger sister, whom she didn't really get along with—surprised by how little there was to say goodbye to.

There were so many potential career benefits to her participation in the *Delany*'s mission that Nalini failed to note the fact that the trip itself sounded like her worst nightmare. That this honor wasn't another abstract academic fellowship, but something she really had to *do*. Something she actually didn't want to do. On paper, cryosleep sounded straightforward, almost relaxing: You simply sleep through the most dangerous parts of the journey. But as soon as her cryopod's lid clicked shut, it became immediately obvious to Nalini that underplaying her claustrophobia during the interview process had been shortsighted. Locked into place and still wide awake, Nalini noticed for the first time how much the pods looked like coffins. Before losing consciousness, Nalini realized she'd been snared by a branding trick: This was not "cryogenic sleep," it was temporarily induced cold death.

Yet it was still worth it, Nalini tried to remind herself the second she woke back up. A historic mission, the first humanned mission to Jupiter's orbit. Traversing the Solar System with a dozen crew members contained within the 7,827 square feet for over eighteen months. From a research perspective, this offered a priceless opportunity for discovery. A chance to compile the raw sociological data that might one day improve interpersonal dynamics for the long-haul space travel needed to escape the planet they were currently destroying. Or perhaps her work could even address humanity's carcinogenic social tendencies in general. So that one day, if they ever did manage to reach another exoplanet in a habitable zone, they wouldn't screw it up like they did their first one.

In those first weeks of floating in Jupiter's orbit, Nalini began to fear that the crew's wariness of her openly monitoring them would contaminate the process. But over time they grew tired of holding up their façades, just as she'd predicted they would. Nalini's probing eyes became no more conspicuous to them than those of a portrait on a wall. It wasn't complete invisibility—they saw her socially. Sometimes they even targeted her as the subject of pranks, behavior she referred to in her notes as "Group Masochistic Bonding." Whenever they were successful in the act of pranking her, the perpetrators' habit was to laugh and encourage others to laugh with them, a tool to define in-group membership. It was that signature human maneuver: forming social bonds around opposition to an almost arbitrarily defined outsider (in this case, her).

On the day-to-day, Nalini functioned as a full member of the crew. Because of the ship's limits on physical space and weight, everything on the *Delany* had multiple uses and purposes—Nalini was no exception. In addition to her core mission to observe crew dynamics, she also served as an assistant to Senior Astrogeologist Dwayne Causwell, coincidentally the only individual on the ship who seemed to like her. Whereas the majority of the crew was conducting research on the planet Jupiter, Dwayne's solitary focus was on just one of its seventy-nine moons: Europa. Its name had always reminded Nalini of some failing nightclub in Prague, but the moon was infinitely more interesting. A bruised ball of ice that hid a revelation: an ocean of liquid water just beneath its scarred crust. The moon was famous for being a possible intrasolar colonization target, but at this stage, even getting near enough to conduct drone surveys of its surface took a miracle of technology and finance. The base on

Earth's own moon was only thirteen years old and still had that new-car smell; an In-N-Out Burger on Europa was a long way off. Still, even the smallest step was a move in a glorious direction.

Researching Jupiter itself was the focus of Bob Seaford, overall mission leader, and his "band of merry pranksters," whose idea of humor included switching the sour cream with toothpaste, then laughing when Nalini bit into her burrito. All ten of "the Bobs"—as she'd come to think of them—were from M.I.T. "The Engineers," they called themselves (even M.I.T.'s nickname lacked imagination, in her opinion). Representing rival Caltech (go, Beavers!) was a two-person partnership consisting of just her and Dwayne Causwell, with whom she also shared the research assignment of mapping Jupiter's most promising moon.

On paper, and as was clear to whatever algorithm assigned them to be lab partners, Dwayne was Nalini's perfect match. Nalini was an applied sociologist with a background in planetary geology; Dwayne was an astrogeologist with a personal history of sociopolitical engagement—a rarity in his field. In addition to an alma mater, they shared the distinction of being the only crew members of African descent. They also shared an intense dislike of Bob; Nalini struggled for scholarly distance, but Dwayne didn't bother to hide his contempt. And they both leaned on humor to combat personal frustrations.

Winner of the Society of Exploration-Geophysics Distinguished Award, Dwayne Causwell was brilliant, and ethical to the point of piousness, with a reputation for generosity among his students, peers, and community. "A *real* good guy, not a creep who describes himself as a 'good guy,'" as one of the references in his psych profile noted. In practice, Nalini found all of his glowing recommendations accurate. The man was exemplary. In fact, Dwayne's only shortcoming as a lab partner, in Nalini's estimation as both a postdoctorate specializing in long-haul-transport social dynamics and also his lab partner, was that the guy just would not shut up. It turned out, a major side effect of holding both the world and oneself to such a high ethical standard was that at times one was utterly insufferable—another theory Nalini had going into the mission that proved correct. After 8.58 months trapped inside a space can with him, Nalini often wanted to reach into Dwayne's ever-open mouth and hold his larynx still with her bare hands till all the pious protestations stopped. But besides that, Dwayne was a joy to be stuck in space with.

When in ranting mode, Dwayne mostly went on about the Bobs, which Nalini found completely understandable. Primarily because the Bobs acted like little shits. Nalini had observed, at around five months post-cryo, that even her own ability to record them with academic impartiality was diminishing. This gave Dwayne the status of a fellow traveler with whom to complain about them endlessly.

Sometimes Nalini asked Dwayne to stop. Suggested "they" (he) take a break in talking about Bobist topics so that "they" (she) didn't go mad. Dwayne would try; he really would. He'd go on for a bit about things like the environmental importance of rejecting fundamentalist veganism in favor of ethically harvested honey. Or about the implied ethnic bias in the choice not to season the *Delany*'s rehydrated food. Or how he wished the *Delany* were one of the newer cryoships, the ones with artificial gravity replicators. But any observations about the quality of their orbiting home would always lead to mission funding. Which would lead to the subject of the trillionaire donor who pushed NASAx to make his literal "golf buddy," Bob, the *Delany*'s lead researcher, despite the fact that any impartial psych evaluator who spent five minutes alone in a room with him would come to the conclusion that Bob was "a complete and utter asshole." And with that, Dwayne was back to Bob again. The topic was unavoidable. For all their time together and occasional digressions, the pillar of their relationship was a mutual distaste for Bob Seaford, the Bobs, and all that Bobism stood for. As pillars went, it was a solid one.

The Bobs hogged the bridge most of the week, partly because of the nature of their research, but also, Nalini noted, as a dominance display. They maneuvered their probes through Jupiter's beige fog, hooting as if they were going player-versus-player in some blood-soaked video game. They were loud. They left chaos everywhere—sometimes out of laziness, other times to make the statement that cleaning up their own mess was beneath them. Soiled and discarded socks sometimes floated through the air. In-group Bobist nicknames were crudely etched into the NASAx consoles. Food supplies and schedules were regularly discarded according to their whims. They acted like they owned the whole ship and everything on it, including Dwayne and Nalini—thereby tapping into the pair's own ancestral trauma, inadvertently or not. But on every seventh day, it was Team Beavers' turn to take center stage, launching their probes, scanning Europa's surface until the moon orbited out of range once more.

Team Beavers' four drones were named North, South, West, and Camden, the latter a private joke Dwayne took pleasure in not explaining to her. On each run, their pilotless aircrafts shot out to the four directions of Europa's orbit, taking the day to meet back at the origin coordinates. There, they transferred their visual data to the *Delany*. "Vacation pics," Dwayne liked to call them. And Nalini did find them to be like other people's vacation photos, in that they showed a place she would never go and after a while they got very boring.

"Oddball."

"Where?"

"Drone South, look. That makes it twenty-three to fourteen: I'm crushing you, lady."

There'd been a lot of "oddballs" during the mission: visual peculiarities from the cam footage that Dwayne then printed and taped to the whiteboard as a nod to whimsy in the workplace. There was the image of the rock formation that looked kind of like a smiley face. Meteor scarring that looked like footprints of a giant running for the bus. In his game, every oddity was worth one point; oddball was the only kind of ball there was room to play on the *Delany*. Nalini collected them, too, and planned to present them one day to Josey, her little sister, so she couldn't complain that Nalini didn't bring her anything.

"A perfect circle, right there on the surface. Look at the size of that thing. That's got to be, what, ten thousand kilometers in diameter? Twelve, maybe? That's insane. There's no new crater-impacts in the record."

"Well, then, that can't be right. It doesn't make sense," Nalini told him, as if this negated the existence of what they were both looking at.

"I'm not saying it makes sense—it doesn't make any kind—I'm just saying that it's there."

The shape the cam caught from miles above was indeed round like a circle. The next image they brought up, taken by a drone roughly two hundred kilometers to the oddity's west, was even more impossible. The circle seemed to be on top of the surface, not drawn into it.

Most of the landmarks they found that appeared to rise out of the planetary mass's surface were, in fact, indentations, illusions of perspective. Scars of a moon abused by the universe. The only way to tell for sure was to have the computer combine all the correlating footage of the area into a three-dimensional model. Dwayne tapped a few keystrokes to create the model. And there it was.

Rising up off the surface of this moon, a perfect circle. Not just generally round, or near oval. A perfect 360 degrees. True in curve. Poking out of Europa's surface like a zit.

Dwayne looked at the screen and started to say something that audibly caught in his throat. The man who would not shut up was, for once, quiet. Dwayne quietly swiped another drone image onto the main screen. Then another. Kept doing it until there was nothing left to contradict the impossible. For almost a full minute, there was not one sound between them.

"A mountain?" Nalini gave in.

"Come on, lady, you ever seen a mountain with that kind of slope? And look. Look at the top. Perfect curvature."

"Reminder: We are looking at a computer-generated model based purely on visual images constructed from a compilation of pictures taken roughly two hundred kilometers away." Nalini was cautioning herself as much as him, and she knew it.

"So what?" Dwayne successfully countered. "The base, where it connects to the level surface—*do you see that*? It curves back in. Its footprint's smaller than the widest point at the meridian. And the surface—it appears smooth, like a balloon, right?"

"Like a bubble," Nalini managed, just to get the idea outside herself, and there it made no more sense than it did in her skull.

Usually, new photos of oddballs were printed and hung on the station's wall, each one replacing the weakest one posted before, reinforcements in the fight against boredom. This time, Dwayne printed two photos. One copy he gave to Nalini with the message "Tell no one. Not even your little side piece." The other photo Dwayne slipped into the top of his shirt as if there were a bra under there to store it in.

He wouldn't look at Nalini in the hours after that. Not even at dinner, as they floated across from each other, munching on unseasoned MREs. And Nalini wouldn't look at him. Because, if their eyes met, it would be real forever.

It took 3.55 days for Europa to orbit around Jupiter, and Nalini used that time to reassess her entire understanding of the universe.

Hours later, it was Bob and his Bobs' turn to "cook," which meant hydrating prepackaged protein. Precious ship space was allocated on the *Delany* for the long communal table that pulled down from the mess's ceiling, an otherwise impractical device for zero-g space travel incorporated on Nalini's own suggestion. It offered enough room for all the members of the crew to latch themselves on and break bread (or at least rip aluminum packets) together. Theoretically, she argued in her initial application, this would keep the crew socially bonded, unifying them after a day of individual and subgroup projects. It was the first of Nalini's experiments to fail.

It didn't work because Bob Seaford and his acolytes didn't want it to work. They were in the majority and genuinely believed this fact entitled them to create new, self-serving rules. Rules like making dinner at 1900 hours on days when Team Engineers were recycling their drones, then moving supper back to 1730 hours when it was Team Beavers' turn to do the same. Meaning, Team Beavers missed dinner. Meaning, Team Beavers had to reheat and clean up an extra time. And even though Team Beavers was just Dwayne and Nalini, it was a huge pain in the ass. Worse, it forced Team Beavers to submit to yet another blatant dominance display while being unable to complain without increasing tensions with Bob's majority group, thus making things worse for Team Beavers' minority. And the Bobs were fine with this, including Nalini's "side piece," Ahmed Bakhash.

Before "side piece," Dwayne referred to Ahmed as "Ahmed the

Emaciated Communications Guy," but he updated that nickname when he realized what was going on. By then, Ahmed, though still a Bob, had begun conducting clandestine hookups with Nalini belowdecks—in the storage compartment behind the water tanks—when the two shared maintenance assignments. This was after month six, during a period when space-cabin fever drove Nalini to temporary nihilism. But for his part, this act of defiance was the very limit of Ahmed's rebellion; his mantra being "I don't want any trouble, okay?" Ahmed recited that phrase every time Dwayne tried to recruit him from the Bobside. Nalini truly admired this about Ahmed: his profound commitment to self-preservation. It was what attracted her to him in the first place—the man was like a one-man neutral country in a world war, a morally nebulous position, but still a welcome break from Dwayne's constant battle-readiness. Ahmed was *chill,* and Dwayne was livid—these were their natural states. And Dwayne never exhausted his own self-righteous rage, because he utilized it for catharsis as opposed to a tool for helping anything. Often, his confrontations made things on the ship clearly and obviously worse. But it didn't matter, because it was a masturbatory act made even more intense by the pride Dwayne took from his belief that it was evidence of his moral purity.

Despite this insight into his character—one she was certain he would be mortified to learn—Nalini's respect for her senior colleague was undiminished. The man was a legend; his accomplishments were absurd in their ambition and variety. As a mere undergraduate, Causwell was profiled nationally for his advocacy of using drone engineering as a force for social activism. While Nalini was still a toddler, Dwayne had been part of a cohort of Caltech phenoms who'd pushed for replacing police bodycams (notoriously unreliable and alterable) with their own drone swarm freeware capable of independent surveillance of the LAPD. When it was adopted, it was considered a landmark in police oversight, providing bounteous new evidence of race-based police brutality. It wasn't until years later, when it became clear that people were just as capable of shrugging off high-def recordings of things they wanted to ignore as they were with the blurry stuff, that Dwayne decided to take his drone research to the stars. He was exemplary. But it didn't change the fact that every time Dwayne confronted Bob on his latest affront, the astrogeologist became intoxicated by his own righteousness, as if his complaints would appeal to some neutral judge who would finally render a decisive verdict on his behalf. But there was no judge—no alien life holding up numbers on the sidelines. Just them, on a small ship, hurtling through a lifeless universe. Instead, every time Dwayne went off on Bob, the pranks only increased in frequency, and severity. The divide between Beavers and Engineers deepened, and nothing changed, yet everything felt worse.

"The universe is a vast celestial necropolis," Dwayne said out of nowhere. Clearly, he'd been thinking about it. They were triple-checking the maintenance logs for the solar sails, going through the process largely by muscle memory as their minds wandered.

"I like how you said that while pensively staring out the portal at the stars, for maximum dramatic effect."

"If you accept the Drake equation," Dwayne continued, ignoring her tone, as he'd become accustomed to doing, "then our universe's most fertile period for generating advanced civilizations ended more than five billion years ago. *Five billion years ago.* The party was over before humanity even got out of bed."

"So we missed sentient life—so what? Have you ever met sentient life? A lot of them are assholes." Nalini shrugged.

"Next shift, we reset the drone's software, eliminate tampering as a factor. Then we halt the regular survey schedule, and send them back to the oddity."

"Dwayne. You're really going to disrupt the—"

"Just one drone," Dwayne interrupted, and Nalini didn't have a good enough argument other than *This freaks me out.*


Before his own conversion to Bobism, Ahmed was once an individual named Ahmed Bakhash, a graduate of UT Austin who largely did his post-doc work at Stanford. Therefore, at the beginning of the mission, Nalini categorized Ahmed as a neutral player in the already forming Caltech-versus-M.I.T. divide. This lasted until forty-seven days after wake-up, when the Bobs replaced all the underwear in Ahmed's storage case with burlap Y-fronts. Scratchy, coarse industrial material meant to hold potatoes, not testicles. It was an act that showed great forethought: These were rare novelty items, bought on obscure fetish sites and ordered months before to add to one of the Bobs' extremely limited personal weight allotments. The morning of the Burlap Attack, Bob Seaford himself shared this information with Nalini. So that he could explain his upcoming mirth and amplify it.

"Guy's gonna be itching for a week," said *the* Bob. His thinning hair was so short that it would have been invisible on his pale flesh if he hadn't dyed it brown. Noticing the way Nalini stared back at him, he added, "Just a little fun. For morale. To keep us from going bonkers." Bob Seaford winked. At first, Nalini was unable to determine if the wink was a friendly reflex or if Bob was acknowledging that what he'd just said about morale was the bullshit she knew it to be. But then he added, "Whatsa matter? Can't take a joke? You one of those? That's the problem today: Nobody's allowed to admit what's funny anymore."

Bob seemed to want to continue the conversation, but Nalini had no intention of hearing more of his philosophy on who should be laughed at without social repercussions.

"Okay," she replied. It was a nonsensical response that was really just an act of submission, and thus she immediately felt tainted by the interaction. Bob looked her right in the eyes and grinned as if he could taste her cowardice and liked the flavor. Pretending not to see, Nalini turned to jump-fly up the portal in the opposite direction to be clear of him.

It wasn't that Nalini feared Bob physically, it was that Bob was so emphatic in his statements, so unquestioning in the validity of his points of view, that his forcefulness demanded either total acquiescence or the social discomfort of direct and open conflict.

Bob was a bully; it was very straightforward. Some classifications didn't require a doctorate in applied sociology.

When Ahmed walked into the mess for breakfast, Nalini could see the bulk of the burlap undies beneath his uniform. That bulging was the only sign that something strange was happening. Ahmed himself made no mention of this private torture. After hydrating his breakfast, with his back to the room, Ahmed floated his slender frame over to the table, buckled into his chair before praying, and ate. There was no hint in his face of the discomfort the burlap must surely be causing him. No indication he was even suppressing a response: To Nalini, Ahmed looked bored, half awake, lost within the maze of his own thoughts. The Bobs' giggles faded into sighs; Ahmed's nonresponse stole the joke from them. But Ahmed's performance wasn't perceived by his antagonists as an act of defiance, Nalini recognized. It was far subtler than that. It was nonviolent resistance for the nonconfrontational. The Bobs recognized it as submission, but Nalini saw that it was submission as a willful and graceful act of rebellion.

Dwayne's initial response to Ahmed's undergarment incident had been less graceful.

"What the hell is wrong with you people?! Do you think this is funny?!" At the time, Dwayne was working on the trash compactor, and when he swung around to the room, wrench still in his hand, lumps of food waste floated through the communal space. "Does this excite you?!" Dwayne demanded. "*Does this arouse you?!*" he repeated, and the Bobs tried to smile, but their spell was broken. They were just individuals again, for the moment. Then Bob himself said, "Chill, bro. It's just a joke," and forced out a chuckle.

"That's the problem with bros like him," Bob added, minutes after Dwayne briskly floated out of the room. "Everything's so serious with those guys. Nobody can have a little fun."

Studying Ahmed in the weeks after the incident, Nalini was overwhelmed by a hybrid emotion of pity and profound respect. It moved her in a way that she couldn't name, but the feeling pulsed under her ribs. This confusing emotional reaction led her to pursue a private interview with Ahmed, to discern the theoretical underpinnings of this new form of "radical surrender," as she began calling it. Conversations that led to the more intimate meetings behind the water tanks in storage during shared maintenance assignments. Because, why not—her best data had already been recorded by month five anyway, so she found it easy to justify the risk of tainting the research. At this point, Nalini's primary objective was just to make it back to the real world without leaving her mind behind.

When the next drone images came back from Europa the following day-span, Nalini and Dwayne saw that the anomaly—what had originally appeared to be a bubble the size of a city—was upon closer inspection a bubble the size of a larger metro area, suburbs, exurbs, and all.

"That's a biodome," Dwayne said, like the word slipped past the censor of his conscious mind.

"You're crazy. You're crazy, that's crazy. I'm going crazy now, too—we're both going crazy, together. But I have to ask . . . how big?"

Their first estimates, based off of the previous photos, were clearly in error. "Size" was a straightforward data point on which Nalini felt comfortable focusing.

"Roughly four hundred thirty-nine miles in circumference. Seven hundred seven in kilometers." Dwayne's voice cracked, interrupting his sentence with his own awe. "Also, it's green."

Nalini looked up at the main screen, at the impossibility displayed there. No, it wasn't green. The surface had no color; it appeared translucent. Or perhaps a naturally forming glass or other crystalline solid.

But whatever it was, it wasn't green. The green was what it contained. The green part was inside of it.

They skipped dinner. They sucked their soup packets below, by the air filters, near storage. Nalini said it was so they could talk, but it was really because there were no windows down there, and she didn't want to look outside again, ever. They did talk, but about nothings. Gossip about professors long discredited. Finally, as he picked his mess out of the air and began to head back, Dwayne started talking in a quieter tone, as if this was the separate, silent conversation that had been happening the whole time.

"All the UAP sightings over the years, all the flashing lights and flying Tic Tacs or saucers or whatever?" Dwayne said, waiting until Nalini finally offered "Yes?" before continuing. "Even if that shit really is alien, I always figured it still wouldn't really be *aliens*— I mean, not like living beings riding inside. More likely: Ghost tech. Abandoned drones still flying around the universe eons after outliving their creators. Like autonomous robotic vacuum cleaners, end-lessly sucking debris from the carpet of a post-apocalyptic house."

Nalini voiced the three-word phrase that had been bouncing in her head for hours. "*It was green.*"

"Yup," Dwayne responded, and, to articulate her implied conclu-sion, added, "Green means life, baby."


"Bullshit!" was the consensus response among the Bobs when Na-lini and Dwayne presented their findings. All the Bobs thought it was a hoax, even Ahmed. Not exactly a hoax, Nalini realized—no, the Bobs thought it was a *prank*. Of course. They thought it was re-venge. A Trojan horse to somehow attack their clan. Nalini and Dwayne were both outsiders, not to be trusted. Worse, Team Bea-vers had motive, given the escalation in blatantly unfunny practical jokes in recent weeks. So the Bobs looked at the digital imagery and analyzed it for evidence of tampering—all while Dwayne hovered over their shoulders to make sure they weren't doing their own sabotage.

"You sure you're okay, *big guy?*" Bob asked, as Dwayne floated, eyebrows raised. Nalini was sure Bob knew Dwayne Causwell spe-cifically did not like to be called "big guy." "This is a little out there, even for you. I mean, holy shit, this is nuts?" Bob burst out with a laugh that was purposely loud and forced and signaled to the other Bobs they were supposed at least to smile as well.

"There is no 'nuts' in science, *Bob*. A scientist is supposed to ig-nore preconceived notions in favor of empirical evidence. I know you bullshitted your way onto this mission with help from the guys at your country club, but, still, I'm surprised you didn't know that." Then it was Dwayne's turn to force a laugh, a solitary sound devoid of the pretense of humor.

That night, far belowdecks and out of sight, sweat droplets floating in beads away from their exposed flesh, Ahmed really ruined the moment by saying, "Little cabbage, I don't know what you're up to with this—and don't tell me, I one-hundred-percent don't want to know. But if this space-blister thing is about you and Dwayne trying to get back at Seaford, it's not worth it. You can't beat Bob in that manner. He's a spiteful and petty man without shame." The last sentence Ahmed whispered in a barely audible exhalation.

"It's real. It's surreal, but real. The only reason Bob can't see that is he's blinded by the notion that Dwayne and I can't be trusted, because, for whatever reason, he's designated Team Beavers as his enemy."

Ahmed nodded politely as he snatched his clothes from the air, waiting until she was done before pushing both feet off the deck. "But, Nalini, you are," he said as he floated above her, pulling on his pants in midair.

The thing was, Nalini, proud Beaver, *had also attended M.I.T.* Technically, she was a Team Engineer affiliate. Between Nalini's graduate degree and post-doc fellowship, she'd likely spent more time on M.I.T.'s campus than most of the Bobs ever did. But collegiate tribal affiliation was based on where one did one's *undergraduate* education, and so, in that regard, Nalini was Caltech through and through (go, Beavers!). As ridiculous as this little war was, the difference in schools wasn't totally meaningless, she thought. Caltech's Pasadena campus was a small, temperate town, not a frozen city unto itself like M.I.T.'s; Nalini found it doubtful that Dwayne would've undergone his latent lean toward progressive activism in Cambridge. Conversely, Nalini felt that in response to living in the hyper-competitive college town M.I.T. shared with the predatory overachievers of Harvard, it made sense for young people to form cliques, defensively.

During Nalini's own years in Cambridge, spent pursuing her Ph.D. at the Economic Sociology Program, she, too, was forced to make unfortunate social alliances to survive the landscape. Hers took the form of a brief membership in a communal-living raw-foods co-op in exchange for reduced room and board. A period of her life Josey found hilarious to bring up at large family events, a malicious act that always ended with Nalini's having to repeat the phrase "It wasn't a cult."

Still, objectively speaking—and Nalini felt that cultural objectivity was essential to her, as a former undergraduate of Caltech and *not* M.I.T.—Nalini knew that both schools were similar in more ways than not. And there were other connections among the crew that were arguably stronger. One of these Bobs even shared a family name with Nalini's maternal line, Patel, with all the shared immigrant experience and regional and ethnic connections that implied. And of course, it was with one of those Bobs, Ahmed, the svelte communications-technology specialist with the emotional IQ so high it was in itself erotic, that she'd been sneaking time in the storage hold behind the water tanks. But it didn't matter. Because of *Bobs.* Or, to be more specific, the patient zero of Bobism: Bob Seaford. A bureaucratic scientist whose greatest distinction was the level of shamelessness with which he endorsed dodgy environmental-impact assessments for energy oligarchs. Appallingly wealthy donors who repaid Bob's decades of soul-selling with the senior research position on this little field trip to Jupiter.

"You want our drones? *Ours?* Really? Your own custom tech's not good enough, huh? How far are you going to take this? Every minute of their time's been allocated for years; you want to *play* with them to research a visual anomaly?" was how Bob Seaford started the conversation. Bob's tone was smug, but Bob's tone was always smug.

Like many who had been awarded positions of power they did not earn, Bob rationalized his good fortune with an unstated belief that somehow he must be as qualified as a person who'd actually earned that position.

Nalini knew the type too well: Bob bullied his way through life because that's what bullies do. But even saying this to herself gave Bob an element of power.

"Don't you see? It's a win-win, *Bob*." Dwayne emphasized the name with disdain every time he said it. The Bobs rarely said it to Seaford's face—he was largely "sir" or "chief" or "gov" with that lot—which was why Team Beavers found petty rebellion in saying his name consistently.

"Either you get to expose me as a fraud and make me a laughing-stock for the rest of my career," Dwayne continued, "or you get in on the biggest scientific discovery since Bigfoot."

"That's a horrible bet: I'm literally laughing at you now." As Bob Seaford chuckled, a vein appeared on Dwayne's forehead so abnormally large that Nalini could see his heartbeat pulse in it. Unaware of how close Dwayne was to physical assault, the other Bobs snorted in support of their leader, which encouraged Bob himself to reiterate part of Dwayne's original statement with mocking incredulity. "'A win-win' to see you lose-lose?"

Nalini's hand to Dwayne's fist. The words "Don't. Not worth the fallout." She made sure Bob saw and heard this, too.

"Whatever," Bob declared. "Tomorrow, six hundred GMT. We'll all get to the bottom of this." And spun himself out of the room casually, as if that were not an act of self-preservation.


The next morning, the male Bobs showed up on deck holding balloons made out of condoms that they called "space bubbles." Bob floated upright with a packet of coffee in hand, yawning his disdain.

When the drone's feed went live, a couple of Bobs began shouting out its coordinates as it moved toward the oddity. The rest of the crew gathered around the drone display, largely jovial, subdued, half awake. The mood was light. This lasted up to the moment when they saw it on the display.

The dome. The blister. That bubble.

Whatever it was, when the Bobs saw it, they *roared* with laughter. They thought that was real funny.

Laughed and laughed and laughed until they ran out of air.

Eventually, though, as they struggled to contain themselves, the Bobs began to notice the look on Nalini's face. She was frozen, staring at the images showing the clearly unnatural structure. Perfectly round from all sides.

Then they noticed the same look on Dwayne's face. The usual scowl, which had taken up permanent residence months ago, had been replaced with a slack jaw of awe. They saw the tears escaping down the grumpy man's cheeks despite himself, saw Dwayne's full lips pursed and trembling.

The Bobs weren't smiling anymore.

After some pointless rechecking of equipment, some zooming in as far as the imaging would allow, the Bobs, too, grew completely silent.

Because, with *their* drone, they didn't just see the bubble. They could see what was inside. Another, impossible world.

"That's . . . I think that's a landing pad." Nalini pointed at a section of the image taken directly above the structure.

"No," Bob Seaford finally said into the hush. "That's a football field."

Nalini marveled that Bob, for once, might be right.

What they saw was not the *size* of a football field, Nalini realized as she looked longer. It *was* a football field. An actual American football field. With white lines sprayed into the grass, raised seating, and, just beyond the field itself, a parking lot packed with cars. Then, as the drone pulled back from the field, Nalini saw something that dwarfed the field, spreading miles and miles within the structure.

A city.

An entire city. Then suburbs. Then the green tops of woods beyond that. Highways laid over the ground like a nervous system. A river that bowed, hugging the collection of skyscrapers of the city's downtown.

All within a glass dome on the moon Europa.

The crew of the *Delany* stared at the screen into another world, inside of a bubble.


And then, in a disorienting instant, they were inside of it as well.

# CHAPTER 2

"It was freaking aliens," Chase declared, then sipped his Pistol Pete's to give all the new faces at the meet-up a chance to soak in that wisdom. "Near Valles Caldera, about sixty miles west of Santa Fe. That's right, I said it. I got no problem saying it. Now, does that statement make me look crazy? Sure. But that doesn't mean freaking aliens didn't steal my wife."

That was when the chili-cheese tater tots came out of the kitchen. "Carnitas?" the waitress asked, and Chase reached up like she might drop the plate. There were a lot of "unexplained phenomena" interest gatherings in New Mexico, and Chase was a regular at most of them. But the Allies of Alien Abductees Sunday meet-up at Tres Abuelitas was the gold standard. They had those private dining rooms, they had those pitchers of Bud for five bucks, they turned tater tots into art. Just two bucks more to get meat on top, and then it was a meal you could sleep on.

There were a lot of UFO meet-ups to choose from. Some focused strictly on that military UAP stuff, all the verified footage of little Tic

Tac ships or the long cigar-shaped ones or the silent black triangles, etc., each flying around at speeds and slants that would turn human passengers into applesauce. Lots of veterans of nuclear sites came as guest speakers at those clubs, coming to talk about the wild things they saw, trying to get the feds to disclose more. Some groups were all about that consciousness idea, that you could communicate with the "visitors" if you meditated the right way. Other cliques were into the thing as a larger phenomenon, looking at portals and dimensions and poltergeists and whatnot—freaky stuff that freaked Chase out to think about. And, of course, there was the old-school ufology scene, with a whole mythology laying out the multiple alien species and a galactic tournament in which Earth was just one playing field.

The meetings weren't just good; the meetings were important. Sometimes it was years between leaks of any solid data, so if you were interested in the topic the best you could do was talk to like-minded others about what little you all knew. And, sure, there were tons of UAP podcasts featuring UAP podcasters talking to other UAP podcasters, but it was always better to commune in person, looking one another in the eye while destroying a steaming plate of chili-cheese tater tots.

But for abductee experiencers? Sweet Lord. That was a unique social situation. It was just different.

All those believer camps—as varied and contentious as the members could be with one another—had one thing in common: Once you started talking about abductions, everyone got real uncomfortable, real quick. All of a sudden, everyone was looking at you funny. You were either crazy, or crazy for bringing it up. A uniformed four-star general could interrupt a sincere discussion about dog-men versus hybrid dinosaur-pigs and reveal his abductee story and everyone would look at him like he just crapped his pants.

It was not a huge leap, at least for Chase, to go from believing there were alien craft flying around to believing they might pick someone up. The UFO scene had all types of people, with all types of beliefs. But once you told people you were an experiencer of abduction, a lot of them figured you were either nuts or a con artist. Or they did believe you, and it made them majorly uncomfortable, because it went against their pet theories. Or simply because the idea that there were forces above that could snatch your ass whenever they wanted, do whatever they wanted, then make you forget if they wanted, was some seriously fucked-up shit.

But not at Tres Abuelitas. Always a nice crowd at the Allies of Alien Abductees meet-up, and always all types of folks. People willing to open their minds. And professional types, not just kooks. Sometimes actual scientists would show up. Or tourists who flew into ABQ before driving north to Santa Fe. But tonight was special, because, for the first time, Chase's boss, Harry Bremner, was finally in attendance. After a decade of declined invitations, here the old guy was, coming out to see what Albuquerque's unidentified-phenomena scene was really all about.

Having the boss in attendance—it was mind-blowing, that's the only way Chase could describe it. Such an honor: Harry Bremner was considered the Michelangelo of the military-training-compound industry. Getting him there was a huge accomplishment on Chase's part. A vindication of all those times he'd tried to get the old man engaged in a conversation on unidentified aerial phenomena and bombed—all those attempts that Harry shot down with "Chase, don't start with that shit again." After each failure, Chase accepted the brush-off, waited a few months, then once again rolled down the limo's privacy window to tempt Harry with his latest theories and research on the UAP issue. It was Chase's duty to the cause, he felt: The issue could use the addition of Harry and his strategic megamind, his military experience, and all that. His connections. But even Ada was like, "Chase, if you don't cut it out, he's going to fire you." Or she'd say, "Nobody wants a chauffeur who won't shut up about freaking aliens." But look now where they were: Harry and Chase, to-gether at the Allies of Alien Abductees' Sunday meet-up at Tres Abuelitas. Chase just wished she was here to see it.

"When I said your tab's on me, I didn't mean you could get drunk and dump me into a goddamn ride-share. I pay you to drive my car, Chaz. That's the basis of our relationship. So stick to Cherry Coke," Harry told him, though Chase already assumed as much. Harry himself never drank—or not in the limo, at least. Harry was an up-right guy, and a good boss. For instance, he let Chase call him "Harry" and not just "Mr. Bremner, sir." In exchange, Chase never told him to stop calling him "Chaz," which he hated, but he could never envision a way to tell that to his boss that wasn't terrifying. The old guy could be a bit prickly; everybody knew that, he was fa-mous for it. And, sure, Harry got worse with every year, with every divorce, every process server, each time he got audited. And, wow, there were a lot of lawsuits coming in from all sides, more all the time—it was like they were breeding. It made sense that the man was a little testy. But, big picture, Harry Bremner: straight shooter, decent boss, decent guy. End of the day, the man paid Chase damn near double what any personal driver was getting in all of Bernalillo County.

Harry brought a friend—which was fine, which was cool. Chase thought it would just be the two of them, but at least he came. Har-ry's guest was stiff in his fancy suit and his perfect posture and did not look like a lot of fun. He was the only one in the room not smil-ing, besides Harry. But they were at the bar, and that's what alcohol was for.

Harry's posture shifted and he leaned in close to Chase.

"Tonight, I want you and Mr. Talbot to become acquainted. I think you'll hit it off. No, let me rephrase that so you don't miss the nuance, Chaz: I insist you hit it off."

Chase had just picked Mr. Lloyd Talbot up from the airport the hour before. They hadn't shared words other than "Can I get your bags?" and "Thanks." The only reason Chase knew the guy's first name was because Chase had written it on cardboard and stood holding it in Arrivals for way too long. Besides that, Chase didn't know what to make of the guy. Dude wore a tailored suit like it was as comfortable as pajamas. Even his posture was on point; he was fit and fancy, like a middle-aged underwear model. But that was a common style among Harry's lawyer army. "They take the food out of my mouth, then regurgitate it into frivolous nonsense like personal trainers," his boss once explained. In contrast, Harry could pass for a shopping-mall Santa and liked to brag about how when you're rich you can let yourself go to seed and still score hot dates.

As to why Harry brought Talbot with him to the Allies of Alien Abductees' Sunday soiree, Chase had no clue—Harry wouldn't say. Talbot was checking him out, though, he could tell that. Not in, like, a romantic way, but not in a way he could put a finger on, either. It suddenly occurred to Chase that Talbot might not even be a lawyer—he'd just assumed. Could be an arms dealer or something. Harry owned the largest private military training ground in the American Southwest, so it was common for him to take clients out on the town. But Chase usually drove those guys to fancy restaurants or high-end strip clubs or concerts, not to UFO salons (this one sometimes discussed cryptozoology, too).

"May I?" Talbot had returned and now sat down on the stool beside him, pushing by some regulars to do so. "Mr. Eubanks, I mean no disrespect—I am sincerely and genuinely intrigued—but I heard your earlier comment and . . . well, I'm not doubting, but I am curious as to what evidence brought you to that conclusion? What makes you so certain it was, as you put it, 'freaking aliens'?"

"*There was no evidence*," Chase told Talbot, and let that sink in. Chase looked over to Harry and tried to send the message with his eyes: *What's wrong with your boy?*

"Right. Okay. But what—" Talbot kept going.

"Nada. Not a goddamn thing. That's the point. See, let me tell you the whole story."

The regulars, they'd heard the whole story. Many, many times, they'd heard Chase's entire story, and so those closest began to drift away to other parts of the bar. Chase noticed but didn't care, too much. As long as there was a new guy, he could tell the tale—as therapeutic for him as it was illuminating for them. And that's what Chase loved the most about the Allies of Alien Abductees' meet-up: There were always fresh faces to initiate into the true nature of the universe.

Ada Sanchez's obsidian-blue 2029 Honda Odyssey was last recorded on May 8, 2032, headed due northwest on Route 16. Traffic cams showed the van's back windows were obscured by cardboard boxes and miscellaneous possessions. And then—she vanished. Despite significant effort, New Mexico state troopers could not trace her. Local police in Guadalupe, Bernalillo, and Los Alamos counties found no signs of her, either. Various bands of empathetic volunteers, immediate and extended relatives, spread out and traced every conceivable route, from highways to dirt roads to mountain passes mostly frequented by goats. All hoped to find some clue of where in the world Ada Sanchez was. But zilch.

They thought Chase did it. At least in the beginning. A couple drunk-and-disorderly citations in his twenties, a charge for hit-and-run on a parked car that was bullshit and didn't stick, but otherwise his record was clean. The state troopers, and Ada's family—who never liked him and had literally called him "white trash" on multiple Thanksgivings prior—swore he must be some kind of monster. When they found her divorce application ripped up in Chase's trash with his own fingerprints on every single piece—that didn't look good. Didn't help that, the night Ada went missing, Chase didn't even come home, and was off grid for about ten hours—the cops got all worked up about that. Fortunately, when they called to check up on his alibi, someone at TD's Eubank Showclub (no relation) actually vouched for him. Turned out a bouncer remembered him sucker-punching someone for some slight Chase himself could not recall. And then some beat cop remembered having to tap on Chase's limo's window the following morning to tell him he couldn't park there. On top of that, there were three consecutive days of security footage of him showing up at Eveningdove Memory Care to visit his mom—which of course she didn't remember, but he was there. And also on the vid clips of the 24-Mart across the street from it, buying Cool Ranch Doritos and Pistol Pete's to wash down his sorrows, because at that point he thought she'd just left him again.

On the fourth day of her absence, Chase went back to work driving Harry around, and picking up bigwigs from the airport and bringing them out to the desert for their grand tour of the Theater of Operations (TOO) campus so they could see Harry's miracle for themselves. "TOO: The Greatest Immersive Tactical Training Facility in the World" sounded like just a tagline until you rode through the gate and found yourself in the Disney World of war zones. After Chase was cleared, the investigators got all worked up about TOO, too. Made sense: It had tons of people, places to hide. Cops thought there might be some kind of link there.

"Meticulously designed Potemkin villages, with every detail considered, all the war zone has to offer without the war," it said on the website. What that meant, Chase would explain when on and off the clock, was that, if someone was blindfolded and dropped in the middle of one of Harry's fake cities, chances were they'd think they'd been kidnapped to whatever hellhole was being shot up at the time. Each village looked like the city it was copying, but it was more than that. Each sounded like that place, with native speakers roaming its streets. Each one—and this got Chase every time there was a new one—*smelled* like the real version, with local food being cooked inside its functioning buildings.

The "Caracas" was built by actual refugees from Venezuela. Three years later, Colombian refugees built "Bogotá"—Harry's recruiters even hunted down an architect from Medellín to design the place, some political dissident he found now delivering pizzas in Minneapolis. Or was he just a migrant? Migrants, refugees, dissidents—Chase could never remember who liked to be called what. But there were always new ones coming; that Chase knew for a fact. An endless supply. Cameroonians, Saudis, North Koreans: people from whatever place was worth running from. There'd be a war or an invasion in some country, and then the lucky ones would make it into America. And then the even luckier ones would end up out in the New Mexican desert at Theater of Operations, building hyperrealistic life-sized replicas of the cities they'd run from. So that, when they were done, those fake cities could be used to train soldiers and translators and spies to go back and invade the original places. Of those lucky ducks, a handful of fortunates even got to stay on after the construction was done, as actors, given the roles of "locals" to populate the fake versions of the war-torn cities they'd barely escaped.

"The Circle of Strife," Harry would joke to prospective clients, without smiling. Harry didn't joke a lot, but when he found one he liked, the old guy would repeat it for years. And if you said anything about it, he'd get real snippy. Lot of times, if you said the wrong thing around the old man, he'd stop talking to you altogether—which was tough, because what "the wrong thing" was constantly changed. Chase had seen that go down with other employees a few times—cold shoulder for days after, then, next thing they knew, they got canned. For all his UAP talk, and despite what Ada thought, Chase did know when to shut up. And for a limo driver that meant most of the time.

So, when Ada went missing, all those TOO people had to be searched. State troopers were all over that. Backgrounds were re-checked, alibis cleared. They poked around the buildings, repeat-edly. But, again, nothing.

In those first days, before Chase knew how gone Ada was this time, he wasn't even mad at her. She wasn't running away from him, he understood that. She was running from their admittedly shitty apartment with a kitchen so small one person could barely slide inside. Ada was running from her gallery/kiosk at Coronado Mall, where half the time she spent more money on rent than she made selling her framed original and signed desert landscape paint-ings. Ada was running from the fact that—and this was the biggie—they were always flat broke.

They were not without hope. Chase stood to inherit a damn near fortune, actually—in the form of a dry-as-hell plot of 5,739 desert acres forty minutes outside town. A failed family cattle ranch they'd still managed to keep up the taxes on. A piece of land that, thanks to the expansion of the suburbs, was worth big millions last time Chase checked—which he did weekly. Even split with two meth-head brothers and three viper-mean sisters, then gutted by the IRS and probably the inevitable lawsuits between said dirtbag siblings, that was still a lot of money. But not until his mom passed, and though the sweet old lady's mind had gone, her frail body seemed to have forgotten to leave with it.

Arguments about "When is your mom going to die?" never went well, even when the question was not asked aloud. Chase didn't take it too personally, even though he was the one Ada yelled at. It wasn't about him, or his "goddamn raccoon-tail mustache," or even his "shitty little chauffeur job." Sometimes, he would talk to Ada about one day betting on himself, buying a whole fleet of town cars for the luxury airport-transport market. Possibly even (although he would never ask directly) getting Harry to throw him a TOO contract for the sake of old times. It could work. He knew the business.

Ada always started talking about how he needed to go back to school and train for a *real* job, whatever that was, but Chase loved driving. He used to be in roofing, in New Mexico, in the summer— holy shit, did that suck. Driving, he got air-conditioning, he got to wear a suit and tie. He got to meet some rich people, sometimes even famous people. Interesting folks that he liked talking to, on the sneak. Big shots like Harry—powerful people who liked his auto- motive companionship so much that sometimes they even went for a cerveza with him and picked up the tab. Chase just found the gig relaxing, out on the open road, sitting on cool leather with the radio on. "It's honest work and I'm lucky to get it," he always told her. But after a few years of marriage and struggle and debt, Ada wasn't try- ing to hear that anymore.

The night before she took off, as they lay in their undies in their bed in the dark, Ada whispered, "I just want more, okay? I just want more. I'm not saying that's all your fault. I'm not blaming your mom for not dying—it really hurts me when you say that. I just want more than *this*. We're both too good for this dump." And Chase said, "Okay, okay, okay," which was what he always said when she got like this. Which stung later, when he realized that possibly the last sentence he'd said to her was two letters repeated over and over to blow her off.

The next morning, Chase slept in, even though Ada was up early and making a racket in the kitchen, cable news blaring as usual. When he finally got up and headed toward the bathroom that after- noon, he looked in the hall closet and saw that all of her luggage was gone. Again. And he figured out the obvious: Yeah, Ada left me. *Déjà vu*. Wasn't the first time. But she'd be back, like always.

A few months later, when his mom finally gave up the ghost, Chase realized that part of him thought Ada would take the occasion to reappear. As prophesied, the land money was all tied up in the lawsuits with his useless siblings, but Ada couldn't know that. Not that she was a gold digger—Ada wasn't like that. She just wanted their life to start, was all. So he caught himself waiting for her to show up at the wake, then at the funeral. Waiting for the sight of her minivan to wind through the cemetery roads to meet him as they put his mamma into the ground. He would never stop waiting for her, and by now he'd accepted that little fact about himself.

"No cellphone pings, no credit cards used. No credit change at all— I'm the one that paid off her cards. No sign of her minivan. Nothing. Not one trace. Not one single one. Absolutely nothing. That's my evidence. Because my wife would have never left me for good. We had plans. Had a spot on the acreage picked out—going to get one of those high-end prefab houses. With a big porch, and a garden. Get a condo in the city with no lawn to take care of, and then head out there when we want the fresh air. Get old like that."

"But you said she was your ex-wife?" Lloyd Talbot interrupted, and Chase startled at the reminder there was someone besides himself that he was talking to. Talbot was polite and all, but Chase figured he was definitely messing with him.

"With all due respect, sir, can I ask as to the nature of your inquiry?" Chase wanted to sound as formal as this Lloyd guy looked. But the other man apologized immediately and gave him not just an answer, but a business card. "Special Envoy of the Secretary-General, Lloyd Talbot, United Nations." Paper stock so thick he could use it for drywall. Shook Chase a bit to see how right he was about the guy being a big shot.

"I'm a professional associate of Harry." Talbot smiled at him like this was supposed to explain everything. As if "a professional associate of Harry" was some kind of secret code for an exclusive rich-guy club. But then Talbot followed with: "I'm working with Harry on some related business, and he told me about your misfortune. Suggested I check you out directly, to see if you'd be interested in getting involved. That's why I'm here—because we share similar interests."

Chase looked over at Harry. The old man had his readers on at the bar and was staring at his phone, ignoring the cheers as the room watched the *real* Aggies take down Fresno State at home in Las Cruces.

"Well, shit, if Harry vouches for you, you're good with me," Chase said, but thought, *Cash money.* That's what this was about. Because, though Harry was not yet a full-fledged fellow traveler of the unexplained, he had been a generous benefactor to the Ada Sanchez Rescue Fund—that was the thing about Harry people didn't get. He could be a mean SOB, sure, but he was good people. He'd even encouraged his rich buddies to hit the page's donation button as well. And, clearly, this Lloyd Talbot guy was loaded; his watch would be an even trade for a used Harley Softail.

"Yeah, technically, sure. Ex-wife. *Technically.* But my Ada? Never filed the papers. See, what you got to understand about Ada is: She just likes to run away. That's just her nature, I guess," Chase told the United Nations Special Envoy of the Secretary-General. "Got a wandering spirit. Always did. Always wanted to travel—and we would have, someday, when the money cleared. But these little unannounced trips? She always came back, so, technically—"

"I understand," Talbot said to him.

Talbot looked back across the room at Harry, and nodded. And Harry looked up from his phone and nodded back. And Chase watched this and pretended it wasn't about him in some way that he had no idea about.

Talbot leaned in closer to him. Motioning for Chase to come in closer as well, so that a whisper could travel through the bar noise between them.

"Chase, I'm going to show you something. A picture, okay? And I want you to really look at it, really take it in. And then I would appreciate it if you would tell me honestly what you see."

"Is it something gross?" Chase did not like blood or jump scares or sicko stuff. "If it's something freaky, just give me a heads-up."

"Not at all, I promise. I just need your expertise. And keep in mind: This photo was taken recently. About eight months ago."

Talbot held up his phone, swiped to an image, then asked in a matter-of-fact voice, "Do you recognize this person?"

First thing Chase thought, looking at Lloyd Talbot's cell, was that he'd never seen *that* photo of her before.

And he didn't remember her in that outfit, either. Or that hairstyle.

Next thing Chase thought wasn't words. Just the abstract muddle of confusion.

Ada Sanchez, his wife. Standing at a bus stop Chase was also unfamiliar with. Holding an umbrella he'd never seen before, wearing glasses he was pretty sure she'd never needed. His wife or ex-wife or whatever, Ada Sanchez. But years older.

"Where is she?" Chase just wanted to get it over with. Just to know. Goose-fleshed and nauseous, he still wanted to know. Fine, she really had left him, maybe even without aliens involved, but at least she was okay. Lloyd Talbot was staring at him the whole time, and Chase knew his own face must look like he was launching into Crazy Town. But the Lloyd guy let him go through all the feelings without saying one word, letting him soak in this image of her.

Staring at it, Chase couldn't even think of a good question, let alone an answer. "If that's really her, how come she didn't tell any-one? Not even her own people? Why didn't she call?"

"That would have been impossible," Lloyd told him, then waited for the harder questions.

Liquid bowels, tunnel vision, headache.

"Well, where the hell is she?" Chase asked him.

"In an artificial ecosystem the size of an American county, con-structed meticulously to look like an American city, located on the surface of a moon of Jupiter called Europa."

Chase stared at Lloyd Talbot, taking in the full measure of the man before replying.

*"I freaking knew it."*


By the time Chase slowed the limo to a stop at the Kirtland Air Force Base security gate the following morning, he'd already let doubt overtake him. He peeked through the rearview at Harry, looking for some clue of betrayal back there. A setup, maybe. *Deep fakes.* Or, worse, *False flags.* Or like a reality show or some such nonsense. If there was a joke, Harry was in on it. Chase squinted hard, trying to detect any sign of deviousness in his boss's face.

But Harry Bremner was just staring at his tablet as per usual, watching golf. Chase felt himself untense a little. Harry was harm-less, as long as you didn't report to him, marry him, or do business that remotely interested him. Just under fourteen years driving for Harry, and Chase had never seen the old man pull a joke on anyone—that just wasn't Harry's MO. He couldn't even be both-ered to look at most people. Not that Chase hadn't seen him be cruel, in that way only rich people who'd never been anything but rich could be. But if this was a joke, it'd be the first time Chase had seen the man put real effort into anything even humor-related.

The guard at the kiosk searched for Harry's name in the database, then handed Chase a tablet of nondisclosure agreements to sign before sending them through. As he drove on the base, looking for the building, a nagging part of Chase's brain pointed out that he'd actually seen Harry do some cold-blooded stuff here and there over the years. Roll his eyes at true tearjerker stories on the car radio, laugh about famous people he didn't like when he heard they'd died, things like that. And there was his genuinely creepy habit of calling homeless people "roaches," which was so bad Chase had never even told Ada about that. So what the hell did Chase know about what his boss was capable of?

"There it is," Harry said, not even bothering to point. "Now, listen, Chaz: When we get in there, we're going to continue our discussion from last night. And I want you to hear them out, and be professional. No little-green-men crazy talk out of you, okay? Just listen, let them do the talking. I vouched for you, Chaz—don't embarrass me."

When Chase held the passenger door of the limo, Harry paused before getting out. "We're going to the office of this NASAx Admiral lady, a real hard-ass. But don't worry about her. You just follow me." Harry stopped again before Chase could open the front door of the building for him. "Look, I know that was a bit of a shock yesterday— Talbot's whole photo shtick. That's not on me: I wanted to tell you as soon as I knew about your Ada being found." Harry sounded like he was delivering his part in a conversation they were having, one Chase didn't even know was going on. "Really, I wasn't trying to do you like that—I have a heart. But the goddamn government— bureaucracy, that's all they know. They've got to have their hooks all the way in you, like parasites. Talbot insisted on coming out in person, kicking your tires first. But I told him: I'm not going anywhere without my driver. And if I don't go, my money doesn't go anywhere, either." Chase nodded silently. None of this made sense, but he followed Harry's advice and shut up and hoped that eventually it would.

"I'm sure you heard about the SS *Delany* tragedy?" The woman asking him this question had introduced herself as Admiral Ethel Dodson, NASAx Division, which was the same thing it said on the plate of her door. The office itself was bigger than Chase's apartment, so huge it even echoed as she spoke. That was likely because it was nearly empty, stripped down to a desk, a couple foldout chairs, and a few packed boxes waiting to be taken somewhere. "Recently retired, at least officially," she said, when she caught him looking. The Admiral was taller than Chase, or maybe the same height but taking up more air in the room. Nearly as old as Harry, but didn't wear it like a comorbidity. Her red hair made no attempt to look natural and looked pretty damn gutsy that way. When she reached out to shake Chase's hand, her grip was like the blood-pressure monitor in the back of Walgreens.

"Oh yeah—I got several theories about that one," he told the Admiral, but he didn't elaborate, because even for Chase these theories were pretty wild. There were none he felt confident enough to share with the three people staring at him in this fancy office suite. But they looked at him to continue, so he added, "The *Delany*. Yeah, that cryoship disaster. I know all about that. The Jupiter-mission ship with the $CO_2$ leak last year. Where they all, you know, died." Adding with a somber nod, "Or so they say—I'd like to do my own research."

"Little more than three years ago," Lloyd Talbot began before he could elaborate, but Chase didn't mind. Talbot seemed to know what he was doing. Chase liked that the suited man didn't talk down to him, didn't echo Harry's tone. It was a nice way to say that he knew Chase didn't work for him and would be deserving of equal respect even if he did.

Admiral Ethel flicked an image to the wide screen. It was that picture that was everywhere—the one of the *Delany*'s sleeping corridor. The one where they were all lying in their hammock sacks. You could see their faces. Eyes staring off, all blank, unfocused. They looked so peaceful like that: dead as a doorknob. The pic almost made it seem like a good way to die.

"What a mess. I read all about that, of course."

"Excellent," the Admiral told him, and it occurred to Chase that there was some test happening here of which he didn't even know the subject.

"Chase, I'm going to show you another image. And this image is part of why you had to sign those waivers. Because it's the actual, undoctored photo of the inside of the *Delany* when it came back."

The Admiral flicked again: the exact same picture, but empty. Same angle, same shot. Except there were no crew members in the sleep bags this time. The ship's hull was completely empty. Not one person, dead or alive. Nothing.

"Okay, that is some weird shit. But what's this got to do with me and Ada, specifically?"

And that's when they started telling him the kinds of crazy ultra-classified secrets Chase had been waiting his whole life to hear.

They showed Chase the drone footage, swiping the photos and vid clips to the main viewscreen. They made wild claims any normie would have laughed at. An American city of at least a million. On a freaking moon, 444 million miles away, for chrissakes. In a bubble. City streets. Expressways. Parks. Cargo containers of supplies that arrive into the bubble from who knows where, floating out from a cave with a river flowing out of it. Convertibles sitting in rush-hour traffic, the red blaze of their brake lights. All with brand names anyone on Earth would recognize.

Finally, they showed him the population.

"Who the hell are these people?" Chase asked. He had many questions, but thought this was a safe place to start. He knew he was no rocket scientist (which it turned out the Admiral lady literally was), but he considered himself above average in intelligence. Which was why it pissed him off when people assumed, for whatever reason, that he was stupid. Which he was not. Whether it was because he was a thirty-nine-year-old limo driver, or because he'd rarely traveled to places outside Mountain Standard Time—whatever the reason, Chase had always felt he was a man whom people liked to take liberties with.

"Facial-recognition software came back with multiple hits," Admiral Ethel explained. "In addition to the *Delany*'s crew, a veritable lost tribe of America's missing persons. Hundreds have been verified. People born right here, like you and me. And others, as well."

"This is what I've been saying!" Chase pointed and looked to the others as if they were the ones who hadn't believed him. "This is it, the gold mine. El Dorado. They're all there, aren't they? All living in one place, all this time. I knew it. Alien abductions."

"*Some* form of abduction, clearly. By whom, we simply don't know. We haven't seen anything to indicate the captor. Whoever it is, they have tech far beyond what we're even theorizing." Lloyd's voice was calm; his words were delivered in a slow tempo in total contradiction to Chase's thumping heart. "But, yes, a sort of detention center. That's one working theory. We have footage of grave headstones with names and birth dates that match missing persons. Going back over a century. And then there's people like your ex-wife."

Chase was about to say "*legal* wife," but Harry interrupted him.

"Chaz, you've heard me mention 'Potemkin villages' before, correct? In relation to TOO?"

"Yeah, of course, sir," Chase said, because he'd heard about it pretty much every weekday for the last fourteen years, but Harry just kept going into his set speech anyway.

"The name 'Potemkin village' comes from a story about Prince Grigory Potemkin of Russia, charged with governing newly annexed Crimea for Catherine the Great. As such, he was responsible for accommodating the Empress when she came to tour the war-ravaged 'New Russia' with her foreign allies. The goal was to show off Russia's latest acquisition. But the place was a dump. So, to meet her needs, Prince Potemkin created a mobile, life-sized village, with his soldiers dressed as fake peasants, and erected it at every riverbank where her barge landed. When her boat took off again, he'd pack up the whole damn thing, take it farther downriver, and set up again before Her Royalness could land."

"I heard you tell that story to clients so many times, I could tell it myself," Chase told him, but Harry ignored his response and kept going. Chase had seen him do this to clients, too.

"It's a myth, probably. But the larger concept of re-creating cities for strategic purposes is a reality. Theater of Operations is basically a collection of Potemkin villages used for military training—you know this. We let new recruits get a feel for a place before being dropped down into the real shit-show. Nobody can touch us, as far as realism or innovation, but it's not a new concept. In World War II, there was a mini-Germany in Chicago built to test tanks. In the Cold War, the Russkies had a spy-training ground in the Ukraine identical to an American suburb. Every detail, down to the fire hydrants."

As Harry talked, Chase realized the man couldn't even imagine that his chauffeur had been listening all this time.

"That's why Mr. Bremner is so important to this project, Chase," Talbot interrupted. "He's a leading expert on this issue."

"Really, the *only* expert in both theory and execution," Harry corrected before continuing. "And keep in mind, there are a number of nonmartial Potemkins as well. Disney World: Main Street, U.S.A., is Walt Disney's platonic ideal of American small-town life. Las Vegas, all those places pretending to be other places. So, in and of themselves, artificial life-sized environments are not inherently military."

"So what kind is this one?" Chase thought it was a simple enough question, but none of them answered him. The Admiral looked off, and Lloyd Talbot looked to Harry. When the older guy didn't offer anything more than a shrug, Talbot tried.

"Honestly, we don't know. That's what we're going on a trip to find out. A very long trip, with some unknown factors," was how Talbot put it. "To Europa," Talbot added, when Chase looked at him blankly.

"No, to *New Jersey*—I think he gets the point, Talbot." Harry plopped down into one of the chairs before the office's desk. The serious-looking old woman sitting behind that desk paid no attention to him. Her eyes were on Chase; he could feel them. It made him even more nervous.

"My apologies, I should have offered you a seat earlier. Please, forgive me." Talbot smiled politely over at Harry, then turned back to Chase with that look people gave him sometimes when Harry was in a mood and they got a whiff of what he dealt with on the daily. "Originally, we approached Mr. Bremner primarily for his exceptionally rare expertise on reproductions of urban environments. But as things progressed, and we were denied both congressional and off-book funding, he generously offered to provide the financial resources to make this mission possible."

"And accompany the mission as well," the Admiral added.

"I'm old and fat, but I'm covering the check, so they have to take me."

Chase was going to say, *You're not old or fat,* but he'd made that mistake before, and he didn't want to relive Harry yelling that he was a "goddamn liar."

"So, if I'm going to make the trip, I'm going to need a body-man. You see where I'm going with this? And I figured you'd want to get in on it whether paid or not. When I saw the database found a match with your Ada, I knew it had to be you—someone with skin in the game. Unlike whatever rock-jawed government merc they wanted to set me up with, I know I can trust you." When Chase didn't say anything in response, Harry added, "That was a compliment, Chaz."

"Thanks, boss," he managed by muscle memory; it was all becoming too much for him to think beyond that.

Ada used to say Harry talked to Chase like he was Harry's dog. That wasn't fair, and Chase had told her to cut that out every time. "He's like a dad to me," he'd hit back, and it was an exaggeration, but kind of true. Dads could be complicated, and sometimes they acted like monsters—Chase's sure as hell had. But that didn't mean they didn't mean well, overall. And that's just how it was with some rich folks. Chase had driven tons of them long before going full-time with Harry, so he knew. Ada never believed him on this, but, swear to God, Chase felt sorry for them. When you were a fancy billionaire type, nobody ever called you on your bullshit—an essential ongoing lesson in a person's life, in Chase's opinion. When you were that powerful, nobody pointed out to you when you were being horrible. Everyone just smiled and nodded, and then resented having to smile and nod. Lot of rich types had no clue that everybody they had power over hated their guts for it. Walking around with your head up your ass was no way to go through life, mountain of cash or no mountain of cash.

The Admiral continued: "All we know so far is from microdrones, which passed in and out of its portals without problem. We don't know the *who,* or the *why.* When we arrive, we'll find out. We'll have cams embedded in our attire, we'll record everything. We go, we deliver a multi-year plan for them to manufacture their own cryoships to escape, we recover the *Delany* crew, and then we return immediately.

"I'll be spearheading diplomatic first contact on behalf of the UN. We'll offer the weightless gift of our knowledge, ready to download right off my wrist." The Admiral held up her smartwatch, and tried to smile.

"The goal is to get in and out. Especially *out*." Talbot said it like a joke, offering a strained smile with it, but the other three's faces were unmoved.

"Mr. Eubanks, do you understand what's being asked of you?" Admiral Ethel asked him. "We're requesting you be on board with this, literally."

"Yup, I got it." Chase nodded, looking at all three to convey his comprehension, which did not actually exist. The Admiral said nothing more for a moment. Just kept staring at him. Chase would be damned if there wasn't pity there—that's what that was. He would have been insulted if he'd been able to focus on one of his current feelings in the internal swirl.

"Let's not beat around the bush anymore, okay? The government bigwigs are petrified about all this getting out—they can't even handle the shit-sandwich already on their plate."

"Unfortunately, that's a fairly accurate political assessment," Talbot added. "When the world's going to hell in a handbasket, nobody wants to hear about an interplanetary picnic. Understandable, but frustrating nonetheless."

Harry swatted the notion out of the air with his stubby fingers. "They're too busy fighting back all the usual bullshit. The climate refugees, the seawalls, the riots and terrorists and militia wackos, all those damn forest fires. So it's private industry to the rescue, once again. We're going rogue."

"A black-ops mission," Chase thought out loud, barely audible.

"Jee-zus—don't start with your fantasy bullshit, Chaz. Be a serious person. Listen, Talbot's going on this mission to rep the government, okay? I think he figures, if he pulls this off, he'll go down in history. The esteemed NASAx Admiral over here is coming out of duty to the *Delany* crew, and for a hell of a way to begin her retirement, am I right?" Harry turned to look at Admiral Ethel, who seemed surprised that he was actually correct. "And I'm going because I'd rather blow my fortune on this than let the leeches sue me dry, one by one. They can kiss my empty bank account. And that's why it's no biggie to me if we make it back. I guess I got a death wish to do this, but, hell, everybody dies, and I'll get to die rich and old. And you got your Ada. So I'm running this by you."

"I appreciate it, I appreciate it." Chase nodded and kept nodding, in a way none of them mistook for his agreeing to anything. It was important to show them he was taking all this in stride, Chase felt. But, really, he was taking in the words "death wish" over and over.

"Mr. Eubanks, there is an immense amount of risk in what we're intending," the Admiral warned. "There are no guarantees, or backup: If something goes wrong, no one will know what happened to us. There are few *knowns*—that includes the feasibility of returning. Over the last few months, the three of us have all had time to digest that before making a decision. Your friend Harry wants you to join him, but this is your choice. Do you understand me?"

Offhandedly, Harry said, "Travel-wise, we get on a ship, we go to sleep, that's it. When we wake up, we're there. Place looks like Seattle. It's actually not that big of a deal, you look at it that way." Talbot and the Admiral both turned away from Harry.

"A one-hundred-percent diplomatic mission," Lloyd Talbot said, as if asked for a promise. "We'll be wearing civilian clothes, casual, nonthreatening. No weapons, just the watches outfitted to record and deliver data. We're coming as future friends, to greet our new neighbors. Offer a copy of our entire digital database, as a show of good faith."

Chase was still slowly nodding. And as the others examined him, he nodded a little faster.

"Spit it out. What are you thinking, Chaz?" Harry demanded.

*Ada,* he reminded himself. That was what he should be thinking about.

"Ada." He said it out loud, but it was for his own ears. "I say: Hell, yeah. Let's do this."

There was no celebratory clapping, which was kind of a disappointment. There were no cheers. Harry just nodded, pulled out his phone once more, and started poking at his emails. Talbot winked at Chase in a nice way that made him feel a little less dizzy. But from the response on Admiral Ethel's face, that resigned look that was almost like sadness, Chase wasn't sure if he'd given the right answer.

# CHAPTER 3

Vice Deputy Party Chairman Brett Cole walked out into the downpour without an umbrella because *Good Morning Friends!* said it wasn't raining. And, sure enough, after he caught the subway, then rode for twenty-four minutes, and arrived at his destination station, it wasn't raining at all. The clouds had completely disappeared, and the only sign there'd been a storm was his clothing, which was sodden and dripping.

Brett wore a seersucker suit—tailor-made, pin-striped, powder blue cotton—it was a fashion statement, but a professional statement as well. It said, *I'm essential and comforting, like a pillow.* A retro style to appeal to the aged leadership wing of the party, but also a wink at the pre-geriatric generation—*the future of our nation*—who might perceive a hint of irony in the seersucker's anachronistic formality.

Despite the delayed sunniness, it was a good day. A special day: Vice Deputy Party Chairman Brett Cole had merely been Communications Deputy II Brett Cole just yesterday. But now Brett held a title with "chairman" in it. So everything was about to change around here.

Brett's first flex of his newfound power was insisting on being this year's host of the Thirty-eighth Annual Spring Fling 5K & Half Marathon. To some, a fund-raising event for sick children of some sort may have seemed mundane, but only political novices could be so foolish—which Brett no longer was. If it went well, *Steve Sterling at Midday* might run clips. Very possibly, the clips—Brett—could even appear on *Spectator News at 6,* or on one of the talking-head shows after. And if it turned out to be a slow news day, it was even possible Brett could be seeing himself on *Good Morning Friends!* the following dawn. If God truly loved him.

Yet, as promising as this day was, there was still a lot to be nervous about, and many of Brett's past performance evaluations made a point of noting that being nervous was a central part of his work style. What if the broadcast producers decided he lacked the photogenic glow to be on television? Brett had been told many times that his face was "generic," a word that appeared too often in his life (or at least the life he'd lived before being promoted to Vice Deputy Party Chairman). What if that new usurper showed up to try and take credit? What if it rained some more?

Out of the station and onto the street, Brett was thrust into an unmoving crowd of pedestrians, standing still as if stuck in a human-sized glue trap. Saturday tourists, taking up acres of public walkway, just looking up at the sky. Maneuvering around them deftly (he felt) for a man his size, the Vice Deputy Party Chairman barely noted that many were shading their eyes to stare above. What made Brett start wondering what was going on was something else: a sound.

It went steadily from a distant murmur to a rumble that seemed to follow him as he kept walking. So loud it started to seem rude. Trying with increasing desperation to stay focused on simply getting to the event stage, Brett refused to give it the respect of attention.

Stubbornly, he managed to ignore it for nearly a minute, until that ceased to be a practical plan of action.

High above, the Vice Deputy Party Chairman witnessed what all the other citizens saw: something he had no words for. Unidentifiable. Flying through the air, an object as big as a subway car.

Fire shooting out in bursts from its bottom.

Coming down slowly like an old-timey hot-air balloon. Until it was so close that a burst of its fire caused a wind that pushed Brett and those who stood around him to the grass.

Prone on the lawn, even in this moment of horror, Brett Cole couldn't help but notice that the ship—it had to be a ship of some kind, it had windows—had landed conveniently close to his portable stage. *There are no problems only opportunities. There are no problems only opportunities,* Brett kept whispering to himself as all around him the people of New Roanoke were screaming.

# PART TWO

# CHAPTER 4

What is this place? *New Roanoke.*

Who built it? *God. And God's chosen.*

How long has this existed? *Always.*

Where did all these people come from? *They were chosen.*

Who chose them? *God.*

And repeat, until every inquiry eventually hit the wall of the omniscient nonanswer.

That G-word was thrown around a lot by the staff at the New Roanokan Collected Welcome Center, usually when they didn't feel like relaying information to the new arrivals. Located in a faded downtown office building with chipped linoleum floors that reeked of ammonia, the whole thing didn't seem particularly welcoming to Nalini. Militantly complacent, with an aggressive insistence on indifference to the needs of anyone other than those inside of its own bureaucratic sphere, like a lot of public-facing bureaucracies across the world—hers, and apparently this one as well. When prodded, the faded county clerks typically became mildly irritated with any question that posed a greater challenge than "Where's the bathroom?" Even to that banal inquiry, Nalini's own caseworker robotically replied, "God," before correcting this to "Down the hall, first left."

God. An answer that wasn't dogma or a declaration of faith, but a bureaucratic shrug thrown to shut you up. Repeating on loop until, at the completion of the New Roanokan Citizenship Training Course, the lead supervisor asked, "Any last questions?"—only to sigh in frustration when Nalini Jackson, former NASAx Post-Doctorate Fellow of Applied Sociology, D.A.Sc., and current Lady Stuck on a Moon, shot her hand up immediately.

The beleaguered instructor rubbed his bald head, whispered just audibly, "Why me?," and then, finally, broke from the official party line.

"Listen, I get it, guys. I do. You're scientists, so this has to be extra hard for you. Me, eight years ago I was just a dog groomer from Tampa—and even I had a ton of questions. An entire city in space? I mean, come on. So I get that this is all overwhelming; it is for everyone. It's natural to want more specific answers, especially after such a life-altering event. But you're just not going to get them."

"That's not acceptable—" Dwayne interrupted, only to be stopped again by the clerk, who immediately began making a series of loud nonverbal warning sounds before continuing.

"Listen to me, for your own sake. Even if you did get some answers, let's get real: Chances are they'd just give you more questions. It's an enigma: You can either let it drive you crazy for the rest of your life—and it can—or you can just go with the flow and make the most of this. Do like the locals do: Accept it and live your life. You got no choice; this is your home now. Which I know sounds like a raw deal, but, honestly, I'd rather live in New Roanoke than be back ducking hurricanes in Tampa. Or flooding in Houston. Or stuck in a real shit-hole, like Tallahassee. No offense if any of you are from there, but you know what I mean."

This did little to console the former crew of the SS *Delany*.

Sensing he was losing the room, the bald man added: "Hey, you want a pro-tip? Join the Founders Party! Even if you're not into politics, that's the way to go. Get you involved, and they run everything. Worked for me—that's how I got this job, actually."

"What other political parties are there?" Dwayne wanted to know.

The instructor shrugged. "I don't know, man. There's some little ones. None worth mentioning, really."

After they were released from orientation and moved into their dormlike halfway house, Nalini finally got to go out on her own. Walk the streets of this generic yet impossible city, and explore it for herself. "I've been abducted by unknown forces," she began repeating in her head randomly through the day, hoping that this reminder, along with the irrefutable evidence all around her, would make it feel real. The dilemma was actually rather straightforward: They were on another planet's moon, in a terrarium that reproduced a contemporary American county, with no idea how they'd arrived. When Nalini ignored her emotions and existential panic and broke her situation down to the key moments leading up to it, the story was arguably rather mundane. They were on the cryoship. And then they were sitting in the otherwise empty bleachers of a football stadium. The exotic part was that they had no idea how they got there. And that said stadium happened to be on an alien moon, of course. Within minutes, the crew was met by a group of security officers in militaristic uniforms. They were ushered to the orientation center and given their registration forms. There they sat for new photo IDs, followed by a weeklong New Roanokan Citizenship Training Course. They were provided food, housing, eventually even jobs. But no answers.

In those first weeks, Nalini often found herself driven to bouts of sobbing, but things got better when she decided to let the incomprehensible register in her mind as a dream. Real and unreal, there and unreachable, the world around her like the grass blurring outside a window on a moving train. Upon waking each morning to a life she didn't recognize (for all its uncanny familiarity), Nalini made a conscious effort to take this new reality seriously, but not literally—or the other way around, perhaps.

Her lingering disquiet narrowed to one disturbing observation that circled around her mind: The fact that this world was impossible didn't seem to deter it from existing. If you could ignore basic reality and get away with it, what kind of message did that send to the universe? Or what kind of message was the universe sending? So, because the demands of her clinical mind were entirely frustrated by New Roanoke itself, Nalini chose instead to utilize the tools she'd depended on in past instances of trauma: She dived deeper into her research.

"Rely on your training," they told soldiers and first responders and first-year teachers in public high schools. The mantra was a way of focusing the mind on learned repetitive skills and disconnecting from those parts of the brain screaming hysterically. When Nalini found external stimuli overwhelming, she threw herself into her research. It was the emotional spur of the back-to-back loss of her parents (one of leukemia and the other of heartache soon after), combined with the stress of being left to manage a younger sister she didn't enjoy or understand, that pushed her to write and submit the proposal on the "Effects of Prolonged Interstellar Expedition Isolation on Group Dynamics." Even though doubling down on her career is what got her on that cryoship and into this mess in the first place, Nalini still deemed ignoring the Bergen Work Addiction Scale a solid coping strategy (and also still lacked a better option).

Initially, Nalini's plan was to create a sociological analysis of New Roanokan culture, in book-length form. The indirect implication was that she would one day return home to publish it, and harboring that passive assumption calmed her. As a topic, it was both obvious and incredibly ambitious. New Roanoke, previously unknown and completely isolated, provided endless possibilities for discovery. It was her new life's work, the daunting scope be damned. This isolated population would be her career's Yanomami tribe—without all the ethical missteps of that first contact, she hoped. It was a bold plan, and bold was good, because the scope and ambition of the project was almost enough to distract her from the fact that she'd been kidnapped by unseen forces and stuck in a terrarium.

Unfortunately, as Nalini attempted to slowly insert herself into New Roanokan society, the significant obstacles to actually conducting her imagined grand study became apparent. Very quickly, she discovered a clear, rigid class divide between the people who'd been recently "collected" and those who'd been born in the place: the indigenous New Roanokans, descendants of earlier generations of abductees. Many within the indigenous population could trace their lineage back centuries—and were notorious for letting others know that whenever possible. Nalini found that divide fascinating and had no doubt this caste system would be an excellent subject for further investigation. But the problem was that, as a low-caste new arrival, she never actually met any indigenous New Roanokans. They were all over their television station, but rarely mingled with the "nappies," as the newly collected were slurred (whether its etymological root was a reference to the British slang for "diapers" or a diminutive of "kidnapped" was an ongoing debate).

As in all the other places in which Nalini had lived, the best display of class stratification could be found in its real-estate market. A small, wealthy elite existed beyond the lives of the majority, either high in the air in downtown skyscrapers or behind gates on expansive properties beyond the reach of pedestrians or public transit. Nalini witnessed their opulence as most in New Roanoke did: from a distance, on TV and other media. Together, they presented this privileged lifestyle as if it were the normative rather than an extreme exception. But the reality was obvious and reaffirmed everywhere she roamed: The vast majority of city dwellers lived as she did, in modest apartments, or in simple row houses, or detached homes in the nearby suburbs. The quality of each differed widely, because "middle-class" was not a single stratum but, rather, all the variants between extreme generational wealth and abject poverty.

But Nalini didn't see much of the latter. Though she knew the impoverished must exist in sizable numbers—income-to-rent ratio and scarcity of sustainable jobs implied as much—they were absent from her daily life here. Unlike at home, where tent encampments had become an inescapable part of city living, New Roanoke was devoid of the phenomena. They didn't have random, shelterless individuals, either. Ahmed noted as much, positive this was evidence of a superior society. The streets were empty. Disturbingly so, Nalini couldn't help but feel.

In Nalini's own simple apartment building, the residents were exclusively recent arrivals stretching back just the decade (including the former *Delany* crew members). Down the hall of the fourth-floor walk-up where Nalini and Ahmed cohabitated, there was a commercial fisherman from Nantucket taken after falling overboard, a middle-aged Hertz Car Rental agent whose last Earthly memory was passing out drunk in San Bernardino, and a chiropractor from Bellingham now reduced to doing unlicensed alignments for cash in the building's basement. And even though Nalini did have access to these and other recent arrivals (and noticed shared behavioral quirks among them), she decided to start her research project with subjects still closer at hand: her old crewmates from the *Delany*.

Nalini found the Kübler-Ross Five Stages of Grief to be overused, pedestrian, and absurdly over-applied. They were often taken by the general public as a rigid set of requirements, as opposed to offering a loose framework for greater understanding. But viewing the negotiation of grief and loss as a journey through Denial to Anger, to Bargaining, to Depression, and then to Acceptance provided a solid structure to her work with the crew. The model was initially created in reference to terminally ill patients, but she felt it could easily be applied to a group of otherwise healthy astronauts who'd been kidnapped and held captive in a human-sized fishbowl. As long as she made the point, in both the abstract and the introduction of her eventual peer-reviewed paper, that she held no loyalty to Kübler-Ross as a model, she thought she might get away with it. The same would apply in the introduction to the eventual commercial, public-facing, pop-science bestseller she would publish on the subject post-rescue, which was totally going to happen. She'd long hoped to test her theory that, for a clinical work to translate successfully to the commercial market, it had to be extremely accessible while maintaining an unearned air of intellectual aloofness. Something lightly entertaining made to look dryly academic. "Broccoli-covered chocolate" was what Ahmed called it when she presented the theory to him. She would call her book something like *The Collected,* a good title for a pseudo-scientific opus destined to sell millions and spark an inferno of jealousy and disdain among her academic peers. The dream. In the aftermath, she might become untenurable—even at a lesser Ivy. And that would be okay, because by then Nalini would be obscenely wealthy and they could kiss her ass, intellectually speaking. And this would all happen because Nalini knew, in her heart, that she was totally going to get out of here. Somehow. Because she couldn't imagine that the surreal nature of this whole thing was sustainable— rational reality would surely assert itself, eventually. Until then, it was on well-worn pillars of established academic theories like the Kübler-Ross that Nalini would choose to stand.

# STAGE 1: DENIAL

Despite marinating for weeks in the situation, Nalini initially refused to accept the scientific impossibility that New Roanoke even existed. *Mind control,* she hypothesized, but wouldn't say so out loud, because it sounded silly.

Her first impulse was to deny actively that all this was truly happening. She even went so far as to spend a few days convinced that this was, somehow, the greatest trick the Bobs ever pulled, a willful delusion Ahmed didn't bother arguing with her about. He simply nodded and said, "Okay, my cabbage," as she ranted, until she became exhausted by the effort of upholding the lie. Then, after accepting this was happening, Nalini turned her eye toward the other undeniable reality: That they were truly trapped. That there must be some means by which they could escape, could overcome the logistical challenge of the vast vacuum of space and return home.

Nalini was joined in this defiant hope by former Senior Astrogeologist Dwayne Causwell, with whom she drove through the city on ride-share bikes, searching for the hidden tech maintaining everything. Their initial hope was that, if they located and identified the engine that drove this city, the crew could somehow repurpose it into some sort of celestial life raft (on the specifics of this they were unsure; that wasn't their field of expertise).

Dwayne divided the map of the city into fourteen distinct segments, each navigable in one afternoon. This systematic effort provided a comforting reprieve from panic until the entirety of the New Roanokan map was covered. After this, Nalini powered up to the next level of the Kübler-Ross, while Dwayne began his own process toward a complete psychiatric cataclysm. In the weeks following, from her bedroom window Nalini could see Dwayne roaming the streets at night. Pacing on foot now, alone. In search of some thread he could pull that would begin this reality's unspooling.

# STAGE 2: ANGER

Dwayne was pissed at her. For giving up. He walked faster down the street at ever later hours. Ahmed spent weeks angry, typically expressed as silence. When Nalini asked, "What's wrong?," his only response was "You know." This was true in general, but so nonspecific it became a lie—for every hell was artisanal and individually crafted, and Nalini did not, in fact, know what exact hell he inhabited. They were living together by this point, combining their Newly Collected Housing Waivers in order to afford a studio apartment farther down the block from the dorm and its overwhelming odor of desperation.

"I had an exceptionally promising career that I toiled my entire life to obtain! All gone now. Stolen!" Ahmed finally snapped at her, as if she already knew this was the specific nature of his suffering (she did not; she thought he mostly missed his "mum").

Nalini, for her part, now felt she was angrier than the entire population of the moon of Europa combined. At herself, because she was so utterly useless. Selfish and unserious and just a bad person—the exact judgment of her self-audit changed day to day. And Nalini knew that that was wrong, that she was really mad at the cosmic unfairness of the situation. That her hard-earned life had been stolen from her. That Josey had lost the stability of the last immediate family member she had, for the rest of her life. That, without a nagging big sister, Josey might neglect the parts of her mental health over which she had some control: maintaining her meds, showing up for therapy, sidestepping known triggers before they made things worse. And though, rationally, it was unfair for Nalini to punish herself for not preparing for an outcome that was, still in her mind, impossible, it was far easier blaming herself than some phantasmic unknowable force that had snatched her like an apple off a neighbor's tree.

# STAGE 3: BARGAINING

For a stretch, Nalini became obsessed with the question of which crossroads on her life's path, had she chosen differently, would have avoided this fate. Simply not applying for the *Delany* mission—sure, that would have helped. If a god or devil offered, she would be totally willing to trade all of her past and future accomplishments for an uneventful life spent sitting next to her mom, alive and on the couch chain-smoking menthols. That would have kept her off any cryoships. But, alas, no deity appeared.

A communal crew dinner of the Bobs was called. At a Denny's. Leaping at the chance of distraction, Nalini, who generally tried to avoid the Bobs on principle, surprised Ahmed by asking to join him. The purpose of the dinner was to talk strategy on how to get the hell out of there, but, of course, there was no strategy. Without Dwayne present to commiserate with, Nalini tried to focus on eating the majority of her Grand Slam Pack breakfast (featuring eight pancakes, eight scrambled eggs, four bacon strips, four sausage links, *and* hash browns). When she finally gave up on finishing this and lifted her head from the plate, Nalini watched her colleagues perform the Bargaining stage of the Kübler-Ross as a collective—textbook and obvious. All the "What if"s and "If we'd only"s and "Maybe if we'd"s. Not one mention of God, because they were scientists, and the only socially acceptable display of faith among them was atheism, and even that was an embarrassingly unscientific leap from the safe nonwager of the agnostic.

"We gotta make the most of this," Bob Seaford declared from the head of the table, holding up a glass of milk like it was the Holy Grail. "Do what they ask of us: Fit in, become a part of this crazy thing, and see how that changes the equation." This was one of the rare times Nalini agreed with him. Hearing it, she thought that Bob had skipped straight over to the Acceptance stage, but soon it was clear Bob meant his words in the Bargaining sense.

"*If* we do as we're supposed—hear me out, guys—*if* we play along, maybe whatever brought us here will release us." He added, "As a reward for good behavior," when, uncharacteristically, everyone didn't instantly agree with him. It was a pathetic notion—even the local New Roanokan mythology contained no mention of anyone's being freed for "good behavior," although, practically speaking, that would have served as an excellent social-control mechanism. Still, to a subset of former class pets (which on the *Delany* formed the majority), the idea remained attractive.

Jogging off the calories of her Grand Slam gluttony in Grand Circle Square Park the following day, Nalini saw Dwayne for the first time in weeks. He was in the greenspace's Speaker's Corner, testifying. Standing on a milk crate before passing pedestrians who barely looked his way, the lapsed Baptist preached. Nalini came over and stood before him listening, since no one else was. She did it because she cared about him, and that's also why it was so painful to see him so humbled. This was a man who used to charge a small fortune just to be flown in to a campus to read from prepared remarks, then accompany his hosts to a restaurant specializing in overpriced food. On New Roanoke, Dwayne didn't lecture, he confessed; on his crate, he offered a secular gospel of his personal failures: past subservience to the monster of his own ego, a cowardly history choosing the solitary comfort of the lab over the chaos of marching in streets for a better world. A better world sounded good, Nalini thought. But: *Which world, Dwayne?*

## STAGE 4: DEPRESSION

After three months, the initial welcoming period for new arrivals came to an end, and every member of the *Delany* crew was being encouraged to find gainful employment to avoid the streets.

"What happens if you don't get a job?" Nalini asked that commercial fisherman from Nantucket as they paused at the mailbox.

"Nothing good, lady," he laughed. "You'll end up living in the Cavern with the skid-row basket cases, I guess. Or just start losing it, like your former lab partner."

For a stretch, Nalini stopped seeing Dwayne walking or talking on the streets of New Roanoke at all. When she checked in on him at his apartment, he greeted her at his door with a grunt and the musk of a man who'd denounced and rejected personal grooming.

"Dude, you reek," Nalini told Dwayne, and was surprised to see this seemed to be news to the man, cocooned as he was in his melancholy.

For her part, Nalini didn't experience Depression as an individual stage but, rather, as the fibrous connective tissue that held all the other stages together. There was a night, however, when her despair reached a crescendo. Ahmed was out for Thursday-night drinks with the Bobs at the Blarney Stone; she stayed home alone. No distractions from the crushing enormity of their predicament, feeling the full weight of the emotional burden, Nalini thought about doing something about it. Something bad. Something permanent—something so wrong she wouldn't even name it inside her head. In that moment, this act seemed like a rational response to her reality. An act of power, even. Of defiance. Even though it was the worst form of self-destruction. That Nalini should do as those nineteenth-century West African slaves bound and bound for the New World did: jump overboard rather than endure captivity. It was a rational choice, she felt at the time. The primary reason Nalini did not act on this impulse for self-destruction was the knowledge that her own African ancestors were specifically the ones who didn't jump overboard. Her ancestors were the ones who made it to the other side of the bloody triangle of the Atlantic slave trade by enduring, and kept that up for centuries. If they hadn't been, she wouldn't be here, or anywhere. The other suicide deterrent: Nalini refused to be the first of the *Delany* crew to do so. She would not give Bob the satisfaction. Hell, no.

Although Nalini could also acknowledge that Bob likely wouldn't care one way or the other, this was a strong motivator.

## STAGE 5: ACCEPTANCE

There was nothing the former crew could do to change their situation besides choosing to stop wasting energy trying to change everything. New Roanoke was fine, just another small city, but on a moon. That's it. Whatever had taken them there hadn't hurt them, and maybe never would. If it was hell, it was a hell with a Popeyes Louisiana Kitchen and three Massage Envys. How it all got here, how it was being sustained: not urgent questions next to ones like *How do we make the most of our new lives in this place?*

*I will make it up to Josey,* Nalini vowed. With the bounty of my research. At this juncture, Nalini reached a stage where she was both sure she would be rescued and certain she was stuck for the rest of her life. She had become Schrödinger's Cat. If she was doomed to stay, she decided she would become a middle-school teacher, to work with children as penance for not being there for Josey—the seventh-grade Josey of her mind, the last version of her sister she had connected with. That was fine—there was always a shortage of middle-school teachers in the STEM fields. This plan calmed Nalini for a week before she remembered that she also disliked kids, especially the middle-school ones. *Are you babies? Are you teenagers? Make up your minds.* But even that was fine; penance is supposed to be painful.

Ahmed Bakhash was one of the most adaptive individuals Nalini had ever known, and if she hadn't gotten engaged to him four months after landing, she would have considered him an excellent research topic. They hadn't even been on New Roanoke a month before Ahmed started exploring the job market. Nalini watched him devising a list of possible jobs, deciding which to pursue based on how well his existing skills would translate, and which offered the best long-term earning potential. For, as seemingly identical as this land was to their own, there were some significant differences, the complete absence of any aeronautical presence in the dome being one of them. There were no planes, let alone space shuttles. There was no research science, or need for it, because all the real innovation came from out of town, passed on from Earth like hand-me-downs. New Roanoke was a state of replication, not innovation. So Ahmed decided that—absent any demand for astronautical engineers— a career in broadcast technology was the key to providing him with a lifestyle that would make being kidnapped on an alien planet more palatable. His existing skill set went far beyond the requirements of the job, so, in lieu of a résumé, Ahmed constructed a broadcast-tower signal booster, about the size of a trash can, and presented it to the Roanokan Broadcasting Company's executive-level management. This display secured him a senior engineering management position; always an overachiever, outpacing others in mental acuity and work ethic, Ahmed now had an even greater advantage. Like a city slicker in comparison to his country cousin, Ahmed was up on the latest fashions, technology-wise, while his New Roanokan peers lagged five, sometimes ten years behind. In a matter of months, he'd progressed all the way to Vice President of Communications, acquiring a local financial advisor as well.

Ahmed's corporate audition was arranged by Bob Seaford himself: Bob managed to get that politically connected, that fast. Through the lens of her professional discipline, it was fascinating for Nalini to watch Bob work, a joy radically tempered by her intense dislike of him personally. In the first days of their group citizenship training, Bob repeatedly requested an audience with "whoever's in charge," exasperating several daily instructors until one finally acquiesced to his demands just to get him to shut up. All the Bobs quietly cheered this on when they heard, assuming Bob was asserting power and agency on behalf of their larger collective. The first person in charge Bob targeted was the night-shift manager at the New Roanokan Collected Welcome Center, a petty bureaucrat seemingly selected by Bob because he was the easiest to blindside.

"Okay, that's it—I've heard enough. Let me speak to whoever you report to. Get them in here. Now." The flustered night-shift manager brought in a slightly older-looking administrator, then fled the room. Focusing on the new guy, who seemed half awake and visibly off guard, Bob immediately repeated his routine: "Who is your direct superior? Names, I want names." And then, to his boss, Bob buckshot variations of "What the hell is all this about?" and "No bullshit, someone tell us what is really going on," on repeat. Until whoever was harangued relented and got his boss. Over and over for the course of a week this went, Bob's performance of entitlement too flawless for anyone even to think of questioning it. At first, Nalini took this to be a pointless symbolic act, yet another one of Bob's hollow dominance displays meant to excite his acolytes. After all, these were the same questions they'd all been asking the staff since they landed. But for Bob the question was only a tactic, a runway to his grander performance.

Witnessing his slow-motion infiltration of the indigenous leadership, Nalini soon realized that she'd underappreciated what a rare and skilled Machiavellian operator Bob Seaford truly was. The local society had no natural defenses against his opportunistic maneuvering. Their ruling class was soft from lack of obstacles or resistance. The first-generation abductees of New Roanoke were people plucked from quiet, comparatively unremarkable lives—folks who could go *missing* without the world coming to a halt. Amid this subset of Earthlings, Bob was an anomaly: an overachieving and cunning predator. Like any ecosystem invaded by an alien carnivore, New Roanokan society had developed no natural defenses against being devoured.

Bob's grilling of the senior manager of the New Roanokan Collected Welcome Center was conducted in such a forceful and annoying manner that said manager kicked his queries up to his superior as a way of exiting from Bob's overbearing orbit.

Next up was the Founders Party Communications Deputy II Brett Cole. None of the *Delany* crew had ever heard of him, of course, but the local admins said his name aloud with a measure of gravitas that implied they should. Apparently, Communications Deputy II Cole was someone who'd "taken a break from his senior party schedule to honor us with their presence," their intake counselor offered, his eyes flicking to Bob for a hint that this was finally enough. It was, apparently, because Bob's demeanor immediately switched upon the Communications Deputy II's arrival.

By then, Nalini was more aware of the Founders Party's position in this society. Not only was it the ruling party; their brief history lesson revealed that it had been for a generation. On its surface, posters of smiles and strength and national pride, which Nalini associated with the deniable malignance of soft-core fascism. An emphasis on tradition and "New Roanokan values," which she took as a polite way to advocate for a nativist power structure in a world where foreigners were plopped down on a regular basis. On honoring God, as a way for a party of humans to claim divine rights. The conservative sect closely linked with the party, "Church of the Collected"? That was just creepy; Nalini didn't need to know anything but the name to get it. But, considering all that, when the Communications Deputy II showed up, Nalini was surprised to see that individually he came off like a total sweetheart.

This doughboy of a man (Nalini imagined this is what an adult-sized baby would look like in a suit) seemed to be under the assumption that the crew of the *Delany,* having just arrived from Earth, were as impressed by his presence as was the rest of the Welcome Center's staff. Cole soon proved to be a numbing orator, overly formal and prone to silences between thoughts, and the words that came out of his mouth were just gilded versions of the same nonanswers they'd be fed daily. What was truly different about the occasion was how Bob responded to them.

After some effusive praise that stopped just short of perceptible insincerity, Bob switched seamlessly into a more conspiratorial tone. "Chief, I'm not from here—obviously. But I can see a man of substance when he's standing before me. You coming down here, to talk to us? That's character. Brett Cole. I'm never going to forget that name." Bob walked over to the man and slapped him on the back. Cole startled at the gesture, but an earnest grin flashed across his face, as if he'd waited his entire life for such an audience response. Bob had his hand on the other's shoulder when he leaned in and added, "Just want you to know, if I can return the favor in any way, I'd love the opportunity. My goal is to show just how much a new arrival can do in this great society you got going on here. I'm trying to be like you when I grow up."

Communications Deputy II Brett Cole beamed. And with that perfect balance of fraternal and obsequious, Bob began burrowing himself into the fiber of the primary power structure, the Founders Party. Using his weakness, as a newly arrived outsider in a nativist stronghold, as his greatest asset. Offering himself as a symbol of the recently collected, a prominent token willing to play ball if it kept him on the roster.

Nalini watch all this unfold and was humbled by the brilliance of Bob's machinations. The efficiency and skill with which he injected himself into the local society revealed an expertise honed over decades. Clearly, it had been with a similar method that Bob managed to secure the backing of his high-roller oil-and-gas buddies to get on the *Delany* in the first place. It wasn't long after his charming of the party man that Bob had his first party job himself. The title of this Nalini didn't bother learning, because the role of the job was too clear for her to bother. Bob offered his service as a token immigrant in a fiercely nativist party, historically a highly lucrative position.

Within months, Bob had left the lower-income neighborhood surrounding the New Roanokan Collected Welcome Center altogether. It was less than a year later that Nalini first heard the rumors about Bob's new McMansion on the other end of town. Perfect for dinner parties, apparently. At least according to Ahmed and those Bobs who'd been invited.

In contrast to the overachieving assimilation strategies of Ahmed and Bob, there was Dwayne. Before dawn, when Ahmed first rose to shower, Nalini—always a light sleeper—rose as well, usually to make tea and plan the day as she waited for the "sun" to rise in the artificial sky. It was at the window that she would sit and watch Dwayne, speed-walking in the dark. Some mornings, in circles around their block. Zip, zip, zip. Other times, it was just off into one direction and then gone, down the street and out of sight for the day. Or days. Nalini hoped he was going somewhere specific, somewhere he'd found to get away from it all. His pace, the way he swung his arms, it looked . . . *wacky.* Nalini liked to think of it that way, *wacky,* because she was afraid of categorizing it more clinically, hoping that, instead, there was a logical reason she was missing. Maybe he was just exercising—it made sense that Dwayne, a rabid vegan and disciplined practitioner of Ashtanga yoga, would get into extreme walking after being stuck for so long on the *Delany.* All this was guesswork, because, despite the basic stipend given to him, Dwayne had no phone, and either his doorbell was broken or he simply wasn't answering. After putting it off for longer than she was proud of, one morning Nalini rose in the dark and dressed before Ahmed so she could catch Dwayne the moment he came out for his daily wander.

"Yo, lady" was how Dwayne greeted her on the street, and an unexpected shudder of relief made Nalini aware that she'd assumed that he was mad at her for some grave yet unknown offense. Despite the walking, without the meticulously balanced dietary regime of the *Delany,* Dwayne had already managed to gain enough weight to inflate his cheeks and thicken his neck—slight, but something someone who'd spent months staring at him would notice.

"So what's going on, chief?" Nalini tried to keep pace with him, because he was already launching into his strut and on his way. He knew what she was talking about, and didn't bother with the game of denying it.

"I'm still looking for a way to get out of here," he admitted.

Nalini walked alongside him silently in the time it would have taken to say the obvious: *We've been through this, we can't get back to our ship, they have no ships, and even if we tried to build a ship we lack the technical, financial, and industrial means to make that a reality.*

"I'm walking the length of the bubble in spirals now," he continued, his voice intensifying as he went. "Just to see what's here. What's really here, and not just what they say is here—not just take their word for it. I refuse to renounce my freedom based on the assessments of total strangers. And I don't know if you've noticed, but some of these people are really weird. Walking around smiling, empty-eyed. Who does that? It's creepy. They look like nonplayer characters in a shitty game. I think that's what happens to you if you just give up."

"Lot of people here are dealing with the trauma of being here. Likely, even the ones born here—generational trauma, possibly. It's not a game."

"No. It's a terrarium."

"Sure, okay." She shrugged. When Nalini saw Dwayne's slight blanch, Nalini realized how dismissive this sounded, so she added, "I'm just tired of thinking about it, to be honest."

"I can't think of a damn thing else. I keep thinking: bearded dragons."

There was a vast stretch between how obvious this connection was to Dwayne and how little sense it made to Nalini, and it made her worry about it more.

"I never told you the bearded-dragon story?"

"No. Tell me your bearded-dragon story."

He kept walking, staring down as he talked. "When I was a kid, my pop refused to let me get a pair of bearded dragons. You know, little lizards, about a foot and a half long. He hated them, hated the smell of them in the pet store, thought they cost too much, said our apartment was too small. He wanted to adopt me a puppy, and then that became a whole thing, a stand-in for the larger conflict between my identity and the fact that he was a closeted homophobe. But, eventually, he gave in, for two reasons. One: to encourage my interest in science. And two: to get me to stop begging for bearded dragons." Dwayne's pace slowed a bit as he looked up at her, but he never stopped moving, pushing forward.

"We're all going through versions of the same thing, Dwayne. Come talk to me. If Ahmed's an issue—which is ridiculous, but whatever—I can come to your place."

"The thing about bearded dragons is that you can't just feed them dog food. No dry, bulk buys. They need to eat crickets. *Live* crickets. So it's like you're buying hundreds of pets to feed one pet. Every day. So what does that mean? That means you're at the pet store once or twice a week. That means, no matter how careful you are, crickets get everywhere; random appliances start chirping, because somehow the crickets got inside. It was a nightmare. My dad was totally right, it was a horrible idea, even if he came to that conclusion for the wrong reasons. But I refused to admit it, and kept them until I left for college, because fuck that guy."

"We're not bearded dragons."

"No, we're not. We're the crickets."

The next time Nalini heard Dwayne deliver the bearded-dragon/crickets analogy, it was a year later, and he was standing on a milk crate at the Speaker's Corner of Grand Circle Square Park again. It was one of several theories he floated during the span of twenty minutes in which Nalini watched him. Now others were watching him, too. Not just walking by, but standing attentively to take his words in. Nalini stood at a distance as he railed passionately about things that were never going to change unless everyone present changed them. Dwayne was vague on specifics, but it was still bold: Even publicly acknowledging that New Roanoke was not actually the promised land was an antisocial act of rebellion. The crowd grew for a while, too, until, eventually, there were dozens listening. And they stayed until Dwayne segued to his theories on the importance of discussing the "invisible things" issue. It was the first time Nalini had heard it discussed in the open. At the mention of "invisible things," the crowd cleared out almost instantly. No one wanted to talk or hear about that.

Every human community has its superstitions; typically, they said more about the individual culture or era than anything else. Often, there was a physical component upon which they were based—countless historic ghost sightings had been linked to carbon-monoxide-fueled hallucinations. Mass hysterias were sometimes due to things like well-water poisonings. Succubi to nocturnal emissions. Demonic attacks to sleep paralysis. Chupacabras to wild and mangy dogs. Causes varied, but, historically, the combination of misunderstood phenomena and cultural impulses led to wild theories.

New Roanoke had its own anomalies demanding an explanation, except no one wanted to talk about it. There was a pattern of disruptions, incidents when objects, and sometimes people, would suddenly begin *floating*. Knowledge of this was based purely on witness accounts, passed from person to person, which also happened to be the least reliable kind of data set. But their frequency could be taken as a crude form of evidence of *something*. People had been hurt by this phenomenon—or at least people had been hurt and pointed to it as the cause. Nalini had no idea what was behind the science of how this place was created, how it was supplied, or even how she got here, so accepting the idea of occasional gravitational anomalies didn't seem to be a huge intellectual leap.

What was fascinating to Nalini, intellectually and practically, was the mythology that had grown up around these rumored occurrences. *The invisible things.* It was believed that talking about the phenomenon increased the chances of being a target for it. That public disobedience to the state encouraged it further—a rather convenient social-control myth, akin to the bogeyman, but for adults who should know better. Some mentioned it as if it was a natural force, like tornadoes. She'd heard others talk around it, like it was a person or persons, or some other conscious entities. Angels or demons or some sci-fi version of either. But even this paltry bit of information took a year to acquire, because of the taboo—discerned from mutters and curses. Everything she'd heard about the "invisible things" from locals had been delivered in whispers, outlined by the edges of what they wouldn't say.

Nalini finally found (occasional) employment substitute-teaching in the ring of hell that was the middle grades. But she had no idea how Dwayne was supporting himself. He seemed to have rejected the system while still surviving inside of it, spending his days preaching to passersby and passing a hat to whosoever stopped to listen. Nalini hoped his activism might at least offer Dwayne some peace.

It didn't. In the coming days, Nalini made a point to pass through the park on her lunch break to keep tabs on Dwayne. Day by day, his rants began taking on more of a shape and a worldview. Dwayne's main principles: We were all kidnapped, not "collected"; we needed to find a way to escape, but the first step would be to confront reality and reject the Founders Party propaganda. Ignore the dogma that

New Roanoke was a divine creation, that questioning was in itself a form of blasphemy punishable by the unseen hand of God. We could not improve our situation unless we faced it boldly. People would clap at the end of his oration, and put money in his shoebox.

One night, Ahmed came back from drinks with the other Bobs at the pub they'd nicknamed the "Bob Den" and reported the rumor that Dwayne had been elected to be the head of the Party of the People (PoP), New Roanoke's sole opposition party. Nalini had never heard of the PoP. Apparently, they'd been largely inactive for a few years, because no one had been crazy enough to lead an opposition party against a de-facto autocracy. New Roanoke had a representative government, but what it represented was a skewed system whose leadership was chosen by an electoral system based on acreage, not population. It gave the same voting power to one man living on an acre as it did to a thousand people living on a plot of the same size. Effectively, and intentionally, it allowed the wealthy estate regions and well-to-do suburbs disparate power while neutralizing the bulk of the population, crammed into multi-unit housing as they were. Unofficially, the PoP held no senior elected positions, had no real power, or money, or reputation, and was allowed to exist largely to let the Founders' propaganda claim New Roanoke was a multi-party democracy. Upon further research, Nalini found out that it actually had, in the past, represented an important political faction. Or important enough that several officeholders had been imprisoned or gone missing.

"What the hell does 'gone missing' even mean in a world where everyone's trapped in a bubble?" They were sitting on a bench in the park as Dwayne took a pause between his "lectures." By then he had a phone she could call, but Nalini knew he wouldn't discuss anything of substance on it, because he suspected "they" were listening.

"It means they were too lazy to come up with a new euphemism." Dwayne chuckled at this, as if being assassinated was a joke.

Catching her look, he added: "What do I have to lose? Nothing. What do we have to lose as a community? Nothing. The Founder types don't even care."

"Unless you're effective, and suddenly they're interested."

"Exactly my thinking: It's a win-win for all involved."

The news of Dwayne's new position was soon on all the screens to which the RBC broadcast. Nalini had never been much of a television watcher back on Earth, taking pride in making a slightly disgusted face as she told people, "I don't really watch TV." Of all the TV she did not watch, Nalini really didn't watch the news. And since New Roanoke only had the one broadcast station, the RBC, she found it easy to avoid it altogether as she tried to get on with her new life.

Dwayne she never avoided. There were times when she wanted to check on him. But there were other times—many, really—when their talks gave her a moment of normality. He would start ranting about his latest grievance, and suddenly it was as if they were back on the ship once more, in that last moment before everything went crazy.

One of Dwayne's favorite topics to gripe about was the malignancy of the sole network broadcasting on the outdated TVs. "Turn on the RBC; you have to watch what they're doing now. This is the propaganda the general public is ingesting. A rejection of what they can see with their own eyes."

"I don't know nothing about this. I just teach seventh grade," she'd say. Eventually, he'd calm down again. Or he would switch to his other favorite subject: the invisible-force phenomenon.

"I can't even," she would tell Dwayne, to get him to stop. But it would be too late. Nalini would begin thinking about the thing she didn't want to think about.

Nalini started repeating the things Dwayne said to Ahmed. "How can you work at a broadcast company that spews straight-up propaganda?" she'd ask, to which Ahmed would volley, "The RBC has a unique perspective that serves the larger good." Ahmed countered Nalini's "The RBC is opiate for the masses" with: "We're stuck in a snow globe. Can you imagine the chaos if the RBC and the Founders Party didn't calm things down?" All of which were fair responses on Ahmed's part, but so was Nalini's response when she said, "Bullshit," quit the argument, the engagement, and also their entire romantic relationship at the same time.

"It's just not working for me anymore" is what Nalini said, a bland cliché that Ahmed took offense to on those grounds and others. So she added, "I've come to the realization that I was just with you for emotional stability in a time of uncertainty and not because our specific relationship is a viable lifelong partnership," to which Ahmed took more offense. That was how she felt, though. Or at least it was the closest approximation of what Nalini could discern from her enigmatic cloud of a subconscious.

"Fuck off" was Ahmed's response. It was an understandable one, she felt, given that she was literally in the process of leaving him.

Nalini was still "decorating" her new studio apartment, taping newspaper to cover the blindless windows, when the phone rang. It was Dwayne's voice streaming through the receiver, although what he said was lost in a frantic rush that blurred all syllables. She had to spend nearly a minute listening to him rant before Dwayne paused long enough for Nalini to say, "I can't understand a word you're saying."

This got him to pause. She could make out the sound of Dwayne taking a deep breath before screaming each word individually. "I said, 'I told you so!' Nalini: They're here! Grab that manuscript of yours. *The Collected* is about to find an international audience."

# CHAPTER 5

Nalini had to push her body through blocks of shoulder-to-shoulder gawkers, all the way to the final police barricade, just to see it for herself. The SS *Ursula 50*. A cryoship, in New Roanoke. It sat on the grass, still. A portable stage with a movie screen and sound system, already in place for a now canceled race, was quickly moved directly next to the vehicle. The city workmen made sure the stage sat level to the ship's door, moving fast, and then eagerly hustled away. Ignoring the risk of the unknown, the crowd stayed, growing ever larger as more kept pouring into Grand Circle Square Park to witness this historic miracle. The stage was decorated with red, white, and blue streamers and balloons and Founders Party banners, and with one big sign that said *Thirty-eighth Annual Spring Fling 5K & Half Marathon,* which a worker on a ladder was attempting to dislodge. In the packed crowd around her, she could see the cryoship from the best angle available: the one being streamed directly onto her phone. Handheld screens floated above the crowd like plasma flowers.

It wasn't a typical crowd for a Grand Circle Square rally. These people were not, for the most part, Founders partisans, or their wealthy backers, or the employees of the wealthy backers sometimes coerced to attend events. There seemed to be a significant number of what she'd now officially termed in the book as "Floaters": that majority of militantly apolitical citizens whose New Roanokan social strategy was just to keep their blinders on and trust that everything would be fine. They were like passengers on a bus, unquestioning of both route and driver. She'd intended for the moniker to invoke images of them gliding along, letting the current take them where it would, but when she'd mentioned her categorization to Dwayne, he'd laughed and said, "I love it: like dead bodies in a lake."

"Welcome, guys and gals!" A familiar man in a powder-blue suit had climbed up to the microphone stand on the podium and was waving to the sound engineer to lower the volume. "My name is Vice Deputy Party Chairman Brett Cole, and, on behalf of the great state of New Roanoke, welcome to the ranks of the Collected! You have been selected!" Vice Deputy Party Chairman Brett Cole paused to look behind him toward the ship as if awaiting a response. The people around Nalini were cheering wildly, presumably just at the spectacle of the event. But the cryoship itself seemed unmoved. Its lights off, its portal door immobile.

"You have been delivered! Welcome to your new life in the promised land! Welcome!" Brett Cole kept going, until the crowd began chanting "Welcome!" with him, as if this could coax whoever was inside to come out.

To Nalini's surprise, it worked.

The roar of applause as the cryoship's main hatch started lifting forced Nalini's hands to her ears. It was the loudest thing she'd ever experienced, and got louder still when the cell screens in everyone's hands displayed a close-up of an older red-haired woman walking slowly and deliberately out of the portal, to greet them.

The woman had a military bearing but no uniform. She sported a jogging suit, clean and crisp but informal. Cerulean blue with white stripes, as if she were disembarking simply to speed-walk some steps onto her pedometer. Before Nalini could fully take that in, she saw the next person to leave the ship: a sunbaked white guy in a muted gray power suit, followed by an old, chubby man—so chubby that Nalini's first thought was: *How the hell was he cleared for flight?* As the portal began resealing behind them, one last male emerged, dressed in jeans and a plaid flannel shirt, like he was this band's roadie.

"Welcome to New Roanoke!" Brett Cole told them. As the crowd signaled its approval, he motioned for the visitors to come over and meet him at the podium.

"On behalf of the Founders Party, I—" was as far as Brett Cole got this time before the red-headed woman reached out for the microphone.

"I am Admiral Ethel Dodson of the SS *Ursula 50*. Accompanying me are United Nations Special Envoy Lloyd Talbot, esteemed philanthropist Harry Bremner, and his assistant Chase Eubanks. We arrive among you on a mission of peace, understanding, fact-finding, and assistance. We come with one cryoship, but also with the technology and strategies to build a fleet of ships like this one. We offer you our aid. We offer you rescue. We are here to give you the chance to come *home.*"

"Holy shit, they have no idea what is going on here," Nalini said out loud, a mutter fortunately muffled by the simultaneous gasps of thousands.

Before the crowd could react further, Vice Deputy Party Chairman Brett Cole leaned in to the microphone and tried to push past with: "On behalf of the Founders Party, I welcome you to New Roanoke! Founders Party Be Praised! Founders Party Be Praised!"

But it was too late. There were many cheers, there were even some boos, but mostly there were screams. Lots of screaming. What they were all yelling individually, Nalini couldn't make out. Not until a good portion of the voices coalesced around one simple chant, "Home." Or, rather, "Home-Home-Home-Home-Home," with the repeated bass and bellowing of a steam train.

Onstage, Nalini saw a disoriented Vice Deputy Party Chairman Brett Cole struggle to say more into the microphone. "No need for 'home.' I mean, we have a home, this is our home, our only home. We don't need to go anywhere for that," he tried, but barely anyone seemed to register this over the chanting and some of those who did replied by loudly booing.

The first shoe came from fairly far back in the crowd. Nalini saw it flying over her head and wondered if an actual person threw it, or if it was being moved by the you-know-whats. It hit the side of the elaborate stage, bounced off of Brett Cole, and landed with a flat thud, seemingly unnoticed by anyone but the absurd seersuckered bureaucrat it glanced. But within seconds, there was a flock of footwear in the sky. As Nalini started chanting "Home! Home!" with everyone else, she wondered how many people would have to walk home with one shoe on.

Regardless of how the riot was reported on *Good Morning Friends!* the following day, Nalini was not a "planted insurgent paid by the Party of the People to sow unrest against the greater good." This was a lie. In fact, though Dwayne was indeed Nalini's best friend in this whole world, she'd never attended a single PoP meeting, let alone paid dues. And, personally, she found the whole PoP thing to be a tedious hamster-wheel for malcontents; Nalini preferred to do her malcontenting from bed.

Nalini was, of course, not the first person to publicly say "Home!"

that day—that was Admiral Ethel, everyone saw it. Nalini was just the first to yell that word into a bullhorn. This wasn't planned: The police officer next to her just happened to drop his megaphone after being hit in the head with an oxford. When he ran off to assault the perpetrator or the nearest facsimile, Nalini picked it up on impulse and simply yelled what everybody else was yelling. So the riot was all Admiral Ethel—something Nalini would always respect her for.

But the injuries suffered by so many that day were not the Admiral's fault. There was no way she could have known that misuse of this single word, "home," was considered an affront to New Roanoke's mainstream political, religious, and philosophical sensibilities. Or known of the essay "On Home," written in 1623 by the founding mother Virginia Dare, and considered the seminal text of both the Church of the Collected and the Founders Party. Or that this essay essentially laid the groundwork for the belief that New Roanokans were Collected by God to inherit the New-er World. Or that the reason it was rare to hear the word "home" uttered by locals was that it was believed that even saying the word out loud was blasphemous and might possibly (maybe probably) rile up those invisible things it was best one avoided. Or that, as Nalini and the rest of the crowd understood, committing this blasphemy amid the safety in numbers meant those invisible things couldn't go after everyone. Nalini forgave the Admiral's mistake; she herself had just spent the last twenty-nine months adjusting to her new life on a moon 444 million miles from *home,* and was still learning.

"Home! Home! Home!" they chanted. It was exhilarating, giving Nalini a pulse that matched the beat. The cops providing security for the event had a much more practical response to the intoxication of the moment, and they had the billy clubs to express their emotions. To his credit, the senior officer directly in front of Nalini did bellow "Stand down!" to his visibly distraught fellow officers. It was a clear

and admirable attempt on his part to de-escalate the situation; whoever he was, he was a good cop. But then he got hit with a shoe, too,
and, upon recovering, said to no one in particular, "Last warning.
Disperse!," in a rather perfunctory tone, before transforming into a
bad cop. He started swinging.

Under cover of air assault, Nalini lifted the discarded megaphone
again and let everybody know what she was really thinking. "Everybody! Chill out! We have a ship! We're getting out of here! We're
going *home*!" And though this did not spark another chant from the
crowd, preoccupied as they were by being beaten, it was enough to
gather the attention of the seersuckered bureaucrat onstage.

"Arrest that woman!" Vice Deputy Party Chairman Brett Cole
yelled into his microphone, pointing right at Nalini.

Immediately, a police officer snapped his head in her direction.
He met Nalini's eyes, and there she saw his relief at having a simple
command to follow in an otherwise complex universe. The officer
approached with his hands out before him, as if preparing for a hug.
Nalini closed her eyes and braced for the impact, but it never came.
And when she opened her eyes to look again, Nalini saw the officer's
feet where his head had been.

He was floating. About a foot in the air. Upside down.

*Oh, shit, it's real* was Nalini's first thought.

The cop seemed to be dangling by his right ankle, as if caught in
a rabbit trap. But nothing was holding him that Nalini could see.
The officer was silent, his face perfectly still, as the chaos of the riot
spun around him. His eyes, wide, met Nalini's, and pled uselessly in
the moment before he was flicked up and up into the air, until he
was so high Nalini could no longer hear him screaming.

*Oh, shit, it's real* was also Nalini's second response.

She lost sight of him up there in the sky for a second, before he
reappeared, moving now in the opposite direction. He fell back to

the ground at the other end of the park like a discarded chicken bone. Nalini was thankful he landed too far away for her to see the impact.

There was no time, in this moment, to dwell further: A riot was in full bloom now. What Nalini *could* see was three specific fights in the general landscape of brawling around her. And she could see little kids, crying, clinging to terrified moms. The elderly people nervously trying to weave their way to safety. And when Nalini looked back to the stage, she saw that the seersucker man was now missing. Gone, too, were the disembarked crew from the cryoship SS *Ursula 50*. All but the one woman, the Admiral, who crouched below the wooden lectern for cover. Without impediment, Nalini pushed her way to the side of the stage and climbed its steps. *Dwayne should be here,* Nalini thought. But he wasn't, so she grabbed the now discarded microphone.

"Yo! Everybody! Listen! I am Nalini Jackson of Pasadena, California, Collected on Earth's March seventeenth, about thirty months ago." She stood in the same place the Founders Party rep had just minutes before. Remembering the stage's projection screen, she turned and looked behind, and there she was, fifty feet tall, on canvas. "I was kidnapped off an identical cryoship model, the SS *Delany*. And I need you to hear my message."

Some of them out there in the human sea actually paused. Some looked back at the phones still in their hands, to see if what was happening was officially happening in broadcast form. Even the police officers just below her slowed their club swinging. Some out there looked up at her onstage, directly.

"You need to chill. The hell. Out. You have to calm down. That's what we're supposed to do, right? Because something's going on and it's not safe. That's pretty clear."

Fortunately, though Nalini was still a newbie on this world and also not a representative of the Party of the People, the crowd mo-

mentarily accepted her authority enough to recall their predicament. Like air escaping a blow-up mattress, Nalini could almost
hear anger vibrate off the riot. Her last thought before she was
yanked from behind was: *Dwayne is going to be so jealous.*

An older woman in uniform appeared before her. "Want to get
moving?!" she yelled directly into Nalini's face. Nalini understood it
to be a rhetorical question as other hands started pulling her away.

In the clutches of a group of masked people, all wearing black
hats and gloves, she was dragged off the stage and past the chaos and
moved toward a windowless van.

Nalini thought, *I've never been arrested before,* as if this would stop it
from happening. The van door slid open, and she was shoved inside,
and she could never say she'd never been arrested again.

There, already seated, was Admiral Ethel. The woman actually
smiled when she saw Nalini. "Dr. Jackson, I presume."

# CHAPTER 6

Amid screams and projectiles, United Nations Special Envoy Lloyd Talbot, the investor and philanthropist Harry Bremner, and the driver Chase had also been shoved off the stage, but, in their case, into the back of a stretch limo. As the three men struggled to untangle their limbs, the vehicle's tires screeched and it accelerated forward. For a moment, it felt to Chase as if they were driving through a tunnel of sound: besides the screech of the tires, the sound of something crunching, the sound of protesters screaming in pain and horror and also banging on the window.

"This is very unpleasant, and I am very uncomfortable," Harry declared, looking to Chase to do something quickly that would change all this. In lieu of that thing, Chase yelled to the stretch limo's chauffeur, "Dude, that is not how to accelerate a commercial passenger vehicle." The driver didn't bother responding. Even with all the chaos unfolding, Chase could hear Harry's increasingly heavy, labored breathing beside him. "Can't we open a window?"

Chase said to no one in particular, almost begging. The old man seemed to have aged ten years since they'd landed.

The blur outside the car's windows: ground floors of office buildings, sidewalks crowded with lunch-breaking pedestrians who appeared totally unaware of the chaos just blocks away. Billboards for national American products Chase had in his own pantry. The horrible chauffeur almost swiped a beggar, and then leaned on his horn like that near homicide was the other guy's fault.

"Hey! Slow down, cowboy!" Chase yelled to the back of the guy's head, then went back to trying to crack a window. Chase wasn't used to riding in the rear, his hands off the wheel. He wasn't used to being in a bubble on a moon, either, but being in a back seat felt odder at the moment. Through the rear window, Chase saw the guy they'd almost hit. He was still standing in the street, holding a crude cardboard sign in his hands, impossible to read at that distance.

After making sure Harry was buckled, he told the boss, "Sir, try to relax! Deep breaths! In through the nose, out through the mouth!" This was Chase's go-to advice for all difficult situations, the beginning and end of his crisis-management skills.

"What, are you a redneck yoga instructor now?!" Harry's face actually was red, his eyes bulging. The go-to advice was less effective when he was screaming each word, Chase figured out.

"No panicking," Lloyd Talbot added. His voice was singsong, playfully casual, as if this were simply another day in the life of a UN special envoy. Flying for months in cryogenic sleep to a moon with a fake American city in a bubble would one day be just a line on his résumé.

"I use a meditation app. It really helps." Lloyd leaned forward and whispered in Chase's ear, for only him to hear, "Remember, you just have to watch out for our VIP here. That's it. You worry about Harry, and I'll take care of everything else. Including finding your

Ada." And that sounded damn good to Chase. Just looking at Lloyd slowed Chase's own breathing. Focusing on that, and the fact that all he had to do was follow Lloyd and make sure Harry didn't have a cardiac arrest, helped.

They passed a digital clock hanging in front of a jewelry shop, and Lloyd turned back to Chase and added, "One-thirty-eight P.M.; set your device," and started adjusting the data recorder on his wrist. Harry, though clearly weak, began pointing at things, muttering, "Chase, look," again and again. "Chase, look, there's a car wash," and "Chase, look, a Chick-fil-A," in a hollow tone Chase had never heard from the man before.

Outside his window, Chase took it in. "They got a goddamn Chick-fil-A."

"Where's the Admiral?" Lloyd Talbot was turned toward the rear. "I don't see another car."

"We could only fit the gents," Brett Cole told him. "Your lady companion will be along shortly. I'll call when we get to the State House, but I'm sure she's in good hands," he added, eyes and attention focused on the traffic outside. Chase could see Brett Cole gripping both hands on the dashboard, as if that gave him some control over the vehicle.

"Respectfully," Lloyd continued, "Ethel Dodson is an admiral. And she's the ranking officer—the only officer on this diplomatic outreach mission. *She's* the VIP. Perhaps we could go back for her? Immediately?"

Brett Cole turned back from the front passenger seat to let Lloyd see him visibly wince at the suggestion. "That's . . . not a feasible option for the moment."

Completely disconnected from the discussion, Harry whispered, "Do you see this place? It's a wonder. Truly a wonder." He was leaning back in his seat, not looking at anything but the limo's ceiling.

"Mr. Cole, is this polity currently in a state of political unrest?" Lloyd had a pocket notepad out, on which his pen rested in anticipation.

"It's fine. It's always fine." Brett seemed offended at the suggestion. "That reception was . . . Well, it's never like this. Rarely. Very rarely. It's just . . . sometimes . . . *unusual circumstances.* That's what I would call it—I mean, we've never had an arrival like yours before, with a ship. And smack-dab in the middle of town, no less!"

Lloyd Talbot wrote something down on his pad. "Just for context, how would you describe your form of government: (A) monarchy, (B) constitutional, (C) democracy, or (D) dictatorship?"

As they sped through a commercial area, Chase could see advertising screens broadcasting images of the stage he had been standing on just minutes before. They were everywhere. *He was everywhere.* Standing there by the Admiral, unaware the camera was on him at the time. *I'm on the TV,* Chase marveled. From the passenger seat, Vice Deputy Party Chairman Brett Cole erupted with "New Roanoke is a peaceful democracy that thrives on the unified vision of its citizenry." A paper cup smacked the front windshield, spreading a thick pink-and-red substance across it that Chase suspected strongly was a Sonic Strawberry Cheesecake milkshake. The crowds outside seemed to have caught up with the news and were eyeing their speeding limo with new interest.

"In short: It's the promised land," Brett added.

Lloyd Talbot leaned in closer to Brett. "And, Mr. Cole—or Vice Deputy Party Chairman Cole, I should say—just one basic question. Logistically, where does all this come from?"

"Where does what come from?" Brett Cole seemed genuinely confused.

"Well, *everything*? The shipping containers that provide you with your supplies?"

"I just said. This is the promised land." Brett Cole turned back to give an incredulous snort at Lloyd Talbot's lack of comprehension. "Promised by He who provides, obviously."

"Right. But, for our upcoming discussions, can you be more specific?" Lloyd kept looking down at his pad, his pen stilled there as he waited.

"Fine, for the record. *God.* God delivers. Obviously."

"Holy shit," Chase said quietly to himself. "It really *is* freaking aliens."

Chase noticed that the metal gate surrounding the State House was ornate and fancy but also nearly twice the height of most men, and thick enough to stop a horde of zombies. It was on a hill, too, which, besides giving the brick mansion sweet views of the city below, also gave it a great siege position: high ground in the front, and a cliff drop-off at its back, where they pulled in to park. When Chase and the others got out, he could see over the edge, past the sheer rock face, that massive U-shaped river, like on the maps. Beyond that, the bubble's surface, a perfect haint blue that reached up until it became sky. The color was right, and there were clouds, too, but Chase could see the faint reflective outline of the bubble's curvature behind it all.

"I think he needs your help," Lloyd said, and it wasn't until he repeated this that Chase realized he was talking to him. That's when he realized Harry was still in the car. Sitting in the back seat, staring forward, as he waited for Chase to get the door, per usual. Ignoring Chase's apology when the younger man helped him get out.

" 'Look down,' we say," Vice Deputy Party Chairman Brett Cole cheerily declared to them all, then guided the men toward the entrance. " 'Look down, and let your faith lift you up.' " The way Brett said the second sentence, in a different, rote tone, made Chase think it might be a song lyric, or a proverb or something.

The State House was even more impressive up close than from a distance. A big old brick mansion, with white columns and a dome on top. Feet-worn dips on its marble stairs, ripples in the blown glass windows—old stuff.

"Monticello," Lloyd Talbot said, staring up at it. Lloyd turned to Chase and kept talking to him as if Chase knew what he was talking about. "Jefferson's triumph, but without Jefferson. Without Sally Hemings."

"But with everything that makes Earth's America what it is, they say. Even an Indian population. Though, you know, not as many anymore," Brett said, drifting off into silence, then cheerfully added, as he held open the building's door, "I myself am one-sixteenth Croatian."

Though the exterior of the mansion gave the impression of a grand private residence, the interior expressed the building's primary purpose: bureaucracy. It reminded Chase of the Bernalillo County Tax Assessor's Office, if not in appearance, then in spirit.

After passing through the metal detector at the security gate, they were greeted by a team of five identically blue-suited men who reeked of private security. From behind them emerged a shorter man, sporting a polo shirt and plaid pants. He appeared to have been plucked off a golf course. Armed with the biggest smile-to-head ratio Chase had ever seen, the little man grabbed Harry's hand before Chase could stop him.

"I'll take it from here, Bretty boy," the small man said.

"*Wonderful*," Brett groaned, and Chase marveled that he could put so much disdain into one word.

The man grabbed Lloyd Talbot's hand next.

"Robert Seaford," Talbot said to the man.

"You can't be, that's my name!" he replied, then laughed at his own joke. "Just kidding! No formalities here. Everyone calls me Bob."

# CHAPTER 7

"What the hell was that?"

Just from that tone, Nalini could tell what the Admiral was talking about, and reflexively deflected. "Your forehead, Admiral— that's an ugly lump you got there, no offense. I'll get some ice." With that, Nalini scooted from the booth they were sharing in the vacant nightclub, got up, and walked behind the bar to grab another bottle of free booze.

Club RIO was the worst bar in the entire universe. Or *had been:* From the outside it appeared to be just another derelict husk of a failed business. They'd been dumped there by their Party of the People escorts and literally told to "wait till the coast is clear," whispered in an overly dramatic fashion, in Nalini's opinion.

RIO's interior walls were a patchwork of salvaged plywood blackened unto death with matte paint. The name itself, *RIO,* was announced in hazy gold spray paint over the vacant dance floor. *Good Times!* and *The High Life!* were declared on tattered, dust-covered banners longing to fall. Crudely rendered images of champagne bottles and confetti were painted on the flat wooden surfaces connecting the dining booths. Over the entrance, in chalk and without a hint of self-awareness, read: *Strict Dress Code!* Nalini had passed the place several times before and always found its façade instantly depressing: Someone had a simple dream, to open a bar, but this was what they got. Maybe they didn't have enough money, or expertise, or whatever, but something definitely went wrong. There was no way this place could accurately represent their ambition, because no one would ever aspire to own a shit-hole. Or be stuck in one.

"You saw it, right? I'm not crazy."

At the freezer, Nalini reached into the ice tray, then dropped some into her glass. She brought a bucket of ice over to Admiral Ethel for her head. "The riot?" Nalini asked. "It was a riot. I've never seen one here before, but I've never seen a spaceship park in the middle of town, either."

"I've seen a lot of riots in my life. What I've never seen is a man thrown a hundred meters into the air."

Nalini poured two fingers of bourbon for each of them. When she didn't get a response, Ethel asked, "Did I imagine that? Am I going crazy—I mean, that happened, right? You saw it. What the hell was that?"

"I don't know anything about it," Nalini said, which was technically accurate. But from the Admiral's expression, it was clear that this would not be enough of an explanation. "But I think I know what you're talking about. There's some kind of—I like to call it a 'gravitational phenomenon'—in this place. Sometimes—very rarely, but sometimes—things float. So, yeah, I've seen that."

"That police officer didn't look like he was floating. The man looked like he got *chucked*."

"I wouldn't pay it too much attention; it's not worth it. We can wait to examine that issue when we're home again. Also, heads up: People get really weird if you talk about that specific phenomenon here. I had to learn that repeatedly during my research."

"But, come on, how do you not discuss—"

Nalini talked over the Admiral until the older woman gave up. "There is a commonly shared superstition that if you talk about it, it increases the chances of, you know, the *phenomenon* recurring. That it just makes things worse. Granted, I've found absolutely no empirical evidence that discussion of the topic increases the chance of an event. But—and here I side with the mainstream opinion on the subject—why tempt fate when there's nothing to gain? I like to think of it as just a sort of a Pascal's wager. So, when in Rome . . ."

"This is not 'Rome.'"

"I'll drink to that." Nalini smiled, lifting her glass in the air before taking another swig.

"Well, then, what is this place?"

"It's a fake city in space. But if you're here, you already know that."

"Okay. So what are your theories?"

"I have no idea. And I'll do you one better: No one does. There are no clues, and apparently there's never been any—at least, that's what the historical record indicates, and, trust me, we checked. Whatever it is, it's 'technology beyond our current understanding.'" The last bit Nalini delivered in Ahmed's deep voice and the manner in which he always said the phrase. This meant nothing to the Admiral, but Nalini couldn't help herself.

"There have to be working theories, correct?"

"Nothing that isn't just guessing. You know, it sounds crazy, but, actually, nobody talks about it that much. Not even among the *Delany* folks. Not after the first year. We stopped, just like everybody else. It was just too much to deal with." Nalini could see the Admiral assessing her sanity in real time, preparing her words carefully before responding.

"I don't understand how you could talk about anything else."

"Monumental Muting." The liquor was kicking in, and Nalini was already tired. She should have eaten something before partying. This was all new for Admiral Ethel, but it really wasn't for her. And even though Nalini understood that the first days on New Roanoke were the most confusing ones, she had no desire to relive those feelings with the Admiral.

"Monumental Muting: the societal habit of avoiding topics so monumentally intractable that discussing them has no positive outcomes and countless negative ones. If there're no definitive answers, and every time you talk about it you risk offending or alienating others, why bother? Monumental Muting—that's what I call it in my field research. I have footnotes—I have a lot of footnotes. That's just one of the many original terms I've coined to describe this experience. I've been very busy."

"I bet you have," Admiral Ethel murmured, exhaustion in her tone.

Despite RIO's aesthetic deficiencies, under the dust its interior was pristine, and everything in working order. The walls of the booth they now sat at were largely graffiti-free. The shelves were fully stocked with liquor, and not just the cheap stuff. All the appliances were plugged in. It was the Party of the People's clubhouse; all those pamphlet sales had gone to a good cause. A dive bar.

"Lot to process, Admiral. I get it."

"It's Ethel."

Nalini watched the woman take her own swig before she spoke again.

"I can't believe I'm on a goddamn space colony of unknown and possible extraterrestrial origin and I just got kidnapped."

"You mean the guys who brought us here? They're just the Party of the People volunteers. They're toothless—I mean, that's part of their problem. They're the Washington Generals to the Founders Party's Harlem Globetrotters." The image of the old Founders types in basketball circus gear was enough to make Nalini literally shake her head to get it out. "But we can leave whenever. Wait for them to come back, leave—whatever works for you. Pretty sure I know how to get to the bus stop from here. But don't worry about the PoP—my former lab partner is the nominal head, the public face, I guess—"

"Dwayne Causwell. I know who he is. I know who you are—I know about everyone from the *Delany*."

"Well, look at you! Yeah, Dwayne. So he runs the PoP. They'll come get us soon. I mean, yeah, it's probably worth waiting. I'm too tired for the bus, anyways." Nalini gave an exaggerated and booming sigh that indicated to herself that she was already a little drunk. Or at least on the verge of it, if she didn't slow down immediately.

Admiral Ethel paused as she gave her own, lighter sigh. "I have so many questions. I wish you were willing to answer more of them."

"Okay, fine. Boring answer: Underneath the impossibility of its existence, New Roanoke is just like a lot of places back home. Creepily, nauseatingly the same—take it from an applied sociologist. The rich hate the poor because they're scared the poor will take their money and make them poor, too. The poor either hate the rich for hoarding everything or love them because they think they'll be rich someday, too. That's the basic outline. Hilarity ensues."

"Hilarity," Ethel repeated, holding the tumbler with the ice to her head.

# CHAPTER 8

"Welcome to the fifty-first state. I kid, but can you believe all this, am I right? You get what I mean." And with that, former Chief Mission Science Officer Bob Seaford started the film projector, a pre-digital antique the likes of which Chase had only seen in old movies. When he caught Chase staring at it, Bob added, "Just FYI, they're a little behind tech-wise, but I look at it like this: That just means opportunity. For innovation. This little outreach film here is one of the upgrades I've introduced in my current role as the newest Vice Deputy Party Chairman."

"Outreach to whom?" Talbot's notepad was still poised in hand; the man leaned back in his chair, legs folded. Chase noticed Lloyd's socks, which looked like they were there to be noticed: poinsettia red that glowed so bright they looked plugged in. *Oh, wow, that's what fancy socks are for,* Chase marveled. They're for looking strong when you sit cross-legged in a business meeting, like Lloyd Talbot.

"Excellent question. I'll tell you whom: whomever the cave spits out. We want to get new arrivals started on the right foot." Bob kicked his own right foot a bit forward for emphasis. Chase was starting to remember the guy now, from the *Delany* personnel files. He'd been the only one to tell jokes in his recorded psych eval. And Chase had been the only one in the briefing room to laugh at them. Chase didn't get too far into the *Delany* profile files, because they were boring, but he saw enough to get an impression of that digital Bob, and this Bob standing before them was totally that guy. Most people Chase met in person after encountering them primarily online were entirely different in the flesh. Something in the way they moved or talked or even how tall they were—it never matched up to Chase's mental image. But Bob was just like that Bob. A guy who would remember your name. A guy people shared crazy stories about. Like there was an actual center in the universe, and this guy was damn sure he was standing on it.

On the screen, there was the cave system they'd flown through when they entered New Roanoke hours before. But this time, Chase saw the area from the view of someone standing on the river's bank. Beyond, a gaping hollow in a granite hill. The river itself was way bigger than it looked from the air, and running faster. What Chase had first taken to be a large stream was actually damn near the size of the Mississippi. From the cave's utter blackness emerged a full-sized, fully loaded container ship, just floating through. Coming from nowhere, because there was nothing on the other side of that cave but the open vacuum of deep space, and not even Admiral Ethel knew how the air in the dome wasn't just sucked out into space. The image of the freighter edged slowly across the screen, the opening credits appearing over its top. *Welcome to New Roanoke!* Chase could see markings on the rusted metal cargo, in a language he was pretty sure was Chinese. Lloyd Talbot was scribbling on his pad like crazy, so Chase figured it meant something to him. After scenic pics of all the "fifty-first state" had to offer, the voiceover kicked in, talking about the entire history of New Roanoke.

"That's me talking," Bob said. "That's my announcer voice. I've always wanted to dabble in voice acting."

For a "state" the size of one county, New Roanoke had it all: diseased invaders and their land grab, an eighteenth-century war over whether it thought it was a British colony or a whole new deal, race-based slavery and an abolitionist movement to get rid of slavery, a war when they couldn't work it out, and all the stuff that followed. Women getting the right to vote, a civil-rights movement, the whole shebang. Staying up-to-date on the real America via all the new abductees. A slow but steady supply of fresh immigrants, plucked from their lives on Earth and deposited on a barge with the rest of the goods.

When the tourism vid's credits ran, Bob's name was all over the screen. The man himself started talking before his men could get the lights on.

"Trust me, guys, I know what you're wondering. You're asking, *How is all this possible?* Lloyd, am I right? Right?"

No one said anything until Lloyd realized Bob was waiting for an answer. "You are most certainly right."

"Specifically, you're wondering, *Who created and maintains this place?* Of course you are. And you've probably heard the official Founders Party position? God? And, I don't know, maybe that's right, or not: Again, I don't know. But I do know this: It ain't people. Okay? Let that soak in. It'll take a minute. Trust me.

"But, whatever it is, to create all this? It's basically a god, in comparison to us. So, unless you're really into theology, I wouldn't waste my time with that part. Not worth it. There's no evidence to find. No little green men in town. So you just got to roll with it, enjoy it for what it is and don't drive yourself crazy."

Chase wanted to ask if that meant there were tall gray aliens, but Harry, breathing heavily, stared over at him like he sensed the question and wanted to shut it down before it came out of Chase's mouth.

With some flourish, Lloyd Talbot unfolded his legs and leaned forward. "So you're saying you've seen nothing extraordinary since you've been here?"

"I've seen absolutely nothing. And I say that with pride."

"Amen," Vice Deputy Chairman Brett Cole seconded, then immediately covered his mouth with his hand, as if silencing himself.

"Mr. Seaford, I want you to be absolutely clear with me. I want a complete understanding—that's my goal, because we need that. Are you telling me you've seen no evidence of what might be responsible for all this?"

Bob's hands were before him and waving for Lloyd to stop, like a traffic cop's. "Slow down! I showed you mine; time for you to show me yours, right? So—what are you guys doing? What's your plan?"

Next to Chase, Harry opened his mouth but was stopped by the sound of Lloyd Talbot clearing his throat. Pushing himself up, then walking to the front of the table, Lloyd moved with the confidence of a man who considered boardrooms his natural habitat. "Okay. I can respect your caution. I can tell you that, in the hull of the *Ursula 50*, we have the printers and material to make five more shuttles. Immediately. And that, in the onboard computer, we have the plans to build the factories that can reproduce many, many more. A production plan devised down to the number of toilets needed in the warehouse. I come prepared to offer the leadership of this society an option that would allow them to get every human being off this moon in under five years." Lloyd stopped, stepped back, folded his arms, and, with no expression resting on his face, waited for Bob's reaction. They all waited. But the room was quiet. "Any questions?" Lloyd finally asked, but still nothing. Up until the moment Bob and Brett looked at each other and burst out laughing.

"Gentlemen, gentlemen." Bob waved off his own mirth as he composed himself. "You don't get it yet. I understand—you just got here. The thing is, we're doing really great, as is. We're doing amazing, actually. What's not to love in New Roanoke? The housing's luxurious, the schools are fantastic, there's low crime. None of that global-warming BS. No pandemics, no war, no nukes other than the one on your ship. This is the place where the American dream's still alive."

"But, *Bob*, you can go back home now. This is why we're here. This is an exploratory operation, but we're also here to bring you and your crew home."

"I hear you, I hear you. But wait until you see our restaurant row—you're gonna flip." Bob was already shutting down the projector, clearing his things off the conference table.

"Mr. Seaford," Lloyd Talbot started. "*Bob*. Are you seriously prepared to throw your life on Earth away to be stuck here? And do you think everybody else trapped here feels the same way?"

"You're looking at it all wrong, buddy." Bob's words disagreed, but he was never disagreeable. It was just a difference of opinion between pals. "New Roanoke isn't a prison—it's a new frontier. We shouldn't be talking about leaving, we should be talking trade routes! Or tourism! Or, even better, figuring out the tech that makes all this possible, right? Forget who did it, the more important question is, how do we harness it? Can you even imagine how much that would be worth?"

"The man does make an excellent point." Harry's voice was now fuller, but still weaker than Chase was used to hearing. "I can think of a legion of investors who'd be willing to venture on that."

Lloyd looked at Harry, then looked at Chase to see if the old man was joking. Chase had no idea, no idea at all. So Lloyd gave a sigh. "I respect your impulse, and your instincts, but the issue of commerce can wait until—"

"Word to the wise—folks here are very strong on tradition," Bob said in full voice before dropping into a softer, jovially conspiratorial tone. "But they're even stronger on making money. You want to butter them up, this is the best way forward. I will gladly serve as a liaison."

"I'll need to see more of the architecture," Harry offered, as if remembering why he was there. "The military—"

With a snap, then a finger pointed, Bob lit up as he turned in Harry's direction. "Wait till you see them: They march a lot. Pretty damn solid for a place with no enemies on the planet."

"To your point," Lloyd continued, "there actually has been some discussion on our end, just theoretically, that it might be feasible to run a series of satellite way stations for communications and supplies. Extending the Mars route, possibly within—"

Mid-sentence, Lloyd Talbot's head snapped sharply to the right.

It was jarring and instant; it looked like the guy'd been slapped. Chase even thought he heard the crisp clapping sound of a slap.

"What?" Lloyd stumbled on his feet for a moment and looked at Harry like he'd done something.

"You okay?" Springing up from his chair, Chase went to Lloyd with his arms out to catch him, because that's what the color of Lloyd's face implied: fainting.

"I'm fine. Just a muscle spasm, I think. Hit me out of nowhere."

"That's nothing, it happens here. Pay it no mind," Brett interjected. "Do you need some painkillers? We've got aspirin, acetaminophen, ibuprofen—"

"Really, I'll be okay," Lloyd insisted. But the look on his face sent a whole other message. "As I was saying: Normalizing relations between our governments is possible. But let's not get ahead of ourselves. First we have to get a better notion of what exactly is going on here, at least to establish safety. Then, sure, it's possible to set up a string of way stations to evacuate—" Lloyd's head shuddered. Chase saw it move. Like a vibration. Like a hummingbird. Like faster than any person could imitate. Lloyd paused again, holding his temples, grimacing.

"Dude, maybe you should take a break," Chase told him, but the man waved him off like he was being modest. He loosened his tie. Unbuttoned his shirt. Then Lloyd reached for the pitcher on the table. Chase grabbed it first, though, and poured Lloyd a glass of water, handed it over.

"Not you, too, Lloyd? Keep it together, man." Harry seemed confused that someone else was allowed to be sick. They all watched silently as Lloyd swallowed the full glass in one go. One big, desperate gulp.

"Bit of the jet lag?" Bob asked, so low Chase didn't know if anyone else could hear him.

Harry snorted. "*Cryogenic sleep.* It's not natural."

"Exactly. Just a long trip. That's all." Lloyd, flinching, stopped him. "As I was saying, creating a commercial partnership would be no small feat, but—who knows—eventually? If you think it would smooth the evacuation, then, sure, eventually, it is possible. On behalf of the United Nations, let me just officially state that I would like to offer escape for all who—"

That was the moment when UN Special Envoy Lloyd Talbot's head exploded.

# CHAPTER 9

When Nalini and the Admiral were finally picked up from Club RIO, enough time had passed that it was dark outside and they'd sobered up. There was a knock on the door, and then the sound of keys opening it, and all of a sudden there was a cowboy hat covered in purple sequins. Under that hat, a little lady old enough to be Admiral Ethel's mother.

"Dwayne sent me," she said. "You can call me 'Doris,' " she added, making air quotes with her hands. "We're going to the secret hideout." Her tone made it clear that this was a big deal; then she motioned impatiently for them to follow her outside.

"Used to be able to see the damn things," they heard Doris muttering as they followed her. She headed down the alley toward a white school bus, *AME Bethel Church of the New Zion* in chipped paint on its side. "If people tried together, they could—or at least make it clearer. But who'd want to try? Even before it got this bad?" It was as if Doris didn't just know what they'd been talking about before she arrived, but couldn't imagine they'd be talking about anything else.

When the Admiral asked, "Could you elaborate?," Doris seemed to jump slightly in surprise, as if she didn't realize she had been talking aloud. She didn't say anything more until she was seated behind the bus's wheel, when she delivered, in an announcement voice: "Just a bit of legend. Bit of rumor. Way, way before my time—what do I know? Nothing, that's what I know. So let me shut up." The last statement Doris apparently meant literally, because, once she started the engine, she ignored all questioning, instead focusing on lighting the first of many in an uninterrupted chain of cigarettes as she drove them out of the city and beyond.

"Where are we now?" Admiral Ethel said in a hushed tone, leaning forward from her seat in the row behind Nalini.

"Just the suburbs." Nalini turned her body back to tell her. When Admiral Ethel raised her hand to motion for more, Nalini continued in her more formal, academic tone. "In most ways, New Roanoke functions like any American city, with a largely bifurcated political culture. But during my study of its social construction of reality, it became clear that—like many supposedly bifurcated societies—it's really made up of a ten-twenty-forty-twenty-ten sociopolitical structure. Right now, I'm trying to give each subgroup a full chapter in my manuscript."

"And this means?" the Admiral said, sighing.

"'Pyramid Partisanship' is the term I'm coining in my manuscript. Meaning, at any given moment you can break down its polarization to roughly: Ten percent Malcontents—consisting primarily of those the society serves the least, as well as a few who were just constitutionally miserable. Then there's twenty percent who just dislike it. Then you have the majority, the forty percent who really don't care, they just want to live their lives with the privilege of not having to think about it—my 'Floaters.' After that, a good twenty percent like it here fine enough. And then the final ten percent, the Beneficiaries—the Founders types—they absolutely love New Roanoke. They've convinced themselves this actually is some kind of heaven, which is understandable, given that it is for them, as the ones the society is structured to most benefit. Members of all the other groups present themselves as true believers, but it's often performed as an act of social camouflage. Pretending to be part of the most powerful social segment, a defensive maneuver. That's the elite that, as soon as we got here, Bob *immediately* lodged himself in, like a five-foot-tall parasite."

"The Bob thing could be helpful, give us an ambassador within the ruling party."

"Yeah, I guess, but whatever." And, regaining her tone, Nalini added: "This suburban landscape is essentially the Floaters' natural habitat, where they maintain their militantly apolitical numerical majority. In that regard, the remote location assists in achieving another Floater goal: strategic ignorance of sociopolitical realities. There are others here, too, of course, but they're outnumbered— although, due to the caste camouflaging, it's clear the Founders subgroup is often clueless as to the limited percentage of people who really buy their bullshit." And because the Admiral finally looked sufficiently bored, Nalini stopped and turned around again.

In this land of finite size, one with a stable population, New Roanoke somehow managed to keep a seemingly infinite supply of newly built suburban homes, constructed so that families could live in newly designed subdivisions with nostalgia-infused names to give them the illusion of history and permanence: Fisher's Rock. Emerald Plantation. The Meadows at Sterling Cliff. They all offered a visual approximation of the New Roanokan ideal: securing a nuclear family surrounded by an abundance of wealth and space. McMansions so big they could house normally communal entertainments— restaurant-sized kitchens, home movie theaters, personal pools. The focus on private versus communal distractions was essential because of their remote location, chosen because decreased land values meant more money could be invested in the luxury of the house. They were far removed from the city, which had these same amenities in abundance, but you had to share them.

Living out there made all those stressful issues feel, literally, so far away. And though "floating" implied not making any effort at all, even this quick drive through their breeding grounds betrayed the tremendous effort that went into maintaining willful ignorance. Passing the seemingly endless stream of nearly identical subdivisions, Nalini could see from the road the artificial nature of the oversized residences. Plastic faux-wood window shutters that presumably would guard windows if they weren't functionally unable to close. Façades of hollow brick made to look solid, an illusion betrayed by vinyl siding on the sides and backs of the bloated structures. Beautiful porches not actually wide enough to place a rocker upon. So big, so close together, the structures looked like they were in a sales lot for life-sized dollhouses, all so the developers could squeeze the most profit possible from their finite land lot. Would-be homes silently waiting to be chosen by a buyer and placed on acres of proportional land. While ostensibly offering social permanence, these single-family homes were likely to be single-generation housing as well. Instead of offering the community promised by smiling neighbors in stock art advertisements, these subdivisions offered the opportunity to never have to leave the house and deal with the social horror of talking to others. Maintaining blindness to these glaring contradictions took an act of faith that Nalini found impressive. Even more intriguing, of all the segments of New Roanokan society, the willfully apolitical Floaters spent more energy than rabid Founders or Malcontents to maintain their political stance that they didn't have a political stance.

"Recognize where we're going?" Admiral Ethel asked from behind.

"Northeast? Toward the industrial end, I think. Southwest's agricultural, rural-ish. The west is mostly forest." As Nalini talked, the road became rougher, and the tires rumbled over the gravel. "Doris," who'd been lightly singing something to herself, now began coughing as well, the sound combining into a phlegm-filled yodel which continued until they'd passed through the suburbs to the barren, industrial land beyond.

"The secret hideout," Doris said.

*Horseshoe River Sewage Treatment Plant,* said the sign over the entrance, and they turned left through its rusted gate and headed down a dirt driveway. They saw an old radio tower on the slight hill. Tall and rusting. It held progressively newer broadcast dishes seemingly randomly attached to its frame.

"Used to be, Party of the People was the workers' voice! Or aimed to be. There was no paid weekend here—Party of the People got us that. Same with children working, and forty hours—that didn't drop off the barge, we had to fight for that. We did it. Those were the days. Before they legislated the teeth out of them."

The windows of the building they approached were boarded up and painted the same dark gray as its cinder-block walls. Desolate, unlit, it looked to Nalini like a place you would go to get murdered. No front doors, just slabs of plywood, thick metal chains looping through two sawed-out holes. Doris came to a stop right by the door, and when she opened the door and got off, the other women followed. For a small woman, Doris had a big knock, hitting so hard she had to hold her hat so it didn't fall off.

When the chains dropped and the doors opened, Nalini saw men with rifles standing guard just beyond. But what surprised her more was how many people were inside. How crowded the seemingly abandoned building actually was.

"This way." Doris walked ahead, in the lead. The others in the room stood as the women passed. Dozens of them, staring silently. Turning to examine Nalini and Admiral Ethel as they moved

through their crowded lobby as if this were a wedding proces-
sional.

"What's up?" Nalini said to a gaunt college-age kid she passed,
because the young woman was staring so intently at her that it was
really awkward.

"You were . . . totally amazing," the kid said back, and banged
her fist on her chest in a display of heartfelt respect, a common gesture among younger Malcontents.

The others in the crowded room, frozen silent before, burst forth
with their own calls of "Yeah," and "Fantastic," and "Totally," which
totally freaked out Nalini even more. Made her speed up to reach
the stairs at the back of the room just to get away from it all.

"What the hell was that?" she whispered to herself, but it was
Doris who responded.

"Your little speech at the rocket ship: Somebody pirate-streamed
it, sweetie. Live. To every free screen in New Roanoke. You're a celebrity now." Nalini had no idea if she was being sarcastic or, terrify-
ingly, accurate.

In Nalini's last life as a post-doc applied sociologist who'd do anything to raise her academic profile, she'd had occasion to visit several
broadcast studios, offering unpaid but expert analysis on sociological
phenomena in America's ever-fractious partisan cultural conflicts,
in exchange for getting to be on TV. From this experience, Nalini felt
she knew what a television studio floor was supposed to look like:
loud, crowded, dozens of stories being built at once. But the second
floor of this building was just abandoned recording studios and hollow office cubicles. Obsolete equipment, a general state of disrepair.
Only one of the glass-walled rooms even had its lights on. And
Dwayne was inside it.

Doris turned back to Nalini and Ethel when they reached the
studio door, silently motioning for them to wait while she went in
first. She even extinguished her cigarette for the occasion, choking it

out under her sneaker right there on the grim carpet. In the broadcast room, about a dozen people surrounded Dwayne, clearly trying and failing to offer counsel—Nalini recognized that intransigent expression he wore all over his body when he was being a pain in the ass. The PoP members looked up before Doris walked back to invite Nalini and the Admiral in.

First thing Nalini noticed in the room were the posters, all declaring *DWAYNE,* as if this name was a sacred mantra in itself.

"What, no statues?" she asked, pointing at the image of his massive head, the bloated words *PARTY OF THE PEOPLE* beneath. It wasn't her first time seeing the images; they were pasted illegally across town, usually half ripped down. It was just the first opportunity Nalini had been given to mess with him about it.

"It's about brand building, lady. It's not an ego thing, okay? If anything, I'm turning myself into a mascot for the cause of freedom." Dwayne had apparently been doing a lot of stress eating since those photos were taken.

"That's what Mussolini said." One of Dwayne's entourage audibly stifled a guffaw at Nalini's crack, but Dwayne just rolled his eyes.

"By the time I got out to the park today, it was over. Dozens were hospitalized. I heard a police officer even died. What a mess." Dwayne sighed, then turned directly to Nalini, pointing at her. "But you? You were great. They didn't see that coming. Now, I knew you'd be great, but still: You were even better than my limited imagination."

In his time in New Roanoke, Dwayne had become a collection of circles, from his nose to his belly to his inflated arms and thighs. Despite the PoP ads, he looked less like a freedom fighter than a newly divorced dad. Not just a father, but a dad—a man who brings his own foldout chair to soccer practice.

"Ethel Dodson, Admiral of the SS *Ursula 50,*" Admiral Ethel said with her hand out.

"I heard. Do you know who I am?" Dwayne asked as he shook it.

"Of course." Ethel nodded. "You're part of my mission."

"And that mission would be?"

"To get you out of here. To get everyone out of here."

And with that, the others—Dwayne, and his sycophants or lieu-tenants or whoever they were—let out a collective cheer too loud for the little soundproof room.

Nalini took a seat at the soundboard, hungry and thirsty and so-bering up. "Lovely cult you have there."

"Way you were out there today? You should start your own." Dwayne offered Ethel another swivel chair and, when she sat, asked her, "How much do you know? About this place? About our situa-tion?"

"After the space shuttle *Delany* returned, unoccupied, we sent back drones; we've been monitoring the city—"

"*Camp*. The Party of the People prefers to refer to it as a 'camp,' as in 'refugee camp.' Also, 'camp' implies a more temporary nature," Dwayne interrupted.

Admiral Ethel took a good look at him for a moment before con-tinuing. "We've been monitoring with drones, starting over a year ago. We've mapped the exterior extensively, and the interior to a lesser degree."

" 'We'?"

"NASAx, in partnership with the UN and the support of a private donor. Without public report or commentary."

"So nobody else knows we're here? This isn't national news?" Na-lini interrupted, because she was genuinely surprised at that part. It seemed like being kidnapped by aliens might make a blip in the daily news cycle. Her fantasies for the future of *The Collected* did not in-clude anonymity.

"Not at this point. It is still classified, for now. We're considering this first contact before we—"

Dwayne stopped her by waving his hands frantically. "Let me get this straight: You've been flying little cameras around our heads, gathering info on New Roanoke for who knows how long, and that thing let you fly the drones back out again?"

" 'That thing'?" the Admiral asked. "I'm sorry, I don't follow."

Nalini didn't realize how much movement there was in the room until everybody froze. Dwayne noticed, too, and, without looking, said, "Folks, I understand your anxiety, but it's time for some real talk. So I'm going to need everyone not comfortable with that conversation to clear the room."

In moments, all but Nalini and the Admiral quickly excused themselves out the door, with nary a protest.

The three stood silently. Even Dwayne, who insisted that discussing this topic openly was essential, seemed hesitant to take it further. "Nalini, come on. You ain't tell her? How is that not, like, the first thing you debriefed her on?"

"Because I don't know enough to." Nalini turned directly to the Admiral. "Because it's not something New Roanokans speak on. Sometimes they do, but even then, they usually just talk around it."

"I don't like vague conversations that hint at essential information being withheld from me," Admiral Ethel declared as if this were a mission statement on her website.

"It's not a big deal," Nalini muttered.

"It's a very big deal," Dwayne added before Nalini could continue. "I would argue that—"

"Just tell me what's going on here. Please," Admiral Ethel interrupted before they could continue. And so Dwayne told her.

The Admiral took it all in like a trouper. Or like an admiral, Nalini assumed. Dwayne kept going, recounting anecdotes, explaining his theories—some Nalini herself had never even heard before—and she watched the older woman grow more horrified as he went. Seeing her distress, feeling her own, Nalini reached out to gently put her hand on Admiral Ethel's to comfort her. It was immediately clear that it was too intimate a gesture for both of them.

"Wonderful. Just wonderful," Admiral Ethel said when Dwayne was finally finished. "This was supposed to be my last adventure. This was supposed to be my glorious final send-off. So what are we supposed to do about"—she paused, caught herself before continuing—"*them*?"

Nalini noted that the Admiral was already adjusting to local traditions nicely.

# CHAPTER 10

When Chase looked down, slack-jawed, at what remained of Lloyd Talbot's head on the carpet, he realized his initial analysis was totally wrong. Lloyd's head hadn't exploded. It had gotten crushed. Like a raw egg squeezed in a bodybuilder's hand. All the stuff inside Lloyd's head had become outside stuff. It was really hard to look at.

Chase's own head exploded, too, but only metaphorically. Not the kind that got bone and skin and blood everywhere, like Lloyd Talbot's head did.

*So Lloyd doesn't have a head anymore,* some part of Chase told himself. Lloyd's body still had pieces of a head, but not in the proper arrangement. Chase couldn't get over how Lloyd's athletic and immaculately dressed body kept standing there for a second after, as if it were considering its post-head options, before falling down.

The conference room suddenly became very loud, and, to Chase's surprise, not all of the screams came from him.

"He had a heart attack!" Brett Cole started yelling, pointing at

Lloyd's decapitated body like it had cheated at something. "A heart attack!" he yelled again, like someone was about to fight him over the point.

"What are you talking about, man? His head just blew up!" Chase managed. He couldn't bear to look at the parts of UN Special Envoy Lloyd Talbot that remained. "Can we get him some help?" Chase really wanted to know. Realizing the person in charge of their mission had left the position, Chase looked to Harry to see what to do next. Harry was at the far end of the conference room. Somehow, he'd fallen into a chair, then rolled in it as far away from the now gushing body of Lloyd as he could without leaving the room.

"Harry?" Chase hurried over to him. The big guy's eyes were staring up at the ceiling. All whites, his pupils barely making an appearance.

"Harry? I got you, man." There was no response. Chase caught himself thinking, *But Harry always has the last word,* and in a flash felt guilty for it.

The old man's pupils fortunately popped back down, but they stared off at nothing. His arms shot forward, and Chase thought Harry was reaching for him, but the guy's hands went to his heart instead. Harry's lips were the blue of dead whales; his usually pale-pink face was now one big sweaty maroon ball.

"What kind of bullshit is this, man?" Chase heard himself ask this out loud. No one answered him. Bob wasn't even in the room anymore; the door to the hall was now open.

Chase yelled, "Come on. Don't you all got nine-one-one?"

"A heart attack," Brett Cole said once more, pointing at Lloyd on the ground, with less energy this time.


To Chase's dismay, a doctor in the ER said Harry actually had had a heart attack. Also, a big knot behind his left ear from pushing his chair back so fast to get away from Lloyd that he'd accidentally slammed his head into the wall. It was the biggest Chase had ever seen: like those gargantuan corporate peaches they sell at Costco. But Harry was finally in a bed and being seen to, at least.

"Chase, a sip."

Chase grabbed a Styrofoam cup of water off the hospital bed table, then aimed the straw into Harry's mouth. The old man looked as white as copy paper. Water dribbled down into the hairs of his chin when Harry released the straw, his wrinkled lips sucking air like those of a newborn off a teat.

"I called around." Bob Seaford was back, after disappearing for what felt like hours, standing guard beside Harry's hospital bed. "He's going to be taken care of by the best doctors, the absolute best. I made sure of it. I can't believe they let him do a cryo-jump with that cardiac profile. But, for now, the docs say he just needs medication and rest. And nobody's bothering him here."

"All this fuss. Absurd," Harry muttered, his eyes closed and his voice growing fainter with every syllable. "Take me to a hotel, goddamnit. And make sure it's a nice one." That was the last thing he managed.

"Harry, I don't think that's the best idea," Chase said to him, because he didn't want to go anywhere but back on the cryoship and get out of there. He wanted to get Ada, of course, sure, but he didn't want to do anything else. He didn't want to *see* anything else: specifically, something else like Lloyd Talbot's head getting crushed like a maggot under a thumb. He was already seeing that, on loop, in his mind.

Chase waited until he and Bob were out of Harry's private room and in the elevator before asking, "What the hell happened to Lloyd Talbot? He's like a bigwig at the United Nations, man—what the hell? That was the nastiest shit I've seen in my entire life." It'd been two hours since Lloyd's covered body was rolled out of the Founders

Party headquarters on a gurney and pushed into an ambulance, its lights spinning urgently, as if there were anything anyone could do for him.

"Decompression." Bob shrugged.

"Decompression? *Decompression?* What the hell does that mean?"

"It's a working theory." The elevator door opened on the lobby, and Bob Seaford shot out of there.

"Oh, good, a 'working theory.' That's just great. Is it going to work on Harry next? Or me?"

"My driver should be back now."

"What does that even mean? *Decompression.*" Chase followed him out the front doors. "Is it going to keep happening? To all of us?"

"Well, Chase, you guys didn't arrive in New Roanoke like normal people: by just waking up here. You flew in on your own; that's never been done before. So they're saying it might be like a compression thing. You know, like with scuba diving. Scuba diving kills people all the time. Totally normal—but it should be safe now."

Standing in front of the hospital, Bob waved his hand in the air, and Chase could see a limo in the distance pulling out of a parking spot to head toward them. "Yep. All the time. These things happen."

" 'These things happen'?" Chase was prepared to repeat every nonsensible thing Bob said back to him. He caught himself turning to see Lloyd Talbot's reaction to this craziness, but Talbot wasn't there because of the fact that his head had imploded. "One second, he looked fine . . ."

"He looked pale."

"Lloyd was a pale guy! Like, Icelandic or something—something Viking. Then it was like he got slapped. And then . . ." Chase stopped, breathed in as he saw it once more. "I mean, come on."

"Yeah. Listen, an FYI: You gotta just ignore the slapping thing."

Chase snapped his own head to look at him. Bob opened the back door of the limo himself and hopped inside. Chase kept staring at him in confusion before giving up and getting in as well. "What are you talking about, 'the slapping'?"

"Not trying to freak you out. It's nothing, really. But, occasionally, just so you know, you might be minding your business and you'll feel something. Something that might feel like a pat. Or even a slap, let's say. So don't freak out, it's nothing. Very rare. Not even worth talking about."

" 'A slap'?" Chase didn't really know if he wanted the answer.

"Yeah, but that's it. In the face, usually, but not often. Not, like, bruising-level hard. It's nothing. Don't even mention it; apparently, that makes it worse." As they pulled forward, Bob put a hand on Chase's shoulder. Whether this was to hold his attention or to reassure him, Chase wasn't sure.

Suddenly aware that during his captivity Bob Seaford might have lost his marbles, Chase spoke carefully. "Bob, I don't understand what you're trying to tell me. Who slaps you?"

"Nobody. But here's the thing: It's a taboo to discuss it, so you don't want to bring it up in public—nobody wants to deal with that. I mean, what's the point? Not a damn thing you can do about it. Superstitions and all that. Just makes people upset."

Chase remembered Admiral Ethel going over Robert Seaford's file. The way she'd talked about his psych profile made Bob sound like he could be an asshat, but not a delusional asshat. "Okay, fine. Whatever. No biggie, then."

"Exactly. No biggie. We got better stuff to talk about anyway." Bob paused and nodded, as if he were tucking a somber reality into bed. Then, in a completely new, energized tone, he announced, "Drinks at my place!"

# CHAPTER 11

Despite the reaction of the Malcontents who comprised the Party of the People, Nalini did not consider her part in instigating a riot to have been an effective way of addressing the critical issue of mass exodus from New Roanoke. In fact, Nalini knew she would have likely labeled it counterproductive if someone else had done it. It was an act of impulse and catharsis, and it was very successful if judged by that criterion—yelling at that tubby, certified grade-A Founders Party hack had felt transcendent. She couldn't stand those assholes. But she also knew there were far more effective actions she might have taken instead to increase the chance of reaching her goal of, effectively, blowing this town.

Nalini was not surprised, however, that the PoP members, and Dwayne himself, saw her behavior as a win. In her time studying the Malcontent subgroup, both in casual encounters and in talks with Dwayne that derailed into the political, Nalini had identified a tendency to value cathartic acts over practical ones. In slogans, protests, and sometimes even in their platform itself (given what she could tell from their pamphlets), actionable goals were presented as the sole motivation for their actions, but in practice, ideological purity was considered sacrosanct in comparison to all other concerns. Instead of focusing on building alliances and membership by attracting people from the other roughly 90 percent of the population, the PoP members were more concerned with perpetually criticizing their existing ranks to increase each subgroup's purity. In fact, Nalini had often heard Dwayne reject possible allies (Ahmed, repeatedly) largely because they only agreed with PoP principles 60 percent of the time. So, although the Malcontents relied on a self-aggrandizing mythology that their sole motivation was to further the cause of the majority (and for some this was so), it appeared that their own majority was more focused on winning the argument for their ideas than on actually getting to implement them. The Party of the People was, and had always been, by definition, a "lost cause" movement: an exodus cult that had no means of leaving. As Dwayne gave Admiral Ethel his complicated and likely overwrought explanation of New Roanoke's practical realities, Nalini was struck by the notion of how invaluable it would be to her research to witness the effects of having a real chance at total success on a group founded on nihilistic romantic impossibility.

When Dwayne finally paused to take a breath, Admiral Ethel ran a presentation of her NASAx Europa Exodus Action Plan from her tablet. It was simple, it was well thought out, it was easily explained. There was a main video outlining the goals and processes of mass immigration, from industrial cryoship production to reintegration of ex-abductees into real American life. Even for NASAx, it was very ambitious. In fact, it was everything Nalini could hope for, which is why the lack of visual change in Dwayne's demeanor annoyed her so much.

"What? Come on, this has to be good news, right?" Nalini said directly to Dwayne as if Admiral Ethel weren't in the room. "If they were able to send drones in and out, and nothing stopped them?"

"Nalini, you can't ignore the invisible things. You can't just write them off because you are repulsed by the idea. That's how it got this bad."

"Gravitational fluctuations," Nalini quickly said in an aside to the Admiral.

Dwayne gave up on Nalini and spoke directly to the Admiral as well. "They ignored it, like everything else here that's contradictory, inconvenient. Pretended it wasn't there for so long that now it's out of control, and they're totally unprepared to deal with it. The Founders aren't prepared to admit it's even real. They can't: Too many lies are built on its foundation."

"Well, that's unfortunate," the Admiral agreed, patiently. "But that's also not our immediate problem. We need to focus on one thing: getting out of here."

"You mean it, huh? You really think you can just fly us out of here." As he talked, Dwayne looked off and scrunched his face in confusion as he tried to imagine it. "I mean, how?"

"Same way we got the drones out," Admiral Ethel told him. "Follow the waste barges through your river, into the cave and into orbit. Whatever brought you here, it didn't stop us from entering, so I assume we'll be able to get out."

"Okay. Let's say we go by your assumption. If so, we should definitely distribute this info to the people as soon as possible. But I'm going to be real: If we're really trying to bounce with the *Delany* crew, we should probably just go immediately, while the establishment's still disoriented. Longer you wait, the trickier it will be. Trust me." Dwayne started pulling out drawers from the ancient metal desks that surrounded them, not stopping till he found both pen and paper. "First issue: Nalini, where, even, is everybody? Ahmed is still selling out at the RBC building, I know that. I heard one of the Bobs got placed as an eighth-grade biology teacher at Falling Springs. What about Sasha—have you seen her? And AJ, can you get to her now?"

"Now? What are you talking about?" As Nalini watched, Dwayne drew a crude map on his scrap paper, writing down names on one side of it.

Ignoring her, Dwayne continued talking to himself if to no one else. "This time of day, they should all be back from work. But we could spread out, maybe gather the crew by midnight, get everyone on that ship before these zealots pull something. Everyone but Bob, of course. Because fuck Bob."

"Mr. Causwell, that is not the plan." Admiral Ethel was perfectly composed, and unmoved by his increasingly frantic demeanor.

"Okay, fine, we'll take Bob. But tell him last so he doesn't pull something. You know what? Forget that: We should throw a pillowcase over his head and sedate him. We can tell him when we're in the air. No, even better: Throw him in cryo and tell him after we land in Boca Chica—that's the safest."

Dwayne was still writing names down when Nalini put her hand over his pen to stop him. "You're not listening to her. She's thinking bigger picture."

"Okay, whatever." Dwayne put the pen down, looked at Admiral Ethel directly. "So how long, specifically, is this grand plan of yours going to take? Hypothetically speaking."

"Long term, this is about assisting everyone. Delivering the information needed to adjust the industrial facilities here to produce enough cryoships to evacuate every human who wishes will take time." And when Dwayne just stared at her, the Admiral offered, "Five years, give or take. Schedule permitting."

" 'Five years, give or take'? Unbelievable. Who's the UN bureaucrat who thought that was a brilliant strategy? 'Give or take,' she says. You hear this?"

"Show some respect." From her chair, Nalini kicked him lightly, but hard enough for Dwayne to end the performance.

Admiral Ethel looked to Nalini, who shrugged and offered, "I'm sorry. We've all been through a lot."

"Don't apologize for me." From a desk drawer pocket, Dwayne pulled out a pack of Marlboro Reds, and held it up to them like it meant something.

"No disrespect, Admiral, but see these cigarettes? I got a whole case from a guy down the hall in my building when I first got here. Guy smoked this brand since high school. So, fourteen years ago, he was diagnosed with cancer. Not even lung cancer, which would have been easier to swallow, but skin cancer. Stage Four melanoma—and this was a Black dude from Portland, where it rains nine months out the year. So you know he was pissed. So he jumped off a bridge, and guess what happened?"

"He woke up here," Nalini said, just to speed him up.

"Yup. Woke up here. There's a lot of that—a lot of people here who were probably about to die anyway. Hell, we might have been at risk on the *Delany*. Who knows? The life support was cranky, I kept saying that, but Bob—"

"Who took him? The would-be suicide on the bridge?" Admiral Ethel asked before Dwayne could go off on a tangent again.

"I have no idea; none of us do, you must know that. But here's the thing: Old boy said, when he got to New Roanoke, he didn't have cancer anymore. He was *cured*!" Nalini wasn't looking at the Admiral, but out of the corner of her eye she could see Admiral Ethel startle at what Dwayne had just said.

"A cancer cure," the Admiral said back to him, slowly, to make sure she was clear.

"That's what he said. Said he didn't have cancer no more. Felt great, he said. Said God delivered him from sickness, so, to give thanks, he went full believer, joined the Founders Party and everything. Had to be the only Black guy there. Testified at their little rallies that the force that brought him here also cured him."

"Is that true?" Admiral Ethel asked Nalini, being the more reliable narrator of the two. "What happened to him, where is he now?"

"The damn fool's dead. He died of cancer. That's how I got his smokes."

"Don't be a dick," Nalini told him, and he nodded, like he would seriously take this under consideration.

"Point is, he chose to believe. Believe he was getting better, despite the weight loss. Believe he was one of the chosen ones, even though, when he got sick, the Founders kicked him out—that man was living in the Cavern by the end."

"That's where many of the shelterless end up, unfortunately. A cavernous tent city populated by a permanent underclass. I refer to them in my research as the 'Casualties,' as an opposite to the Beneficiaries, although I don't give them a designation within the Pyramid—"

"Nalini, please stop. Nobody wants to hear that right now." To which Nalini rolled her eyes. "As I was saying, dude was dying in the damn Cavern, and *still* he chose to believe his fairy tale instead of accepting he got kidnapped and left to rot in a space bubble. That's how this place messes with your head."

"It's what I identify as the 'Jenga Effect,'" Nalini began, ignoring Dwayne's sighing. "Once you decide to invest in the uncomfortable reality of the situation—that we have effectively been placed in a planetarium—and buy into the larger New Roanokan mythology of being collected by God, etc., it becomes impossible to let even the strongest of empirical evidence alter your worldview. No matter how big or small."

"Because, as in Jenga, if you pull one piece, the whole thing could come crumbling down." Admiral Ethel nodded at her.

"Exactly," Nalini said. "It's the perfect name for it." And, like

that, she was suddenly thinking of Josey, with whom she had sometimes played the game when home on her winter break. Played until
the girl inevitably became bored and, without warning, knocked the
tower down.

"People like me, we want to go home or die trying," Dwayne explained to the Admiral. "We see this place for what it is. We want to
get out before the bubble bursts, literally. But the rest? Even some
of my own Party of the People members, the moderates: They just
want a chance at the New Roanokan dream, not an exit. Then you
got the others, the descendants, the ones born here with generational wealth and property and investments and power. You think
they're going to trade all that in to live in a cardboard box under an
overpass on I-Four-oh-five? And if they stay and let everyone else
go? Their world disappears, overnight. It would reshuffle the entire
social order, and they like being on top. So we only got one real
option—we need to leave right now."

"You're the main one always talking about *organizing this* and *fighting back* that."

"So you can trust me that I know this place. I've fought for its
people, and I'm just being realistic. You're always saying I'm an impractical romantic, so here's me getting practical. The time, the
money, the level of commitment needed? Nope, sorry. They'll never
adopt your evacuation plan. Their coping mechanism is denial. I
been trying for two years, and I can't even get the general population to take the first step of acknowledging how bad things are. Or
even talk about the invisible-things phenomenon in public—and
that's literally a monster out to get us."

"You don't know that. All we know for certain is that it's a
gravitational—"

" 'Phenomenon.' Yeah, lady, I get it. But the reason we don't
know more is because everybody's too scared to talk about it. Even
you with your 'gravitational phenomenon' bullshit—don't think

it's not obvious that it's another way of indulging in the superstition of not talking about the thing."

When that shut Nalini up, Dwayne looked directly at Admiral Ethel. "We don't just leave them, we leave them with the tools they need—when they're ready. Because I'll tell you right now, they're already planning to steal your ship. Those Founders types are looking at all that tech and licking their chops. That's just how they roll."

"As long as I have the codes for the *Ursula*, I control it." Admiral Ethel tapped her wristband, smiling at it as if it were a precocious grandchild. "I could even ignite the fuel tanks and scuttle it if need be. I love my ship; obviously, I don't want to do that. But anytime I want, I can put in some numbers on this screen and the *Ursula* is over. That buys us time."

Dwayne stared at the monitor hanging above the console, mutely streaming RBC's alternate universe. "The key is controlling the messaging. If we do this, we need to make a statement. Could you talk to Ahmed, see if he'll let us get on air?"

Nalini started shaking her head immediately. "No. Absolutely not. Please, no." Although she knew she could, or she could at least try, but only if it was a final option. "What about on *Steve Sterling at Midday*? I mean, he's kinda fair, compared to the rest, and—"

"Steve Sterling has a job so that when people point out that the RBC is a propaganda network they can go, 'Oh yeah? Well, what about *Steve Sterling at Midday*?' There's a reason he's on at midday: He's got the lowest-rated time slot on the RBC. No, we broadcast this ourselves." And then, smiling, Dwayne added, "Nalini, you're about to be a star."

# CHAPTER 12

When Chase arrived at Bob's place, it turned out to be a vast Mediterranean mansion surrounded by a bunch of other vast Mediterranean mansions. His subdivision wasn't as cramped as some of the others Chase drove by, ones where you could jump from one porch to the next. And it was out there, too, about a half-hour from the hospital and center of town. But talk about "worth the drive." It had a wine cellar bigger than Chase's living room back home. Multiple choices of guest rooms on multiple floors, providing Chase with the opportunity to choose one of each and drink until his pulse chilled out—which he did. It had been a very long day, and he felt well within his rights on that.

When Chase awoke, the alcohol was still hanging around in his bloodstream, and his body was not happy about that. Worse, aside from an extended conversation about the recent post-season results of the NFL, Chase had no idea what he and Bob had talked about the night before; his only certainty was that he had shared too much, because that's what he always did when he got in the cups. Likely, he'd discussed what he usually did when lit: Ada Sanchez. His wife was out there on this moon, Chase could feel it. And he had to find her—if he left without her, he'd return to no life at all.

At breakfast, Chase tried not to get nauseated by his unwanted fried eggs while listening to Bob ramble on.

"Now, the economy here's a trip. They really make nothing. Just a couple factories, nothing essential. And not a lot of local agriculture going on, either. I mean, there's some, but when you look at the numbers, it's basically just for show. No, everything of worth here? It comes in off that barge. Spoon-fed, basically. The real money is in who owns it the second it arrives—and the old school's got that on lock. Once I figured that out, I knew Founders was the way to go."

Chase listened to this and other insights Bob offered, and just waited for enough of a pause to say, "I need to find my wife."

"We'll get on that, we'll get on that, trust me. But, see, what I'm trying to say here is that, if *all* the money and *all* the power comes from just one place—owning the supplies that come in constantly off that barge—and that's controlled by the same people, the same families, over generations, then they basically own the place. The only thing that could change that would be, you know, if someone brought in something of value in some other way. Now you see what I'm saying?"

Chase, who most certainly did not see what Bob was saying, nodded yes, because Bob was getting all excited and loud as he went, and Chase's head was killing him, and he just wanted Bob to shut up. Bob leaned forward and gave him the answer.

"The cryoship, Chase. I'm talking about the cryoship, your *Ursula*. There's billions in tech in there, maybe trillions. And it's cutting-edge military-grade stuff. They don't have anything like that here, and they aren't getting any, either, from what I can see. The supplies they get, it's nothing you can't walk into a Costco and buy back home. Not hologram displays, cryopods, drones—they have no drones here that I've seen. There's not a single commercial field here that couldn't take a leap forward with something on that cash bucket. It's a priceless haul, Chase. And the best part? We own it! How crazy is that?" Bob said, and when he saw the look on Chase's face he added, "By 'we' I mean us representative NASAx-employed American citizens. You get me."

Chase nodded and said "Okay," and nodded some more and said "Okay" some more, until he felt he'd spent the respectful length of time pretending he was interested, and then he asked, "So you going to help me find my wife, right?"

"You mean your ex-wife?" Bob said, confirming Chase's worst morning-after fears. He got a big mouth when he got drunk, and who knows what else he'd said before passing out last night.

"*Ex-wife,* sure. Why I came. You gonna help me or what?" Chase didn't want to sound desperate or needy, but he was, and so he did.

"Just messing with you. Don't worry, champ: You're talking to the right person. I'm going to help you, and you're going to help me. We're going to do great things together. Eat!"

Chase looked down at his plate. Soft yolks hidden under an oily opaque skin—they looked like edible pimples. No way he was putting that in his mouth.

"Wait, check this out." Bob hopped from his seat and grabbed the remote to the kitchen television. As the volume rose, Bob's voice got louder. "You gotta see this; they're running it every hour. You're the lead story, big guy! Here less than twenty-four hours and you're already famous."

Chase had never been on the TV before, but there he was. On the television. Images from yesterday. Chase onstage. Next to him, the greeter, Vice Deputy Chairman Brett Cole, who stood beside Chase like he was giving him the keys to the city.

The voiceover said: "This monumental occasion—the first time

Collected have arrived in their own vehicle—has many people saying it signals a massive sign of approval for the Founders Party."

Then they showed a familiar brown lady standing in the crowd, yelling into a bullhorn. Chase thought he'd seen that woman in those last moments before he was whisked offstage. On the screen, she was yelling something, but the only audio he could hear was the anchor's.

"Despite attempts to ruin the moment by a planted insurgent paid by the Party of the People to sow unrest, it was a great and beautiful historic day."

"That's that Jackson lady, right? From the *Delany*—she was on the crew with you?"

"Shhh, you're going to miss the best part."

After the anchor talked about how the *Ursula*'s technology might mean "a boon for the nation's economy," she ended with "The ship's commander, Captain Chase Eubanks, is currently in negotiations with Founders Party leadership for the betterment of all New Roanokans."

"Oh, dude, I am so not a captain," Chase told the TV anchor like she could hear him. He was about to protest some more but caught himself when the next images hit him.

There, Chase saw himself again. And this time, he was talking. Except his lips were barely moving, and someone else's recorded voice, bass and steady, played over Chase's image as if the words came out of his mouth. Saying, "There's only one way forward, that's calming down and working together. We have to all join as one, for the future, with the Founders Party!"

That was it. The segment was over. The announcers were off to the weather report. There were no shots of the riot. No images of the flying-shoe brigade. No video of the crew—except the Admiral—getting shoved into a limo and plowing through a sea of humans to escape the scene. That history was gone, edited from reality.

"You see?" Bob motioned for a high five, which Chase slapped only because his conscience was trained never to leave someone hanging. "You're a goddamn noted newcomer. Cream rises, baby."

"But I didn't say any of that. And that's the Admiral's ship, not mine. I ain't no captain."

"Well, if she'd asked you to say those things, would you have?"

"I mean, sure. But she didn't."

"Okay. Then think of it this way: I held a senior position on the *Delany*. So just imagine *I* asked you to say that stuff. Which, basically, I did: I pushed my contacts to get that news slant."

"What about the riot? What about Admiral Ethel?"

"Daytime TV, they love a good story. Especially a happy one. Trust me, when the wind's blowing your way in New Roanoke, you can't beat it. This land is made for guys like you and me."

Chase was going to ask what exactly that meant when the TV flashed static and let out a deafening screech of audio feedback.

When the screen regained focus, there was footage of the actual riot. Just as bad as Chase remembered it. The chaos, the violence, all the people screaming.

"Goddamn pirate signal. They're hijacking the feed again. These guys are the worst."

Words flew by on the chyron, but Chase was too captivated by the footage to bother reading. After that, the television opened up to an entirely different scene. Another studio, but not the primary colors of the morning-show set they'd just seen. This one was dark, dull, and populated by people in clothes much the same.

At the center of the group, a spotlight kicked on, and there she was again.

"My name is Nalini Jackson, formerly of the SS *Delany*'s Jupiter mission." It was her, the madwoman. She was calmer than the day before, not screaming. "The SS *Ursula 50* was brought here to rescue *all* of us. Regardless of party, regardless of Church of the Collected standing. Simply, all of us. It comes filled with the plans and added materials to build more ships, enough to eventually take us all back to Earth. That's its mission. It is not the property of *any* political party, or any person but its commander. But it brings us, the people, a gift. And that gift, the chance to leave, must remain the property of all of us. Or of no one.

"The SS *Ursula 50* is currently locked and cannot be opened without triggering its self-destruction. The Party of the People has generously agreed to abide by a truce, and we call on the Founders Party to do the same. It's our hope that, together, we can begin the process of making our freedom a reality."

"Oh, she is so full of shit." Bob turned it off before sending the remote flying toward the couch. "Of course, it's Nalini. Of course."

# CHAPTER 13

Vice Deputy Party Chairman Brett Cole sat in the back of a limousine parked on the side of a country road, waiting to make contact with one of the "Party People" radicals to sort out the whole spaceship thing. He wasn't sure if being chosen as the contact person meant the higher-ups had confidence in him, or if he was being sacrificed because he'd screwed up when he left the rally without the lady Admiral, who had the keys to the damned ship. An honest mistake in a moment of chaos that, yes, led to her being kidnapped by the Party People. He'd made a judgment call: to get the key players away from the riot. He'd just assumed the Admiral lady was more of a spokeslady. An honorary title. Some sort of representative for the men in charge, not the key player. These things happened.

Brett tried looking out the window, but it was too late in the day to see anything besides the outlines of pine trees. Outside, it was scary, and it was dark, and this matched perfectly with Brett's perception of the Party People in general. Their dreadlocked leader was clearly mad and rabid (possibly literally, if the rumors of his odd behavior were to be believed). Brett had never met an actual PoP member in person—or at least no one who admitted to being one—and he was proud of that. If senior leadership hadn't forced him to attend this meeting, he would have blissfully kept his distance from the radicals until death.

After an hour, Brett finally heard tires slowly crunching dirt and gravel as another vehicle approached. "Is that them? Are they here?" Brett asked the Founders Party limo driver, only to remember that the man had already gone. Because Brett was supposed to "come alone," as it were.

Hands cupped to the smoked glass of the window as he tried to peer outside, Brett could just make out some movement. People, shapes. Several of them, slowly pacing around his vehicle. He could hear them talking, too. Not words but the vague sound of speech, muted, and as obscured as their faces.

Even though he'd known it would be coming, Brett jumped when the car door opened on the far side. It was the brown woman from the rally. The one yelling like she'd just witnessed a murder.

"Mr. Cole."

Though Brett had worked his whole life to be recognized by strangers, in practice it made him feel exposed.

"I cannot be intimated," he told her, but he meant "intimidated," a mental error he made because that's what he was.

"Really? That's the first thing you start with? I'm half your size. You've got the unlimited power of the state behind you, and that's your first response?" Nalini laughed, and Brett heard in that sound anger and hysteria, and it made him even more scared. "I'm not here to threaten you. And I'm not here as a member of the PoP— I'm not even a member. I'm here as a good-faith representative to negotiate for the betterment of *everyone*."

"Miss, the duly elected government of New Roanoke is a demo-cratic body which already speaks *for everyone*. I have been authorized to tell you that the pirating of airwaves is a high crime, and those caught will be punished to the maximum extent of the law. That you must cease holding this Admiral Dodson captive, and release her immediately. As for the SS *Ursula 50*, it is in the care of the state. And the state is the law: It does not negotiate."

"And yet they sent you here. To negotiate. And, apparently, the *Ursula* already had a professional negotiator, whom you guys whisked away with its other passengers. So, first, the Admiral asks that, as a show of good faith, you reunite her with UN Special Envoy Lloyd Talbot. Immediately."

Brett closed his eyes, but that didn't protect him from the image of that head one more time, crushed and staining the carpet. "I was about to say the same thing about the Admiral you guys kidnapped."

"How did I kidnap the woman who sent me here to represent her demands? Nice logic."

Brett tried to ignore this, both the contradiction and her tone. "Miss, you need to understand the stakes of all this: That ship is the greatest scientific gift New Roanoke has been blessed with since the industrial age. It means a leap in technology that will bring this world an economic boon. It is a priceless commodity, not a bargain-ing chip."

"N-o-o-o." She dragged out the one-syllable word for at least three seconds, calmly shaking her head at him the whole time.

Brett had more to say, so much more. More bullet points he hadn't hit yet. But he already knew they wouldn't help him further his ultimate goal: getting this over with. So he made a point of sigh-ing loudly, adding an eye roll as well. "Okay, so what is it that you really want?"

"Great." Nalini removed a note of her own from her breast pocket and began reading aloud a bunch of pure crazy.

Brett Cole tried listening. As she continued, he even tried taking his own notes, too, removing a pen from his pocket and jotting down her demands on the back of his folder. But she kept going and going, her dialogue a kite taking wind and disappearing into the sky. These terrorists wanted complete autonomy to control the *Ursula 50* without any oversight. They wanted a dedicated string of warehouses supplied with raw materials and a full-time machinist crew of assembly-line workers with localized housing, to build a fleet of ships to abandon this great nation. They wanted a public lottery system, to be held live on television, to decide the order in which the population would commit this sacrilege, and a dedicated administrative staff to oversee what she had the nerve to refer to as the "repatriation project."

"Wonderful," Brett forced out when she paused to grab a water bottle off the limo's shelf and open it to wet her likely exhausted vocal cords. "That's a . . . very thorough list, Ms. Nalini. And I assume you'll want this to be one of those union things, with full worker benefits and state-provided health insurance?"

"That's a great idea. That's perfect, a union—that would really go far to ensure morale. Write that down," Nalini said to Brett, with building excitement and none of the sarcasm with which he'd asked the question.

"Of course, of course," Brett said, and calmly wrote down "*NO.*" "And, just out of curiosity, if the leadership of the Founders Party was to agree to this, how would you propose all this would be paid for? Is the interior of the *Ursula 50* stacked with gold, for instance?"

"Brett. Gold is a very heavy metal. Of course not," Nalini Jackson said back to him, in a tone that managed to be even more patronizing than his original question.

"Lovely. All right, may I make a suggestion, then? Here's one avenue, for instance: Apparently, the head of our fire department was intrigued by the fact that, despite all of its shooting flames, there are no scorch marks on the grass where your *Ursula* came down. He suspects, or his people do, that there might be some sort of chemical additive that allows for that? Some safety feature we might even be able to use in our cars, perhaps? That would be nice to share, don't you think? An act like that and I might actually be able to get my side to the table."

"I think you're getting a little ahead of yourself there, Brett. Now, funding-wise, we were thinking more along the lines of using taxation to infuse capital directly into the initiative."

"A tax. The Party People want to raise taxes. To pay for this."

"Well, Brett, that's a fairly standard way of paying for large public-works projects, isn't it? At least it is where I come from," Nalini said back to him.

"Madame, listen to me. They're never going to go for any of this. They're never going to go for what amounts to a state-sanctioned rejection of God's plan. And they're really not going to agree to raise taxes to pay for it." It was Brett's turn to laugh now, a nervous snort at the thought of even bringing these requests back to the State House for presentation. "Is that it? Isn't there anything else you can ask for? Something small, maybe? To give me room to at least start this conversation?"

Nalini shrugged and started riffling ahead in her notes, turning pages. "Equal airtime with a new, second television network in exchange for a truce on signal pirating. Also funded by a ta—"

"Don't even say it," Brett stopped her. If she didn't say it, he wouldn't have to repeat it to senior party members later.

"All right. Then here's a free one, directly from Dwayne Causwell himself. Won't cost anyone anything."

"Finally," Brett said, sighing, and lifted his pen to his notes once more.

Nalini paused before this one. Looked around the limo's interior before leaning forward to say the whole sentence. "A public, prime-

time debate about the nature of the 'gravitational phenomena.'"
And when Brett stared at her, completely lost, Nalini leaned in and,
in just above a whisper, said, "You know. *The invisible things*."

"Okay, we're done here," Brett Cole said loudly and started
working on opening the door before Nalini could go any further.
Where he would go once he got out of the limo was unclear. But
Nalini stopped him with her words before he was forced to explore
anything else.

"Fine. But they'll just blow up the ship." The comment wasn't
even made to him. It was made under her breath; Brett shouldn't
even have heard it. And that's why, when he heard it, he believed
her.

"You can't possibly mean that. Come on: Do you really believe
the majority wants to leave? To abandon all we've been given? What
our ancestors have accomplished over centuries? For some half-
baked plan to run away to a planet where we have nothing? That
we'd abandon the New Roanokan Dream?"

"Are you willing to bet they won't?"

# CHAPTER 14

The crowd in Grand Circle Square Park standing around the *Ursula 50* was all male, all in full riot gear, all with the amount of ease appropriate to people standing next to a portable nuclear reactor. Chase watched as one of the men absentmindedly reached for a cigarette from his breast pocket, only to have his co-worker smack the lighter out of his hand. "What the hell is wrong with you?" seemed to be the question yelled, though Chase couldn't tell for sure from his park bench.

*Lease Luxury Lofts!* declared the sign in front of the high-rise behind him. *Scenic Park Views!* it insisted. Its manicured veranda opened right out onto the park, offering a view of Grand Circle's green field and the marble fountain just beyond the *Ursula 50*'s fenced-in perimeter.

"We're a little early for our tour. Take a seat, let's commune a bit." Bob strolled to a park bench and sat down. Chase had no idea what was so important about going to look at empty apartments. Particularly because Bob simultaneously insisted Chase could stay with him as long as he liked, going so far as to offer to repaint the chosen guest room. But Bob seemed to know what he was doing; he seemed to have this place totally down. Chase knew that he, in contrast, had absolutely no clue what he was doing or going to do, so following Bob came naturally.

"If you do find your ex-wife, what will you do then?"

"Get on with our life." It was a simple question for Chase. Every day since she'd disappeared, he'd been a train on the wrong track. "Just get right back on the right track. I got a sweet plot of land to build on, water rights. Do the whole white-picket-fence dream out in the country and let the world rot without us." From his wallet, brought with him because he felt naked without it, Chase removed the picture that'd been there since before she left. "This is her. Ada H. Sanchez. Middle name's Hibiscus, but she hates it."

"Hibiscus. That makes sense." Bob took a sip of his latte, and Chase said yeah, though he didn't know what there was to make sense of.

"She was born east of Taos, but moved to Riverside, California, in middle school. She's trained as a painter, so maybe, I don't know, she could be selling landscapes at the mall here, like at home. Or working as an art teacher, or—"

"Chase. I got it. Don't worry. It's in motion."

Beyond them, a rough perimeter of guards assembled more wooden horses around the *Ursula,* each barrier about thirty meters from the ship itself. In their thick riot gear, they fumbled with the pieces, struggling to manage them with padded gloves.

"Get a load of these guys—they're totally buying into the threat. Nobody's going to blow that thing up, right? You're not going to try to tell me this Ethel lady's that crazy?" Bob took a sip of his Starbucks and stared at Chase for any answer he could find. But Chase just shrugged, because he didn't have one. "Granted, I'm no engineer, but the *Ursula*'s the same model cryoship that the *Delany* was, and I don't remember anybody saying anything about a self-destruct button."

Bob kept looking at him, and Chase didn't know what to say, so he thought about it some more, for Bob's sake. "The Admiral did say something about 'scuttling,' I think? When we were training? Like, something about a 'last resort,' in case we got kidnap—"

"Hey, now! Advice: We don't use the k-word here, chief. It's the C-word, 'Collected.' When in Rome—got it?" Bob turned to look around them, the whole time a wide disarming grin fixed in place. But he didn't see anyone listening.

"Chase, you have to understand, we got ourselves a serious situation here. Your Admiral? We haven't heard or seen her since the arrival. And I hate to tell you this, but it looks like she's in a bit of trouble. The guys at the office, they're saying she's been taken hostage by a rabid partisan element. Terrorists, basically. And who knows what nonsense they're filling her head with. It's all political, this game they're trying to play."

"Is Admiral Ethel okay?" Harry was in the hospital. Lloyd Talbot was . . . squished. Chase was starting to feel abandoned.

"I hope so. But the people that have her, the Party People? I'm not gonna lie: They're fanatics. I'm not saying they're all bad people, but a lot of them are basically stir-crazy in here. And Dwayne Causwell, the chairman?"

"The old Black science-guy from the *Delany*?"

"That's right, the guy from the *Delany*—poor bastard lost his shit before we even landed. Most of the PoPs, they're first- or second-generation New Roanokans, so, basically, they just got here. And they simply don't value working within the system. They're people who never gave it a chance. That little fiasco at your landing, the rioting? That was all their fault. Normal people stay home and comfortably watch things like that on TV. So, now, the PoP? They're looking at this as a huge opportunity. But here's the thing: That could be *our* huge opportunity. We nip it in the bud, we can write our own ticket. Even if your Admiral pulls off the leaving thing—and that's a huge if—it would take time. A long time. How we get to spend those years matters."

"I—I mean, that's smart thinking. But I'm just here to help Harry. Get in, get out. And, most of all, get my wife."

"You think she'll go with you?"

"Hell, yeah! Of course. I mean, sure, she left me, but she left a couple times, and she always came back. And I mean, sure—we had some finance issues, some inheritance stuff. But that's all resolved now, so I know she would have come—"

"What kind of job did you have?"

Bob's question snapped out like a released spring, and Chase had no idea how it was related to everything else he was saying. "What?"

"I said, 'What kind of job did you have?' Back on Earth? You mentioned money problems. You know, when your wife left you."

"I'm an Independent Tour Administrator. Own the limo myself—or the bank does, but almost," Chase said, finding himself reluctant to share more. "Mr. Bremner—Harry—he's my client."

"Okay. And what do you do there, exactly? What are your duties, as a 'Tour Administrator'?"

"Well, a lot of things."

"But primarily."

"I chauffeur high-end clients. I got a commercial license. Bonded and everything."

"So you drive a limo. And your wife left you."

"Yeah, but there's other stuff. I mean, I do other stuff. I'm highly respected in my local extraterrestrial-research community."

"Listen, Chase. I'm going to help you find your wife. But I'm going to help you even more than that. Because this is your lucky day. This is that chance, the one everyone dreams of. Here's the deal:

We can't let them—those PoP radicals who've kidnapped your Admiral—take over the ship. They're extremists. And if they try a power grab, nobody gets the bounty that ship offers. What we'll have instead is a civil war in a fishbowl."

"Sure, Bob. I'm your only hope in the universe. Pull the other one."

"I'm dead serious, Chase. It's all about the Founders Party. They run things: everything. And they're having a generational shift: They need fresh faces. They're old, which is why they need me. *And* you. They don't even have a governor right now, just some nobody interim till the special election. Honestly, I'm thinking of running."

"Okay. Well, good for you, I guess."

"No—good for you. After this morning's broadcast, you— *Captain Eubanks*—are the official face of the *Ursula 50.*"

"Look, I ain't no captain."

"Chase, you can be whatever you want here. It'll be musical-chairs time in the party soon. And I intend to be the one sitting down. Because—you and me? If we play this *Ursula* thing right? We could do big things. I already floated the idea of getting my hands on the *Ursula*'s drones to the higher-ups—you should have seen them salivating. They've got your basic toy-store drones, but nothing like what we have. Policing, surveillance—even pizza delivery—having a monopoly control on those floating toasters would be priceless around here. Hell, with what you guys brought, we could start a tech revolution right here in New Roanoke. Can you imagine that? And it would benefit everybody, but especially you and me. How do you think your wife would like that?"

Chase looked at Bob to see if that was a joke. If it was, Bob didn't seem to know it.

"Man, I'm not trying to be staying around here."

"Of course you're not. But till then, you got to play the angles. You're either swimming or you're sinking, that's how I look at it. So here's the smart move: We get you hugged up with the Founders Party. Nothing crazy, just to show everyone that the *Ursula*'s fate is a bipartisan concern. Which it is, right? All honest. You do that, and I'll see about getting you on the party payroll. In line for the perks. You got something people want—a connection to that ship. Now's the time to turn that into everything you need for as long as you're here."

"But can you get me Ada?"

Bob looked at him for a second, then stood up from the bench. Chase thought he was just going to throw his paper coffee cup in the trash, but Bob kept walking. Back toward the luxury high-rise, motioning for Chase to join him. He entered the building, walked past the elevators to the lobby door marked *Property Manager,* and buzzed an intercom.

"You really think you can help me find Ada?" Chase asked, again.

A voice came through the intercom: "Come right in." Chase heard her, and it hit him, and yet, when the door swung inward, when he saw the woman, Chase still had to ask:

"Ada?"

"*Hibiscus,*" she said. But it was Ada Sanchez standing there. It was Ada who froze when she saw him.

"Ada?" Chase said again. She was there. It was her. Right there in front of him. Not saying anything. Just staring at him.

"Funny meeting you here," she finally said, without humor.

# CHAPTER 15

Vice Deputy Party Chairman Brett Cole assumed the most challenging part of the *Ursula 50* referendum negotiations would be getting the senior Founders Party members to agree to negotiate at all. Despite his reservations, he relayed Nalini's requests by mouth to senior Founders Party leadership immediately, and when no one yelled at him, he spent the rest of the day pondering that unexpected outcome. Eventually, Brett decided that this must mean the idea of a referendum vote was actually kind of good. Possibly, fast-track-promotion worthy—not that Brett didn't enjoy being Vice Deputy Party Chairman. And he was starting to believe that, when you thought about it, the whole referendum thing was actually his idea, and he should put it into a written proposal to ensure he got credit for it, as opposed to some cynical opportunist, like Bob Seaford, who was clearly trying to ride this to the next rung.

Not only could a vote resolve the issue of the *Ursula 50* (and surely in the party's favor), it would also send a broader message to the public that the Founders Party was the true party of the people, and that the Party of the People was their enemy. There was nothing to be gained from using the state power of eminent domain to take the *Ursula* outright when the same goal could be reached in a way that left the voters feeling empowered. And if they lost, Brett suspected the party would eventually figure out another way to ensure that this spaceship was in good hands.

The following morning, Brett woke before dawn to write out his formal proposal. In a public referendum, the Party of the People's position could be presented in a light that focused on the underlying selfishness of the PoP request: To seize property for themselves over the needs of the many. Hoarding valuable technology that had the power to make life better for all the citizens of New Roanoke. Tech that might possibly even save lives, Brett guessed, and therefore life-saving technology. And if PoP's grander plan worked, if they could somehow manage to evacuate all the citizens who would refuse God's love by returning to the purgatory of Earth, how could that not lead to the collapse of the New Roanokan economy? *The economy.* Did these radicals even think of the economy? And how could any *true* New Roanokan stand for that?

Brett put all this into his proposal. He even added a subsection on possibly announcing an across-the-board tax cut based on revenue from any resulting inventions after they stripped the *Ursula 50* for its treasures. Some sugar for the base, in case internal poll numbers looked soft.

Brett Cole put all that in there, then sent the proposal through the appropriate channels. And then he waited. For three days.

No response. There was no "No" from up above, there was no "Yes," there was no anything. The final dossier Brett had submitted, a thick, bound report with a glossy cover, held a detailed outline of what it would take to conduct a statewide election. The cost and logistics of polling stations and organizing volunteers, the proce-dure for certifying Founders poll-watchers, the cost and scope of canvassing before the vote and coordination of phone surveys to judge the effectiveness of party messaging. Brett felt that he'd really put himself into it.

But despite all that, if Brett hadn't hand-delivered copies of his masterpiece directly to the personal assistants of all the committee chairs' offices, he would have guessed they hadn't received the documents.

Then, one morning, after four days without word from the higher offices, Brett's opposing attaché from the PoP called. After offering unwanted sarcastic small talk, Nalini Jackson said, "Tell your overlords to go to the Grand Circle Square at eleven A.M. to-morrow. To the *Ursula*. We want to show you something."

"Ms. Jackson, if it's a threat you want me to relay, let me say—"

"Not a threat. It's an invitation."

So Brett conveyed it as such. Discreetly, back to each of the personal assistants of the people who mattered, one more time. Not even asking if their bosses had read the proposal, just telling their assistants the time, the place, and that they needed to be there. For something.

And, again, Brett got no response. No follow-up call, no office drop-in. Not even from Bob, with one of his trademark ribbings. None of the senior officials seemed willing to acknowledge that they were giving any attention to the situation. And so Brett began to fear that this was because, as long as they ignored it, Brett himself would be the only one held accountable if things went wrong.

The next morning, Brett made it to the Grand Circle Square Park subway stop on time, rising aboveground to see the *Ursula 50* parked where it had been for over a week. But now there weren't just a dozen guards around the ship's perimeter. There was an entire army in waiting.

Hundreds of them: the national guard, which was fairly sizable in spite of the fact that there were no other nations nearby to shoot at.

And Brett looked among them and felt a sense of relief. Not because they could actually protect him from some physical threat, but because he knew that their appearance meant that, even if the elders were not responding to him, they were clearly listening.

At 11:01 A.M., when nothing had happened, when neither Nalini nor any PoP proxy had shown up, Brett knew for sure that the Party of the People was just playing games, as always.

But by 11:02 A.M., he discovered that the Party of the People really wasn't playing.

Without warning, the *Ursula 50*'s aft and starboard thrusters rumbled to life a full thirty seconds before fully igniting, giving the soldiers adequate time to evacuate the area. But they didn't, or at least they didn't get far enough away. The force of the propulsion units knocked their boots from under them, sending dozens of armed men sliding along the concrete until they could get up again to run to a safer distance. It was a smart move given that the thrusters around the rest of the ship soon came online as well, pulsing their energy outward before turning the force down.

In a fury, the *Ursula 50* rose off the ground.

Even at the distance at which Brett Cole himself was standing—which was considerable, and chosen out of supreme respect for his own anxiety—he could feel the gusts of air pushing him back as the explosive force lifted the ship slowly higher. One story, two, three stories above the park's lawn. Up into the air like a child's balloon. And then the ship slowed and stopped there, a hell-storm of fire shooting out directly beneath. Bobbing slightly as it maintained its position in the wind.

All the soldiers remaining stared up, necks craned and arms limp at their sides. With desperation visible even from a distance, their commanders struggled to regain order, to get them back into formation, to get them to lift their rifles and point them high. But there was nothing else the guards could do except witness it hang there beyond their reach. Then watch the ship as it calmly dipped, of its own control and volition, back down to the ground. So precise that the SS *Ursula 50* came to rest perfectly aligned with the wooden stage once more, as the planks swayed and shuddered beside it.

All that, and Brett still jumped when Nalini said from behind him, "You think they'll be open to discussing neutral locations for our referendum planning now?"

# PART THREE

# CHAPTER 16

"It's just really weird, okay? No offense, but it's a lot to adjust to, all at once," Ada told him.

"You don't want to see me, is that what you're saying? I can take it, if that's the case." Chase couldn't take it, but his shock had taken his self-awareness with it.

"Shit, I never thought I'd see you again. I learned to close that chapter when I got here, along with everything else I left in my old life. Then I'm sitting there, drinking my coffee, eating my Cream of Wheat, and my ex-husband's up on a stage on *Good Morning Friends!* Next thing I know, I'm getting offered a free penthouse in a freaking skyscraper, just for agreeing to be some kinda fancy 'super' or something."

Chase looked around said penthouse, the hotel-looking furniture, the floor-to-ceiling windows. "Sweet digs."

"Shit, you think? This place's got four showers." Ada slowly turned in a circle to take it all in. "Can you believe it?"

"How long you been living here?"

"You kidding me? Chase, you still got to learn to listen. I been here, like, seven hours. Movers came and packed me up before dawn, unpacked me just as fast. I mean, I don't have much, but wow. Like little elves, but huge guys. My studio was nice, I guess. I mean, it was a shit-hole, but I made it a comfy one. But this? This is a whole other level. I don't know how the hell you pulled this off, Chase, but, shit, you got my attention."

The ceilings were so tall, it looked like she was squatting in a church. "Yeah, sweet digs," he said again, because this level of luxury was beyond his vocabulary.

"They did this because of you, Chase. They made that real clear. Boy, your number finally hit, huh?" she said, but Chase wasn't really listening to any of it.

"How did you even get here?" he asked her. He had to know. He'd had so many guesses over the years, developed scores of hunches, but never anything concrete. He had to know the real story.

"Not much to say. I was driving near Valles Caldera and the god-damn van breaks down. I was on the side of the highway in the middle of the night, freezing my ass off. Phone was dead. Went to sleep in the driver's seat, then woke up here. Rolling in on the barge like everybody else, with all my boxes right next to me. My luggage—it was all there. No idea where I was or how I got here, or what to make of it at first."

"That must've been some scary shit."

"You'd think, but not even. Moment I landed, I could already feel the emotional baggage floating away. It was like all my stress, all my anxiety, all my student loans, and all my credit card bills . . . just floated away. The second I got here. Not going to lie, it was trippy at first. But I've been happy. I mean, truly happy, for the first time. I can really say that. For the first time, I have everything I need."

Ada must have caught Chase flinching, because she quickly

added, "Aw, don't be like that. Don't get all offended, okay? Me leaving, it wasn't all about us, you know that. It just wasn't working."

"You ain't miss me, though?" Chase finally said it, his voice cracking a little despite his effort. It was what he'd been thinking since the moment he first saw her again. He knew he shouldn't put it out there, make it real. But Chase did a lot of things he knew he shouldn't do.

"Yikes." Ada stopped, put her face in her hands, kept it there for a moment before releasing it, taking in a full breath, and continuing. "Come on, Chase. Don't start acting a fool. Of course I missed you. I mean, it is good to see you. Straight up, no lie."

"You sure? Because if this is too weird—"

Ada squeezed Chase's hand. "You're here now, Chase. And look at you! *Captain Chase Eubanks*—that's so crazy."

He was about to correct her, but then rethought it. Trying to think of something else to say, Chase came up with "I love all the paintings on the walls. They all done by the same guy?"

Ada actually laughed. Chase tried to laugh with her, but it was too late, and she realized he'd been serious.

"You kidding me? Chase, these are all mine. How do you not recognize them? Some of them were in our living room."

"Damn, Ada—I recognized those. I was talking about all the new ones. Those really you? You got good," which he meant to be purely complimentary as well, but knew he screwed up by the way Ada's face shuddered.

Ada righted herself and, in a clearly forced calm tone, said, "Well, thank you, Chase. Yes. I have grown. As an artist, and as a person. And I go by 'Hibiscus' now, please. I finally got time to focus on myself. No deserts in New Roanoke except the ones I paint, so there's a market."

"They worth much?" Chase asked her, and he could not figure

out what he'd said wrong when this woman he could only think of as "Ada" flinched again. "I mean, there's so many. You must have painted a buttload," Chase added.

"Yeah, Chase. I'm making a 'buttload.' "

"I didn't mean it in a bad way. It's just—it's so smart, what you're doing. Landscapes. All these people stuck here, and you sell them the chance to see what things look like in the real world. That's smart thinking."

"This is the real world, Chase."

It was not, but he didn't say anything. There would be plenty of time for arguing.

# CHAPTER 17

The parameters for the accords between the Founders and People's parties to determine the legal ownership and fate of the SS *Ursula 50* were negotiated in just four days, in the basement of a McDonald's. And, compared with the seven other locations in New Roanoke, not a particularly nice McDonald's, either—three cramped booths in a greasy dining room. But the McDonald's on Hastings Avenue was a largely anonymous location set in the business district, desolate between 9:00 P.M. and 7:00 A.M., so privacy was on the menu. Each night, at roughly 10:00 P.M., Nalini Jackson ordered a twenty-piece McNuggets, large fries, and a large Diet Coke. And when the tray came, she breathed in the odor of the fries, as was her pleasure, then took her food past the restrooms, through the door marked *Employees Only*, and down the basement stairs. There, Nalini went to a locked room where she found Vice Deputy Chairman Brett Cole already seated, always waiting for her, always pasty and pale and soft and yet somewhat pleasant, just like her chicken nuggets.

The most contentious point having been resolved—that of

whether or not a referendum vote on the fate of the *Ursula 50* should take place at all—the remaining items for negotiation fell into place at a speed that surprised both representatives. Each political party wanted the vote to take place within the tight schedule of the next ten days: the Founders to eliminate the issue before a public ground-swell could complicate matters; the Party of the People to limit the time the government would have to steal the election. Both parties wanted a public debate of the issue; the Founders Party offered to televise the event even before Nalini could demand this.

"Prime time," said Brett Cole. "The PoP's representative of choice versus ours. On the most-watched time slot of the week, Wednesday at eight P.M. What do you say?"

When Nalini's response did not visually match his excitement, Brett followed with "You don't understand. We haven't had live de-bates for elections in—what?—decades? Certainly not in my life-time. So this is the dawn of a new age! For the great state of New Roanoke!" And Brett looked so genuinely thrilled, Nalini didn't have the heart to point out that if the Party of the People won—which the PoP's own internal polls indicated they could—it would also likely mean the end of New Roanoke as anyone knew it, with a significant portion of the population, if not the majority itself, evac-uating.

"You are my first Party People friend," Brett told her after the second night of discussions. He seemed so pleasantly surprised about this fact that Nalini resisted the urge to question the truth of the claim to friendship, or tell him that only Founders fascists called the Party of the People the "Party People." Nalini was surprised by how much she enjoyed Brett's company as well. She'd originally had him pegged as one of those members of the Beneficiary class that deserved their own subgroup, Opposition Annihilators: partisans whose primary motivation was the degradation of the opposition.

Many Opposition Annihilators were just sadists who'd identified a socially acceptable manner to act out their impulses publicly. But most Opposition Annihilators chose this behavior to avoid substantive personal issues by projecting their own discontent onto *the other*. Brett actually didn't fit the definition, however. He genuinely believed in the Founders Party propaganda he'd inherited as his birthright. He was, simply, just ignorant, and too arrogant to realize he was an ignoramus.

After Nalini reported back about the tenor of the diplomacy thus far, she was instructed by Dwayne himself to insist on paper ballots for security purposes. Nalini made concessions on the debate venue to win the point, only to find out later that New Roanoke had no form of electronic balloting anyway. The next day, Nalini countered with an aggressive bipartisan poll-station monitoring plan involving every voting site. Brett came back the day after that, after checking with his superiors, and said, "Smooth sailing."

Buoyed by this easy win, next Nalini pushed past her pragmatic list of asks to demand that if the Party of the People won the election the government should provide warehouse and construction space, a suggestion at which even Brett, whose negotiation demeanor had become surprisingly amicable, said, "Come on, Nalini. Let's not waste time. No way they'll go for that."

But they did. The following night, Nalini arrived to see Brett beaming, his exuberance lasting through the meeting as, together, they identified possible warehouse locations on a map he'd brought for the purpose. Nalini sat through the conversation while Brett earnestly laid out which factories would be better suited, based on access to raw materials, transportation of workers, and eventual support infrastructure.

"This is fantastic work, Brett. Really. But you realize, of course, we'll still need to finance this whole shebang. This project will be large enough to demand a new branch of government, for oversight alone. So—last things last—we'll need tax revenue."

At the word "tax," Brett's cheerful demeanor drained, as did much of the blood from his usually pink face. "You want me to ask them to raise taxes?" Vice Deputy Chairman Brett Cole whispered, his eyes darting from Nalini's face to the air vent high in the corner, as if his bosses might hear him and strike him dead. Literally. Nalini looked to the vent, then to the light switch, then to the lamp hanging from above. All while following the nervous gaze of Brett Cole's own wide eyes. It was the first time Nalini suspected the room was bugged.

The lights in the windowless basement supply closet went off. Then back on. Then off. Repeating twice. And then all Nalini's suspicion was replaced by certainty.

"Yes. Please ask them about adding a tax to the referendum," Nalini said again, louder. Loud enough that Brett was now visibly cringing. But the message wasn't for him. It was for whoever was listening—she was sure they knew that. Nalini said it politely, too, so it didn't sound like what it was: a demand.

In the seconds that followed, Nalini watched Brett closely. Not with the curious malice of a torturer, although Brett did seem tortured; she wanted to see what the hell he was doing.

Brett rose from the table, rolled down his sleeves, put on the seersucker coat he always left hanging over his chair. As Nalini continued to sit, Brett Cole took a deep breath, buttoned his blazer, exhaled, and, with a nod, walked out of the room. If he hadn't left his briefcase and papers behind, Nalini would have assumed he was gone for the day.

Minutes later, when he returned, Brett was smiling again. "Agreed. A seven-percent tax, no higher. But with that, all negotiations would be completed. As of now." Brett stuck his hand forward.

It hung there, because Nalini knew she shouldn't shake it before checking with Dwayne. But it was a "damn good deal as far as the devil does," as Dwayne himself sometimes said, so she took Brett's spongy McGriddle of a mitt into her own and shook.

When she returned directly from the final meeting with Brett Cole, Nalini found Dwayne in the insulated sound studio of the original home of the Roanokan Broadcasting Company. He was sitting at the remains of the ancient recording studio, blueprints laid out over the looted remains of the soundboard. Admiral Ethel, who hadn't left the building in a week, stood beside him. After Nalini shared her good news about the negotiations, the other two's immediate response was just to look at each other.

"Just the tech, right? Not the ship itself? That's what they're saying?"

"They win, they get the tech, and can do what they want with it. They lose, they have to fund and execute the exodus."

"But they're not trying to put the possession of the ship on the ballot? Really?" Dwayne started wagging his head and grinning in sarcasm. "Does that sound kosher to you?"

"This is what we wanted, right?" Nalini asked into the oddly quiet space meant for their congratulations.

"But why do you think they said yes to so many demands, so fast?"

"How the hell should I know, Dwayne? I didn't even want to do this—I could be substitute-teaching a bunch of delinquents right now."

"Seriously, why? I want to hear your take on their concessions. Think. We asked for tons of stuff. I was thinking they might—*might*—agree to like a third of that. But they caved on almost everything. Even the tax part. The concessions we made? Window dressing. Nothing on our core list was touched. You're brilliant, I know that. But come on, Nalini. Haven't you wondered why?"

"Because they're afraid we'll blow up the ship," Admiral Ethel offered over her coffee cup. She was sleeping in a corner office down the hall, wearing donated clothes that made her look like a reluctant Walmart greeter.

"Maybe. I hope so." Dwayne turned back to Nalini immediately. "Champ, you been studying these folks for over two damn years. You *know* how they roll——"

"Right over anything in their way."

"That's right. So why they all of a sudden all accommodating?"

"Perchance they're finally accepting that their bubble may be about to burst," Admiral Ethel offered.

"They're zealots—it's not that complicated. It's nothing to overthink, Dwayne. It's called 'overconfidence.' Founders Party leadership represents the heart of the Beneficiary caste. They think they've been chosen by God to live in a neo-heaven and thus are effectively demigods. Their delusion functions as justification for maintaining the income inequality that provides for their lifestyle. They were liberal with the referendum concessions because they think they'll win."

"They're not just acting like they think they'll win," Dwayne said. "They're acting like *they can't lose*. And that's a big difference."

The sound of Admiral Ethel putting her cup down clanked through the room. "So—you're saying they're going to rig the election?"

"They're going to do everything they can. We already figured that. They're going to use the law whenever possible and skirt the law when they can get away with it. I've known people like this my whole life: That's what they do. But that level of confidence? This implies something bigger."

"Okay, now you're worrying me." The Admiral's tone was the same, but her voice had grown louder. "You understand you're basically playing poker with my ship?"

"Damn, Dwayne. Why'd you stick me in a McDonald's basement all week to haggle if you think they're just going to take the ship anyway?"

"Lady, you done good. Hell, you done great. And because of that, now we know what they're going to try to pull."

"Cheat," Admiral Ethel summarized. "The second the polls close, we get on my ship—no matter what."

"That's what I'm talking about," Nalini agreed. "Just give them the tech and bounce. I'm not spending the rest of my life in this shark tank, getting smacked around by invisible things."

Admiral Ethel swung toward Nalini and snapped, "'Gravitational anomalies.' I'm more comfortable if we just stick to your original cautionary colloquialism."

# CHAPTER 18

## THE PEOPLE'S FAITH REFERENDUM

On Thursday, June 23, the citizens of New Roanoke will vote in a referendum on whether to initiate a centralized industrial plan to begin mass production of vehicles similar to the newly arrived SS *Ursula 50*. This vote will determine if the Party of the People is given unprecedented access to state funds for the sole purpose of immigrating to Earth and abandoning the New Roanoke dream forever, **OR** give sole ownership of the *Ursula*'s technology to the Founders Party so it can be developed in a manner that benefits advancing all of New Roanoke.

### What will the People's Faith Referendum question be?

The referendum question will be: Should the majority of our wealth, natural resources, and manpower be taxed and the New Roanokan people forced to immediately build a

fleet of ships for the sole purpose of abandoning everything
we have been given as Collected? Or should we use this opportunity to build New Roanoke stronger?

**How can I find out more about the People's Faith Ref-
erendum?**

On Wednesday, June 22, at 8:00 P.M., one representative each
from the Founders Party and the Party of the People will
participate in a live, televised debate on this critical issue, on
the RBC Television Network.

**Who can vote in the referendum?**

Any New Roanokan citizen aged eighteen or over who is a
resident will be eligible to vote if registered to vote, able to
present proper ID at his or her assigned polling location, and
with a signature that is judged to be identical to their previous signature, excluding citizens with felony convictions,
those who are currently incarcerated, and those with out-
standing tax debts and/or fines.

"Why do they hate heaven?" the coiffed man asked, biting his lip,
squinting his eyes at the camera as he repeated the inquiry. Slower
each time, so the television audience got the full effect of it.

"That's an excellent question—I really don't think that's asked
enough," said another man, who was basically the first guy but with
darker hair.

"I'm sorry, but, to me, it's a rejection of all the blessings that
we've been given." The blond woman took a sip from her Jamba
Juice as the other two hosts offered their firm agreement into the
pause. Nalini, watching at home, was certain the female host was
not biologically blond, but fastidiously performing blondness as a

loyalty display, to demonstrate allegiance to the power structure, membership in which was dependent on subservience. It required making a concerted effort to bleach her hair weekly to the exact shade of blond that visually signified she accepted both the benefits and limitations of being a Beneficiary woman in the patriarchal Founders Party. To take her adult hair and strip its melanin until it was reduced to an artificial shade that harked back to the transitory pale hair of Northern European children, simultaneously accomplishing both an ethnic alliance and an embracing of prepubescent-level status signaling. Compared with her male counterparts, the woman's vocal tone was more aggrieved and uncompromising, which Nalini identified as a key indicator of Opportunistic Overcompensation, yet another term she had coined while watching Bob sell his soul for personal gain.

Nalini's social theory of Opportunistic Overcompensation was rather simple: By overcompensating in displays of fealty to a powerful tribe, it was possible to overcome the fact that this tribe was formed around rejecting people exactly like you.

As an example, Bob. If it wasn't completely unethical (or even if it had a chance of making it through peer review), Nalini would totally publish an unauthorized sociological profile centered on Bob. In his pre-debate television appearances, Bob offered an intense performance of Opportunistic Overcompensation—in his case, by rabidly spouting Founders Party partisan nonsense—to counter the reality that he himself was a recently arrived immigrant. Just as the exception proves the rule, inherent contradiction proves the true identity of a sociopolitical group. Bob represented the newly Collected demographic the Founders demonized. Therefore, giving him a public role countered the public perception that, after decimating their political opposition, the Founders had devolved from a moderate democratic force to an all-powerful, toxic, nativist party. This was essential to the Founders, because it actually was an all-powerful, toxic, nativist party. So, ironically, the attempt to hide this inadvertently proved there was something to hide. The blond woman, being the sole female host on a show hosted largely by men, was part of such a bargain: The Overcompensating Opportunist was presented externally as both proof of a group's diversity and a symbolic recruitment tool to welcome more of the same. But it was a bad-faith offer: The unspoken social agreement was that the Overcompensating Opportunists were actually there to guard the door, not to keep it open behind them.

"It's madness!" the blonde declared. "I feel sorry for them, really. For the darkness in their hearts that won't allow them to feel the true glory of God's love that is New Roanoke. But we—"

"But we can't let this happen," one of the other men interrupted her, so she smiled, as she always did when interrupted, further establishing her loyalty to both the party and the values of the Church of the Collected for which it stood. She kept smiling blankly as the coiffed man looked earnestly at the camera and kept going on and on.

"This is the time when we, as the true Collected citizens of this great state, must stand up and show our appreciation and loyalty for all the graces we've been given. The choice is clear: Do we take the gift offered to us by God with the arrival of the first rocket ship to land on New Roanokan soil? Or do we let these Party People seize our bounty for their disgruntled members? And how do we know it's even safe? Are they going to rocket right up *until they break the sky*? That could kill us all. That is so stupid. The selfishness."

"That's it, Phil. That's it right there. They want to ram a hole through the sky," the chubbier man excitedly joined in. "And I'm going to go even further with that—and I know I'll get in trouble for this, but I just have to say it—this isn't just about rocket ships, no matter how spectacular. It's about a way of life. Because they won't stop there—they'll take everything from us if they can. They want us all living in the Cavern. I know we don't like to talk about that place, but sometimes you *have* to talk about it so you don't end up there. So let me tell you, I'm glad there will be a televised debate—"

"Right here on Wednesday—"

"Of this week coming up?"

"Wednesday of this week, at eight P.M., where rising Founders star Bob Seaford will be debating Party People's Dwayne Causwell."

"Bob Seaford, recently Collected—"

"Arrived just two years ago, apparently. People try to say the Founders is just for founding families: If that's so, how do you explain this guy?"

"I know how to explain that guy," Nalini said to the TV screen.

"Some say he's the future of the party. And he's been here just *two years*."

"Two years?"

"Two years."

"Right, but this guy already gets it. Let me tell you: If you haven't seen him speak yet, you're in for a treat."

"These Party People, they don't just want this ship. They want more ships—and they want to raise your taxes so *you* have to pay for their ships, so they can go twirling around in space, on vacation. They don't just want to abandon our great land; they want to force everyone to go with them."

"And break a hole in the sky!"

"Right. A mandatory evacuation, that's what they really want. Destruction of our society as we know it. And we can't let them trick the voters into this sacrilege. We have to make our voices heard."

"And you can make your voice heard, today, at the Rally for Freedom, which will feature Bob Seaford himself, as well as the support of the commander of the *Ursula 50*, Captain Chase Eubanks, starting at noon at the remarkable *Ursula 50* Stage at Grand Circle Square Park."

"Congratulations, Chase. You've been promoted—on behalf of the New Roanokan State Government. It's official now." Bob held the uniform out to him on its hanger, brushing away invisible lint. The way Bob was looking at it, Chase was pretty sure the guy would put it on himself if he was seven inches taller and weighed twenty pounds less. They were in the green-room tent behind the stage, and the door flap was open, and Chase didn't feel comfortable taking his pants off. "On behalf of the New Roanoke government, I salute you." And Bob, smiling, did.

Soon as the older guy walked out, Chase whispered to Ada, "But I'm *not* a captain." It was like none of them outside the green-room tent could, or would, hear him; everybody out there just wanted him to put that uniform on. It was a fancy thing, with shiny gold rope outlining the shoulders, and all types of buttons and badges cluttering it.

"All that time you been working for Harry, without a promotion. Working hard, too. Not cutting corners or taking handouts, either. Don't you think you deserve to be a captain of something? Come on, you got to start valuing yourself at least as much as these people here value you."

And when Ada said it like that, it was hard to disagree with her. Hell, he wasn't trying to disagree: She was right. By now, he should've gotten more to show for years of busting his ass. Something like this. But the problem was, this wasn't just a uniform and respect. It was also a job.

"Baby, you know I do not like public speaking. And it sounds like that's all they want me to do."

"Chase, come on. You start yammering at the bar at the first sight of a free beer."

"Yeah, but that's casual. Not on a stage, like this."

Tying his tie, Ada, who was now Hibiscus, said, "Honey, just chill. This is all new for you, I get it. I know your head's gotta be swirling, and I'm not gonna lie, probably going to keep spinning for a while. This has to be hard. Especially for you."

"What do you mean, 'especially for me'?" Chase recognized a kind of mocking tone in her voice—not mean, but like she was laughing at some joke about him based on something he didn't think was true. He was hurt but still didn't want to upset her, so he added, "Hibiscus. What you trying to say?," using her new name to make sure he didn't sound annoyed. In Chase's Ada nostalgia back on Earth, her way of talking to him like he was a goofball seemed cute. But hearing her do it in real time again reminded him he hated that shit.

"You know what I mean. You don't like change, Chase. Never did—even good change. You like things to stay the same. But this is a once-in-a-lifetime opportunity; you're about to be the face of that spaceship."

"Yeah, but we're not really trying to stay here, right? Sooner rather than later, we're going to be thousands of miles from all this."

"What we agreed is that a discussion will take place down the line, once you get a proper feel for this place." Ada was right about that, so he didn't argue. It felt kind of weird, choosing to stay in some alien ant farm, but he had to admit: They had a real nice setup going on.

"All you really got to do for now is be handsome in your suit— that's what they want. You already look like a leader. Founders just want everyone to feel safe and stable. You got any idea how crazy people been since a freaking spaceship landed in the center of town? There're all kinds of apocalyptic wack-job rumors going around. But you, you're like that spaceship made into skin and bones, baby. So now you—and only you—got a chance to calm everyone down. If that means putting on their Buck Rogers costume, who cares?"

"This is a great new day!" Bob Seaford declared into the microphone, and the crowd in front of the stage agreed heartily. The three of them—Bob, Chase, and Ava—had come onstage together, but at some point Bob got in front of them—which was fine with the other two. It wasn't a huge crowd, or even a medium-sized one, but the organizers kept forcing them to squeeze together for the camera, so it probably looked packed for the television watchers. "We've been given a gift, once again, by the Provider! The bounty of the SS *Ursula 50*!"

A burst of light came from behind, and Chase turned to see a big screen with the image of the ship, the photo enhanced with New Roanokan flags. And there was a new decal stuck to the cryoship; Chase looked at the image and then down at the Founders Noah's Ark logo on his lapel, and, sure enough, they were the same.

"And as a civilized community, a democracy of the people, we will head to the polls to show our appreciation for this bounty, so that it benefits all of society. For we are the Collected!"

The last declaration sent the little crowd roaring, but Chase's response was to squeeze Ada's hand. It was their "couple communication," a simple but effective way of covertly conveying the message: *This shit is crazy*. But Ada didn't squeeze back, so he cut it out.

"Lot of you might be wondering, 'Who the hell is this guy? Who the hell is that?' Am I right? You're probably wondering, 'Why is a newly Collected guy, who basically just got here, representing the Founders Party at such an important moment?' A lot of you have probably heard the talk, right? That the Founders Party is just for the same old families, the big established guys, not new arrivals. Well, I'm here because that's a lie. I did just arrive. And so did my buddy here, Captain Chase Eubanks of the SS *Ursula 50*! The hero of that momentous day."

Ada lifted up Chase's arm in triumph, which caught him off

guard for a second, because he was busy staring at the crowd, start-ing to get freaked out.

"When we arrived in this great state, we had a choice, my friends. We had a choice between joining with the people who work tire-lessly to maintain everything New Roanoke has accomplished, or to side with those who would take it all down. Abandon it. Because I've seen the alternative—that's something that, as a comparatively re-cent arrival, I can surely tell you about. I've seen what's out there, back where I came from. The homelessness. The tent cities. Riots and wanton property destruction. Disease. Crime. The borders over-whelmed by illegal immigrants. Doomed cities that are a Babel of tongues and smells. But not here. What you have here—what *we* have—it *is* a utopia. It will last long after the old place is reduced to smoking ruins, I have no doubt about that. It is a *heaven,* and fighting for that is what this election is all about."

The little group below yelled and clapped some more, and Ada motioned to clap as well, which sucked, because it meant he had to pull his palm from hers, which he was holding like he was hanging off a roof. As the outpouring of love continued, Chase leaned in to kiss her on the cheek and asked, "Am I doing this thing right?" He had to know, because he felt like he wasn't doing anything at all but standing there looking like a jackass.

"You're doing it exactly right." This was good news, so Chase kept at it, waved to the crowd during every applause line. When he finally did talk, it was just to lean in to the mic and say, "Thank you." But the crowd cheered for him, so he was pretty sure he got it right.

When it was over, Chase felt okay. He actually felt pretty damn good. It was a totally new feeling. It felt like power; he was pretty sure that was what it was. Not just being strong, but having strong stuff behind you. It also made him really hungry.

Chase stood at the foldout table a ways behind the stage, choosing among the generous selection of little triangle sandwiches. Bob was still up there, talking about something else now, and nobody was looking, so Chase shoved two into his mouth quickly and carried as many as he could in one hand.

Out of the corner of his eye, he caught sight of a trio of cops. They were coming straight toward him. Chase's first thought was, *Oh, hell, what did I do this time?* But they just gave him the thumbs-up—all three of them at once—and kept walking. "You rocked it," Ada told him, adding a kiss to his cheek before heading off toward the bathrooms. *Hot damn, this is my life,* he thought, watching her go. Grand Circle Square Park was Instagram Filter Hot. Blue skies, every single day, without desert dry. No trash that wasn't already in a can, nobody sleeping on benches. It was perfect. It was like Disney World was a real place and you never had to leave again. Ada was right, New Roanoke was real nice—she was usually right, so no surprise. *This is my new life,* Chase tried out in his head.

There he was, minding his own business, enjoying life, when he spied a white van parked on the street. White vans are made to be ignored, but Chase noticed it because there was that Nalini Jackson woman sitting at the wheel, arm waving in the air, waving at him. Chase waved, and took another one of those wedges of white bread. He was starving—being a celebrity burned calories, which he guessed might be how so many remained skinny. Chase looked back at Nalini blankly as he chewed his prawn-salad sandwich until she exited the van and jogged across the street toward him. She was dressed like a cable guy—which was a thankless job, shame she couldn't get nothing better. Chase put out his hand to shake, but she grabbed his wrist, yanked him—rudely, to be real about it—back in the vehicle's direction.

# CHAPTER 19

"She's here. Ada, my wife. I'm staying with her—Bob hooked it up for me—it's crazy. But it's really her."

"That's great, I'm happy for you," Admiral Ethel Dodson told him. "But, Chase, where's Lloyd? And where's Harry—protecting Harry was your one job, correct?" She was looking back from the passenger seat at him, and Nalini watched him through the rear-view mirror as she drove. Per Dwayne's insistence, Nalini was wearing an industrial one-piece that said *New Roanoke Power & Gas*—which seemed like overkill, but it satiated his hunger for drama, so she went along. The same words were pasted on the side of the vehicle, but inside there were just bench seats like in any passenger van. "So why don't I see him with you?" Ethel spoke in the measured, even tone of someone trying not to yell the words.

"Yeah, *Captain Eubanks*. What is your deal?" Dwayne, his bench-mate, added, by way of introduction.

Chase took a deep breath before saying, "Well, the thing is . . .

Harry? There's been some issues. But with Harry, not the worst news. Not the best, but he's okay now. Just went by yesterday. Brought him some magazines. And chocolate."

"Just tell her what she needs to know," Dwayne snapped at him.

"He had a heart attack," Chase blurted.

"Oh, come on." Admiral Ethel turned back around in her seat.

"But it's okay! The doctors said he'll be fine. They just want to keep him at the hospital for a bit, while he recovers. Honestly, he probably shouldn't have come, you know? I mean, he's not exactly a spring chicken. I was talking about this with Ada, and I don't think it's fair I should be held—"

"I'm no 'spring chicken,' either, Chase. Do you think I shouldn't have come, either?" Admiral Ethel asked him, and before the man could salvage his reply, she followed with "What does Lloyd say about all this? What's the status of his diplomatic process? I've heard absolutely nothing. Is he actively negotiating?"

"Lloyd . . . Lloyd didn't make it." Chase shuddered, thinking about it; he hated even saying Lloyd's name out loud now. Admiral Ethel was silent, but staring at Chase as if her disapproval could alter reality. "He didn't make it. I'm really sorry," Chase added. "I mean, it wasn't my fault, but still."

Nalini adjusted the rearview mirror just to see if Chase looked as cringing as he sounded. Then she watched Admiral Ethel take a deep breath and exhale before slowly restarting the conversation.

"Chase? What are you talking about?"

"Look, ma'am," Chase began, "I don't know what to tell you. But it wasn't my fault! I was just—" Admiral Ethel lifted her hand and put her open palm a foot from Chase's face.

"I know this is a lot. We are all under stress. But I need details. Are you saying Talbot is dead?"

Chase nodded.

"Okay. Now can you tell me exactly *how* he died?"

Chase thought about it. Saw the image again and again, like a looped GIF, and winced. Then he said exactly what he was thinking, to get it over with.

"His head blew up."

"Goddamn!" Nalini couldn't help herself. "What are you even talking about?"

Dwayne yelled up at her, "Nalini, come on. You know exactly what he's talking about."

"Well," Chase continued, "the doctor, he said Lloyd's head imploded, technically. It got squished," Chase told Admiral Ethel. Adding, "Lloyd's head did," for clarity. Staring off, he muttered, "Like two fat fingers on a goddamn grape.

"I don't mean no disrespect, Admiral, but it was some crazy shit. That's just how it happened, trust me on that one. Out of nowhere. Like a . . . like a swatted fly. The doctors said it was some kind of *decompression*-type thing. You know, like the bends or something— Lloyd couldn't adjust to the air pressure, so . . . But, the good part is, the doc said it was an extremely rare, rare condition."

"A *condition*? That's not a 'condition,' that's obviously another attempt—"

"Dwayne, just don't," Nalini stopped him.

"It's not an avoidable conversation. It's about the invisible things. It's always about the invisible things," Dwayne said.

Admiral Ethel's hand reached out again, landing on Dwayne's shoulder. "Our agreement was to limit certain discussions as a precautionary measure."

"He wouldn't believe us anyway." Nalini slowly brought the van to a stop. Outside the van, it was like no place Chase had seen in New Roanoke before. Not on Bob's tour, certainly not on Ada's circular walks around the center of town. So much trash, that was it. It lined the sides of the street in ripped bags and loose piles. After Nalini put the van in Park, she unbuckled and turned around to talk directly to Chase.

"Your wife, she's been in New Roanoke for a while?"

"Four years."

"Good. So here's the deal. If I told you something really wild, or Dwayne did, you'd just think we were crazy. But you trust your wife, right? If you heard something, even something ordinarily un-believable, from her, you might believe her, right?"

"I guess—Ada's a straight shooter. What 'invisible' stuff are we talking about here? What's the big deal?"

"Ask her. Ask your wife. And then we can discuss it from there."

"I don't see the point, though."

"Just ask your wife, Chase," Nalini insisted, before turning around and buckling up once more. She maneuvered the van onto a steep mountain road.

"All right. Whatever. I got a question, though: Where we going?" Chase asked everyone, but it was only Dwayne who answered.

"We're going to the Cavern," Dwayne told him. "You're in for a treat."


Dwayne had Nalini bring the van to a dirt parking lot on a cliff with a view of the Horseshoe River below. In the back of the van, Dwayne pulled out papers from a printer's box, shoving the contents into a worn backpack until it looked bloated and as heavy as one person could manage. "Hey, *Captain*! This is for you."

Chase had exited the parked van and was now standing closer to the cliff's edge, staring down at the river roaring into the darkness of the cave just beyond, the mountain swallowing the current whole. Dwayne had to call him again, by his name, before Chase knew he was being summoned. When handed the weighted pack, he put it on without question, his balance altering visibly from the burden.

He didn't complain until Dwayne told everybody, "We're going to climb down this incline to the sewer line. The best way to get in, quietly, is through the wastewater pipe."

"Sweet Lord." Chase was looking straight down the path, at how steep it was. "How is the front entrance less ideal than going spelunking in a sewer?"

"You can't even get a cop to come to a crime scene, but right now there's two of them posted outside a cave entrance. We're bringing voter registrations, or trying to—they could turn this area into a swing district, possibly. So I want them to actually make it all the way inside."

A battered metal fence separated them from the cliff's drop, its gate sealed shut with chains and rust. Toward the end of the clearing, a flap of fence had been cut open, and gaped from being pulled open so many times. There was trash everywhere: Several mounds of tattered bags and loose contents spewed across the compact dirt beneath their feet. No cans, no dumpster, just heaps the height of NBA centers.

"You really never been here?" Dwayne seemed genuinely surprised.

"Once. Never got past the entrance. I made some errors." Nalini looked around, then added, "I said I was there to study 'Malcontents,' and a group of people took offense to the clinical term."

Chase made a point to hold his hand over his nose. "This place reeks. Why'd you bring us to this dump?"

"We're here for another round of voter registration. But this is your lucky day, Captain. You get to see a side of this place I'm pretty damn sure isn't on the Founders' list of tourist attractions."

"People live here? Really?" Chase was so incredulous, the words came out in a laugh. "Why would anyone want to do that?" He heard himself, and he sounded like Harry. But he couldn't claim he wasn't asking himself the question.

"Because they have no choice. That's why. That's why people live like this, because they don't have anything better."

As they walked down the steep dirt trail, a flat and empty barge floated along the river before disappearing into the darkness at a speed that belied the current's power.

"Somehow I didn't realize this 'Cavern' was an actual cavern." Admiral Ethel pointed down at the dark tunnel of hollow bedrock. "Is that real?"

"As naturally occurring as anything down here. The back entrance is past the slope," Dwayne instructed everyone. "Take your time. No ambulance coming, so, you know, step easy."

Chase paused his descent on the uneven and rocky trail to catch his breath. "Anyone ever float to the end of that river?"

"Dissidents, criminals, tried and sentenced and then sent by an executioner into the dark." Dwayne shrugged. "No one who's come back out."

"Open space," Admiral Ethel added. "That's all our drones found. The barges float into the cave system and eventually out into the vacuum. Then they power off toward some unknown destination— somewhere too far for our best deep-space sensor arrays to follow. I assume water must recycle around subterraneously to the other side of the river."

Nalini marveled at how gracefully the older woman jogged down the rough trail, pausing occasionally to wait for the rest of them. Nalini was half her age and struggled the whole time to keep up with her. She noticed that, as it got steeper, Chase stopped looking down. Instead, he stared up into the false blue of the dome.

Dwayne's back entrance to the Cavern was the spewing end of a sewer tunnel. Old and brick and jutting out like a puckered anus from the cliffside, dumping its waste into the river below. Dwayne removed two flashlights from his pocket, turned both on to check the light, and then gave one to Admiral Ethel. One by one, the four stepped onto the narrow maintenance ledge that hung above the tunnel's putrid stream.

With a gust of wind, they were all hit by the odor at the same time, but Nalini was the only one who gagged. She spit the traces of vomit that rose into her mouth down into the rest of the river of waste rolling by.

"It's worse after it rains." Dwayne patted her back softly until she finally stopped heaving. "But that's why people first started coming down here: It's safe from the Founders types. They avoid it because it's the only place in New Roanoke where they can't pretend their shit don't stink."

They walked single-file and in the dark along that pipe for at least ten minutes. Long enough for Nalini to start to wonder whether they were traveling all the way back to the underside of the city center itself. Then Dwayne finally came to a weathered metal door that shook off powdered rust as he pulled it open and let the light pour in.

Nalini's hand went to her eyes to hold back the glare.

"This is what I've been doing, for over a year: trying to bring the PoP out to here, where it's most needed. Need's the only thing they got a lot of."

As her eyes adjusted, Nalini first thought that they'd come aboveground again, an upward ascent somehow hidden by the length of their walk. But then she saw that the light was electric, bulbs strewn across the ceiling of the Cavern's expanse. They walked through the door.

The Cavern was as vast as an airplane hangar, clearly formed by something beyond human hands. At the far end, a waterfall poured from a subterranean cave, its force slamming into the spinning wheel of a mill. In the space under the ledge they stepped onto, Nalini could see its stream pouring past in the direction of the larger sewer tunnel.

So big, yet still so claustrophobic. Because of all the people. The tents—so many of them and in so many colors, but all filthy. Grime visible even from a distance under the blue tarps hanging over them for water protection. So many vertical lines of campfire smoke, rising past the stalagmites and escaping through the vents opening to the outside. So many bikes and carts and makeshift wheelbarrows in so many stages of disrepair. The stench—it was the sewage line, but it was also of humans packed together in misery. An entire impoverished village, hidden underground.

"These are the people who need to escape this moon." Dwayne turned from the view, looked right back at Chase. "The folks excluded from the Founders Party's vision of society. The ones who get sacrificed to sustain their 'good life.' It's nothing new, but New Roanoke is no different."

"That sucks. But, hell, man, I'm just saying: How's that different from back home?"

"It's not. It's nearly the same, but in some ways, it's even worse. Because the Founders run everything, and they're not going to do anything about it. Because even acknowledging the problem would be tantamount to admitting their dream about the nature of this place is delusional."

Nalini chimed in, hoping she might offer clarity, a little too excited to share her analysis. "It may seem like one little cultural contradiction, but to accept this would force them to cross what I like to call 'the Jenga Limit': the amount of contradictory information a subject can accept before their entire worldview collapses, decimating their initial reality."

When Chase looked at her, silent and confused, Nalini took this as evidence that she should explain further. "Say, for instance, your worldview is based around the idea that New Roanoke is God's heaven. Well, if you then accept that a significant portion of the population is suffering down here, that means New Roanoke is far from a heaven. And then that means you're being lied to by the people you've trusted to define reality, right? And if they're lying to you about that, then what else are they lying to you about? So all of your intellectual foundations come crashing down, right? Jenga! Get it?"

Chase didn't even try to pretend this time. Instead, he looked at Dwayne and asked, "Who the hell even are all these people?" Chase stepped forward to the ledge's edge, looking out at all of them.

"Most of these folks? Newer ones. Came in the last few decades, tops. People not in the system anymore. Got their orientation and housing at first, but after that? This. Not enough real employment for everyone. Even fewer good jobs, for your average not-right-off-a-cryoship types. When those of us on the *Delany* arrived, we got the platinum treatment. But these people? Most of them work for next to nothing, day wages. Gig work, if they can get it. They're the economic lifeblood of the place. Cleaning, cooking. All for pennies, without any social care. The Founders couldn't live the high life without them, but there's always new 'Collected' to replace them, so they're still dispensable. This is the real New Roanoke, not that Founders bullshit. This is who pays the price for the 'shining city on the hill.'"

"Come on, man. That's a bit extra. I've met a ton of the Founders folks—my wife's one. And Bob's been introducing me at the headquarters and such. Decent guys, good people, seems like," Chase said, stopping him. "You're acting like New Roanoke's some hellhole. Let's get real. This town is pretty sweet, am I right?" Chase looked around to find someone to agree with him, and failed. He couldn't help himself, Nalini marveled. Nobody had asked for Chase's opinion on this shantytown, but it was as if he couldn't imagine that his opinion was not essential or desired.

"That ain't right." Chase shook his head knowingly. "You can't write off a whole city because some people fail there."

"They didn't fail. They were *failed*." Dwayne was failing, too, at managing his temper. Nalini put a hand to his shoulder—light and polite, but enough to remind him to calm down.

"I'm just saying. Some people don't have that work ethic, or drive. That's just facts." Looking down at his new shiny military formals, Chase brushed off the fabric, turning aside to make sure he didn't get any grime on it.

"Will you shut him up?" Dwayne said to the Admiral, but she wasn't listening to either of the men. She was too busy looking around, taking in the details of this shantytown. Seeing her do it, Nalini saw it through her eyes. The eyes of someone not whittled down from years of this craziness. But even without that perspective, the place was horrific. Nalini always assumed the Cavern would be bad, like others described it. But it was clear her own previous understanding of "bad" was limited by her imagination.

"They go first," the Admiral said, turning to Dwayne and repeating it. "They go first. We need to make sure they are on the first wave of ships out of here. The ones most in need."

"Admiral, they go first, or they don't go," Dwayne told her. "Because I guarantee you, if the Founders types get control of the tech, these folks here will be left with nothing."

"That's unacceptable." The Admiral motioned for Chase to turn around, and when he reluctantly did, she took the box of registrations out of the backpack he still wore and started walking into the crowd with a confidence that almost made Nalini feel the lady could do something about all this.

"Why you even bring me here?" Chase stuck his elbow over his nose as if the smell was finally too much.

The Admiral turned to take him in before she said anything, not speaking until she had his measure. "Because I want you to remember why we came to this moon: to make contact, retrieve the crew of the *Delany,* and get back out. Not to buy their propaganda. Not to get involved in politics, or pose for the TV cameras, or whatever it is

Bob Seaford's playing at. When the time comes, I need you to get Harry on that cryoship, like we planned. No funny stuff."

"And Ada. You said we could bring Ada back, too. You promised," Chase reminded her, nervous suddenly that this part was now in question.

"Let's all remember to keep our promises," she told him.

# CHAPTER 20

Harry Bremner sat in his wheelchair in the hospital lobby, looking pissed. Or at least it seemed that way to Chase, who saw him and thought, *Shit, I should have come right after breakfast.* But when the old man looked up and saw his employee, he actually smiled, and in response Chase gave a joyful sigh of relief. He looked good, or at least decent, rested. That said, Chase found his current attire unsettling: a cheap generic gown without room for Harry's dignity, let alone personality. But Chase told him he looked good anyway, then started filling him in on the latest with the miracle of Ada and the penthouse and the captain thing and that nasty Cavern, and he would have kept going, but Harry interrupted him with impatient, waving hands.

"Just get me the fuck out of here," Harry grumbled.

"They're saying that your heart can't take it yet. That it isn't safe, Harry."

"I don't care. If I die, I die doing whatever the hell I want to do, when I want to do it. Otherwise, life's not worth it. Just get me outside—take me on a walk or something."

So Chase drove Harry, like always, but this time by pushing him in a wheelchair with a number spray-painted through a stencil on the back. Out the windows, it was daylight, but the sky was a muted white that looked like rain coming, although Ada said it rarely did that outside of the wee hours.

Before they could exit through the glass door, a man in a white lab coat stepped in front of them. The wide grin on his face looked molded out of plastic, his eyes smiling even more than his mouth did.

"Sir, we've been through this. You need your rest."

"Who the fuck do you think you are? Move."

If the doctor was offended by Harry's tone—Chase knew on the wrong day it could really hit you—he did a masterful job of hiding it. Same happy face, no change. "Mr. Bremner, we can't have you running away, can we?"

"Oh, come on. We're literally stuck in a goddamn cage—where the hell am I supposed to run to?!" The last bit Harry yelled through the lobby for anyone within earshot. Chase saw the ones who did hear, watched them flinch. But, again, the doctor registered no response. He just kept grinning as he stepped to the side and cleared their way to the door.

"You know that asshole keeps hitting me up about our cryo-tech? Keeps coming by and saying things like 'We could really use that to keep trauma patients stable when the ER's short-staffed.' Well, hell, bet you could," Harry said as soon as they were outside. "Had another SOB visit, head of some construction firm, wanted to know about the aluminum alloy in *Ursula*'s framework—which is, like, how the hell would I know, I sell war, not spaceships. One of the nurses even slipped me a note from some tech bro trying to buy my NASAx watch—as if. And that's just who got by security. Sweet Lord, the vultures are out."

Harry didn't seem to want to go anywhere in particular, or, if he did, Chase couldn't get it out of him. Every couple of blocks, Chase said, "Do you want to head over there?" And Harry Bremner said, "Whatever." After a few times, Chase stopped asking. Every attempt at small talk was shot down when Harry raised his hand flat and vertical in the air. The old man was observing, that was clear to Chase, although what details he was looking for, Chase had no idea. So he just pushed the chair down the high street, distracting Harry with the store-window displays they passed. All the neat little shops looked cute, but not so much so that he'd go into one of the tiny spaces unless he was planning on buying something—too awkward. That's what Chase loved about the big box stores: Nobody working those floors gave two shits whether you bought or browsed.

They ended up at the park only because that's where the market street let out. Chase was about to turn around—Harry had seen that area when they landed, although today it was sparsely populated and riot-free. When Chase turned the chair, though, Harry instead pointed to a bench, telling Chase to park his chair parallel to its side before motioning for Chase to sit down. Across the grass, a block away, the *Ursula* sat upright, the stage beside it. There were people up there, setting up a sound system—Chase had been to enough concerts to identify the hustle of roadies from even that far away.

After a couple of minutes of Harry not talking, Chase asked him yet again, "So . . . anywhere you want to go? Anything you want to know about this place, from me? For your analysis?"

"Nope," Harry said. And they sat there for nearly a minute in silence before he added, "I've seen enough: It doesn't matter."

" 'It doesn't matter'?" Chase parroted, mostly for himself.

"That's right, that's what I said: It doesn't matter."

"Why—"

"Because anyone—or *anything,* more likely—that's capable of building and maintaining this 'New Roanoke' doesn't need it as a spy or invasion training ground. I thought there was a possibility, when we got here, when I could really examine the details, imbibe the milieu, that there would be an atmosphere of artificiality. But, alas, no. No shortcuts in design, no hint of impermanence. No hollow façades. This isn't just a replica, a Potemkin village, some kind of fake. I know fakes: This is real. It's all real."

"Feels real," Chase offered.

"No shit, Sherlock. Anyone could see that immediately—doesn't take an expert." Harry then shrugged, his way of apologizing, which Chase always took as a signal he didn't mean nothing by it.

"Also obvious: Whoever this is, they're already working on Earth. Unseen, largely—that's how they got everyone. With tech and power vastly beyond our capabilities. Hell, they might be among us as we speak. Unseen, or in our own form—who knows? Some of the dumb-ass medical staff I'm forced to deal with act so odd, I wouldn't put it past them."

"We in trouble, then? Some kind of alien invasion coming?" Chase knew a couple of those obsessive "hostile invasion" theorists from his UAP get-togethers. Constantly arguing about the true threat: little greens versus tall grays. Going on about the UAPs popping up at the nuclear sites. He always thought they were just paranoid wackos. He still thought they were wackos, just wackos who also happened to be right.

"No, no. The opposite—whoever this is could have wiped us out, overnight. Centuries ago. There is nothing we have that they couldn't just take—if you discount silly answers like 'love' or 'a sense of humor.' No, it has to be benevolent. Has to. Or benign, at least."

"So what you thinking? We cattle or something? Like the lobsters in the tank at Pappadeaux's?"

"Jesus. Stop being dramatic. They don't need all this if that's all they wanted. Honestly, I don't have a clue. It's easy to define what something isn't. What it is? No idea. But it has to be here for another reason." And then, remembering something, Harry asked in an entirely different tone, "You get any more about what the hell happened to Lloyd's head? What're they saying now?"

"You know. Some kind of decompression thing."

Harry snorted at that. Loud, like a hog. " 'Invisible things.' Oh yeah, I know all about that shit. I been hearing the nurses gossip about it when they think I'm knocked out. About what happened to Lloyd—what a nightmare. It's creepy, the way they talk about it. Whispering under their breath when the physicians aren't in the room. Like it is some Illuminati conspiracy. Then, when I try to ask for more info? Oh no. Don't tell the old guy. Won't answer any of my questions and just ask more of their own patronizing ones. 'Did you move your bowels today?' Yes, I took a shit, so thank you and fuck you. Very rude, those nurses. So see what you can find out, okay? Ask your Ada. Or that slippery Bob guy. For all the good it'll do us."

"Okay, will do. Ada, she's been real—"

"*Decompression.*" Harry interrupted, staring off in the distance. There were more people in the park than when they'd arrived minutes earlier. Folks walking in and toward the stage. "Horseshit, more like. They might as well have said, 'Magnets.' Never going to forget that one—he was an arrogant prick, but he didn't deserve that."

Chase fell into silence, trying to get the looping GIF of Lloyd's head out of his mind again. When he couldn't, Chase said, "Yep. That was truly some nasty shit."

"Brilliant observation, Chase," Harry said. "So—what else? Update me on your glamorous life on the moon. What kind of aliens have you seen on your travels across this great land? I can never remember which kind are your favorite. You know, there's another patient on my floor who keeps dropping by my room uninvited—old as hell, half dead, won't shut up. Swears they actually used to see the aliens here. Yeah. When they looked in groups—together, at the same time—he swears. At least, they could make out blurry shapes.

Guy blames everybody for not looking anymore. You'd love this guy. He's a complete nutter." Chase had no idea if Harry was messing with him. The words were sarcastic, but his voice had lost its edge. The old man was in pain; that was clear to Chase. He was a special kind of ornery today, but he only got like this around the same time he'd start asking for some ibuprofen or diazepam.

"Haven't seen a one, sir."

"I'm shocked." His voice had one tone, and it was pretty lifeless.

"But I've been thinking on it. And I do have one theory. And the way I see it, that might actually be evidence in itself of something even wilder."

"Oh, do tell." Harry's tone made it clear he meant the exact opposite, but it was too awkward to turn back now, so Chase went and did it.

"What if—hear me out—the aliens are still here, but they're so crazy-looking, so wild, that the human brain can't even comprehend them?"

Harry stared at him, blankly.

"Or maybe it really is on us, that we don't see them because we don't want to. Like, we *do* see them, right? But immediately some part of our brain is just like, *Oh, hell, no, I'm not dealing with that.* Or it's some kind of cloaking thing. Maybe the old guy's right about the groups thing, that having too many eyes on it overloads its system. Just thoughts."

Harry still stared, no shift in his facial expression. Chase assumed he was deciding either to keep saying nothing, or to deliver one of his A-material-level insults.

"That's actually not so bad, Chase," Harry said after a minute. Later, when he'd thought it over, Chase decided that was the greatest compliment he'd ever received from the man.

———

Chase pushed that old man around town for another hour at least. Through the rest of the business district, all the way out to the entrance of the zoo, then back through the residential part, until they got to the hospital. A city on a straight grid with numbered streets was a treasure for somebody who otherwise didn't know where the hell he was. Harry didn't ask for it, but Chase tried to give him the grand tour, because he felt bad for him, even though Harry was an asshole. They'd come all this way, adventure of a lifetime, and the guy was stuck in a damn hospital bed. That just sucked.

For all his protest about going back to his room, Harry really was clearly hitting the wall by the time Chase got him back to the lobby. There was an increasing slur to his voice, and as Chase rode with him on the elevator back to his floor, Harry's curses started blending together.

When they finally got to his room, Chase was surprised to see people waiting there. A nurse, and Bob, too, sitting in the lounge chair like he was at a cocktail party. "Hospital called; I heard someone's been naughty! Took off despite doctor's orders. But it's all good—I talked them down." Chase knew Bob's tone was the kind of thing that set Harry off, but the old man just halfheartedly mumbled, "Piss off," then motioned for both of them to leave as the nurse helped him back into the bed.

"He's doing great; don't you worry about him," Bob said when they were in the waiting room, down the hall. He was staring out the window overlooking the park—Chase thought he could even see the bench he'd just sat on from this angle. There was a real crowd surrounding the *Ursula* now. Whatever event was going on had kicked into gear during the time since they'd passed by. Chase had no idea if those people were there to gawk, or to try and hitch a ride. If it was a protest or a celebration.

"All those folks down there? Founders Party supporters. Our people."

"How do you know?" It was so far away, Chase had no idea why Bob thought he could tell their political persuasion.

"All the Party People sympathizers are home, just waiting for the election to solve all this. Chickenshits."

"Harry going to be okay, you think?" was Chase's attempt to change the subject.

"Relax. You see his nails? Quality manicure right there, I can tell you. Don't you worry, we're taking great care of Harry—he's going to be important. The best: That's what he's getting." Bob looked at his own nails for comparison. "I could have handled everything on the phone, but I came over here because I want you to know I'm keeping my word. Best care on the planet."

"I appreciate it—I'm sure Harry does, in his way."

"And I'm looking out for you, too: Ada, that sweet apartment. I did that out of respect, Captain. It's an honor to take care of that for you."

Chase couldn't tell if Bob was bullshitting him or himself, and readied for whatever ask Bob was building up to in return.

"You see that thing out there?" Bob said, pointing out the window.

"A park, yeah, I know, I was just there. Can't miss it."

"No. That's not just a park, chief. That's a paradigm shift. That's old plans falling apart. This whole place functions on the primary assumption that, if you just shut up and keep your head down, everything will be fine. That's it, that's their whole social contract, in a nutshell. But then this invisible stuff? Apparently getting worse, too? What a shit-show. They look at that cryoship and think, 'You know what? I think it's time to go.' It might as well have *Your World's Doomed, Hop On!* painted on the side."

"Well, Admiral Ethel's got a whole plan for everything. All of it. How to evacuate properly, so things don't get crazy. The specs, the tech: She's got it."

"But, Chase, don't you get it? Right now her plan's on the wrong side. Politically. Do you see the problem we have here?"

Chase, who initially didn't see the problem, was made aware of it the more Bob kept talking.

By the time Chase got back to the penthouse, his feet were throbbing from oncoming blisters, and he reeked of dry sweat from a day in the sun.

"Where the hell you been?" Ada yelled into the shower, her voice amplified by the tile that covered the floors, walls, and even some of the ceiling. Chase poked just his head out—she'd seen him naked a billion times, but pulling the whole plastic curtain back felt too weird. "Bob called—he said something's up with your boss man?"

"Harry," Chase made a point of saying, because she knew damn well what his name was.

"He wants to meet you over at the hospital. ASAP—you gotta go. Now."

Chase pulled his head back in, started rinsing off. "Already did. I talked to him—or he talked at me. Holy shit—have you ever really spoken with that guy Bob? I don't know—that's one shifty SOB, I'll tell you that."

"Then you don't want to get on his bad side, that's all that means. You don't worry about Bob. Hell, Bob getting you into that whole Founders scene's the best thing that ever happened to either of us. That's potential. Look at you: You're a goddamn captain now—don't fuck that up." Chase heard the door close behind her.

Chase got out of the shower, shaved, got dressed, plopped on the couch all nice and clean, but he was still thinking about that conversation with Bob from earlier. Ada didn't ask Chase about his day, or why he'd been a reeking mess, or what Bob said that had him freaked. And he didn't want to tell her that last part. Things were going well with Ada—Hibiscus—and he didn't want to screw it up. Chase was pretty sure Ada actually did love him. He had faith in that. But he also knew he loved her more. That was just the way things were. He didn't have a choice about loving her; he'd given the rights to his heart away to her a long time ago. But her love was conditional. He had to earn it, and keep earning. If that meant avoiding certain topics, what choice did he have but to sidestep them? He couldn't turn his own love off even when he'd wanted to—there was no damn valve.

"You're acting weird. What's your deal?"

"I'm fine, *Hibiscus,*" he remembered to say. "Just tired."

"Bullshit. What is it, Chase?" Ada said from the other end of the couch.

A simple answer: Bob was pulling some shiesty shit, that's what—and let him in on it. But the details in his head would sound even worse out loud. Instead, Chase thought for a moment, then came up with something completely different: what Harry'd been on about.

"What are the invisible things?" Chase asked.

Ada froze. She had a glass of what she liked to call "Homebody Happy Hour Hooch" in her hand, and she immediately put it down. Then she leaned over toward him, arms out. Chase held up his arms for her, too, figuring he must have scored a win and asked the right question and maybe they'd have a little "married people time" before dinner. But Ada didn't hug him.

Putting both her hands over his mouth, she whispered, "Don't say another goddamn word."

# CHAPTER 21

Nalini enjoyed *Good Morning Friends!*, finding the adrenaline rush of hate-watching an energizing way to start the day. Cursing at the screen, at its hosts, its inane and reality-distorting segments, all of it reminded her she was alive; that was the only good thing about agony.

That the RBC would actually have Dwayne on their morning show, live, to promote the upcoming debate was bizarre. For Dwayne to agree seemed obvious madness.

"A truly stupid idea. Possibly the most asinine strategic move I've ever heard in my life," she told him over root beer and French fries, his favorite vegan meal, and a great way to get him to make time to talk to her amid the chaos at the dilapidated and overpopulated PoP headquarters.

"Why?" Dwayne shot back immediately, pulling a straw from his mouth. Nalini hadn't meant to insult him. She'd only said it because it was the most asinine strategic move she'd ever heard.

"You know why: Going on the flagship show of the propaganda

network will only serve to let them portray you as a villain. You don't mess with the RBC—Jesus, Dwayne, you know this. It's state-run media. It's their court, with their game, by their rules. It's not even a trap: A trap implies some sort of surprise."

"It's just a promo. For a debate we *also* want everyone to watch, too. Shared interests and strange bedfellows and all that."

"Sure, gotcha. And you're not creeped that suddenly Bob is going to be your debate opponent? How does that make sense? That, out of all the charismatic sociopaths on their payroll, *Bob Seaford* is the go-to guy now?"

"They want a recent arrival to take down a recent arrival," Dwayne said, shrugging her off and continuing to eat. When the waiter brought the salad bowl of fries to the table, Nalini thought he intended to share, but when she reached in for some, Dwayne lightly smacked her hand. "I'm kidding," he said, with more defensiveness than sincerity. The soda next to him was nearly a pitcher as well. When he was stressed, Dwayne's dietary choices were cruelty-free, environmentally conscious, and aggressively self-destructive.

"*Bob*. They just want to mess with you. Throw you off. It's obvious, and you know Bob's opportunistic ass is down with it. They're going to try to portray you as a monster."

"Sis, they *been* villainizing me. This is our chance to show the Party of the People's humanity to the viewers in the RBC news bubble. It's progress—that's how I'm looking at it, regardless of their motives. Before last week, they wouldn't even play my voice on air."

"Oh, right. Because they're threatened by the seductive rumble of your African vocal timbre."

"Exactly. Excellent point. Also, I got to admit, I really just want to be on *Good Morning Friends!*"

Nalini looked at him, thought about it, and said, "The hosts look like they're made out of wax. When you get close, please poke them with a stick. See if it leaves a hole."

The morning of the debate promo, Nalini came to the Roanokan Broadcasting Company's building an hour early and went up to Ahmed's office out of respect for what they'd once had, she told herself. But also, part of why Nalini wanted to see him was that a small but persistent cohort within the congress of her mind just kind of missed the guy. Nalini wasn't sure if that part of her that missed him was slowly gaining a majority, or if it would eventually be outweighed by the parts of her that felt suffocated by the relationship they'd created. But for now, the romantic lobby had at least formed a powerful voting bloc.

Ahmed's life strategy was working swimmingly. He had attained a rare mythic item in the game of corporation: an office on a top floor, in a corner, with a lot of glass. So much glass that he saw her coming down the hall and immediately started trying to close the blinds and hide. One minute, Ahmed was seated peacefully in his gray herringbone suit at his polished oak desk; the next, he'd sprung to his handmade oxfords and was at the door almost in time to stop Nalini from entering.

"How did you get in here?" was the first thing he asked her, which Nalini took to be a rather rude way to greet a person whom you'd urinated in front of on countless occasions.

"I told the front desk that I was your wife, and I came to divorce you."

"That is really, *really* in poor taste, considering." The literal distaste clear in his voice, as if the mischaracterization of his marital status by the woman who once said, "I can't do this anymore; no offense, but it's so boring," was an abomination.

"I just wanted to say hi." This was both true and a lie, and the pause to absorb the contradiction of that deflated a bit of the tension between them.

Ahmed cleared the way, so Nalini walked into his office, closed the door behind her. Ahmed returned to lowering the walls' privacy blinds, but less urgently.

"If you just wanted to say hi, you could have called me. You have my number. I've invited you many times to my job before. But, no, it's not until you're the poster child for the Party People movement that you've finally decided to visit my office. It's like you're actively trying to get me fired."

"You're still such a *Bob*." She meant it as an insult, but she'd used it on him so many times that he was nearly inoculated.

"Just stop. Show some maturity, Nalini. At least, pretend."

"With your big fancy *Bob office*. You have to know better by now: These zealots are a dead end. It's about to be over. *A rescue ship is here.* Be honest: Do you ever stare at the ceiling at night and worry that you chose the wrong side?"

"No, Nalini. I don't," Ahmed told her. "Because I chose the winning side, like any rational human being would. Choosing the winner is a straightforward task: You see who's winning, and you choose them. Very simple. If that ship actually manages to take off again? Then I'll be on its side. But, unfortunately, that's not very likely at the moment. What's irrational is *you*, Nalini, keeping this rebellious posturing up. We're stuck here. The new ship changes nothing. Do you understand how long it would take to actually get everyone back to Earth? The entire population? A lifetime. I'm doing the—"

" '—best I can given the situation at hand.' I know, I remember. Fine. I'm leaving. I have to go down to the studio now, anyways."

"*Good Morning Friends!* I heard. Please, go."

"How did you know that? You don't watch this crap—is it a setup? Do they have something planned? Some kind of Founders trap?"

"The paranoia."

"You're not saying no. If it was nothing, you would just say no to shut me up."

"Listen to yourself. There's no trap. Regardless of what you think of him, Bob Seaford always has a plan. A long-term one, and an immediate, practical solution. I've heard the Founders may have him tease a new policy position today, something they're excited about, but that's politics, not conspiracy."

"Dwayne was not told—"

"Dwayne hasn't been right in the head since we landed, and you know it. Is that really who you're betting everything on?"

Despite never having his own voice on air before, Dwayne Causwell did have a substantial presence on the RBC Network. Largely, this took the form of one oft-reused photo of him in Grand Circle Square Park, mid-scream, eyes closed, on a particularly bad hair day.

"I'm going to say something about it, on air. They must have a thousand other photos they could use—I've seen them taking pictures of me. It's so childish. It makes me look like a very handsome yet rabid hedgehog."

The Party of the People underlings brought their own makeup person to the studio, at Nalini's suggestion. She didn't trust the RBC not to give Dwayne a clown face. It was a concession the network quickly agreed to; the *Good Morning Friends!* makeup crew discovered they lacked the proper cosmetics for Dwayne's complexion, anyway. The agreement was that this television segment would start with thirty seconds of mutually approved statements from both representatives, followed by three minutes of inane *Good Morning Friends!* banter, concluding with a reminder to tune in to the debate the following Wednesday, on the eve of the referendum's election.

When Dwayne was fully puffed and powdered, Nalini thought his face grossly overdone. But then she saw Bob Seaford himself and the hosts on the stage; she'd never seen so much makeup on people not laid out for their funerals. Caked faces and cotton-candy hair, mannequins brought to life by a curse. Bob, who was practically mounted onto the stage in his lift shoes, fit in perfectly in this setting. Standing behind the cameras, Nalini watched as Dwayne took his seat, and she wondered if the audience would be able to truly see him at all, or if the constant stream of anti-PoP propaganda had created a permanent filter that rendered the real man invisible to them.

"Hey, Ms. Nalini?" Fake Captain Chase Eubanks was suddenly at her side, but facing forward, like he was trying to pretend he wasn't talking to her.

"I heard you talk to the Admiral," he said to her, his tone so comically guarded and conspiratorial that at first she took this to be code, before remembering she really did know an admiral. "I got to get a message to the big boss—we got to talk. It's important. I need to give her a heads-up."

"Fine. What's the message?"

In response, Eubanks literally looked left, then right, then leaned in, once he'd inadvertently broadcast his secretive intent to anyone with a third-grade comprehension of body language. "I was talking to Bob, over at the hospital. And . . . well, we were just shooting the shit, and he was telling me—"

"Shhh" came from the cameraman, who pointed to the red light that had just come on. Chase Eubanks turned back to Nalini, shrugged apologetically, and walked off as the show went live.

Bob and Dwayne both gave their prepared remarks, not deviating from their scripts.

"These are exciting times—a whole spaceship landed in the center of town—how could that not be exciting! But moments like this, they mean change, and that can bring uncertainty, too. The thing is, no amount of information can erase uncertainty. None. No matter how much you think you're certain about, there's still only one thing that can truly vanquish the anxiety, and that's faith. Believing. That's what makes New Roanoke so special: that we believe in its dream. And this is no time to let that dream die. The cryoship can be a part of that dream. Can make the dream even stronger. But only if we hold to our faith, to who we are." A subtle smile framed Bob's face as he talked calmly to the camera. "Our top-notch science team is making the *Ursula*'s technology their number-one priority. We are blessed, but not everything we desire can arrive on a barge. Advancements in building construction, medical treatment, personal security are all within reach. This is tech the rest of America doesn't even have access to. This is the dawn of a new age for New Roanoke. Its positive impact could be felt for decades—centuries, even! As long as we remember who we are: God's chosen."

Beside him, Dwayne rolled his eyes, and Nalini just hoped the RBC's primitive cameras didn't catch that part. "Respectfully, *Bob,* if no one even knows who brought everyone here, or what that barrier protecting us from being sucked into space is even made of, or who's resupplying this nation-state, how can you ethically declare that people should relax, take our time, and not worry? We simply can't know. That's why it's more important than ever that we invest in a viable exit strategy, now. *Immediately.* There is no other rational course of action. It's . . . *time to go.*"

"Couldn't agree more," Bob responded, and instantly Nalini knew they were about to get screwed. "That's why the Founders Party will be unveiling our measured and considered transportation plan at the debate Wednesday night. Hope you tune in!"

The female host brushed back her bleached strands with one hand and leaned forward in her chair in what Nalini took to be a community-theater performance of the word "surprise." "Mr. Seaford, are you saying this isn't just a—as it's been described—a 'stay or go' situation?"

"That's right, Sienna." Bob smiled right into the camera. "Both of our parties are now exploring the transportation option. The *Ursula 50* came with plans, tools, and materials to build. It'll be a massive operation to make that a reality, but it would be completely irresponsible not to explore a lifeboat contingency plan, for future generations of New Roanokans. No one's a prisoner here."

Dwayne snorted, and Sienna paused to look at him in horror before continuing. "So you're saying, if the Founders Party wins, these 'lifeboats' will be built?"

Bob looked at the camera directly once more, squaring his shoulders to the lens before delivering his message. "Of course, that's been our position the whole time. I think we can all agree on that. The only question now is, citizens of this great republic, who do you feel is the best equipped to handle such a massive endeavor? The people who run our great nation, who keep our economy thriving and the New Roanokan Dream available to everyone? Or the people who just complain and graffiti slogans on small businesses, the forces of destruction?"

"You lying-ass mutha——" Dwayne got out before his mic was cut.

"In the meantime, though, our first priority is the immediate well-being of our citizens," Bob continued, talking loudly over Dwayne's futile, un-mic'ed protest. "So let me present to you just a hint of the glory that's in front of us: this platinum voucher we call 'Maker Money.'" With that, Bob lifted what looked like a piece of tinfoil the size of a dollar bill. It was a sight the home viewing audience didn't see until after the pre-prepared graphic of the metallic currency flashed across their screens. "The *Ursula 50* is the greatest technological gift we've ever been given. And the Founders Party has no plans to squander it. When we make use of its bounty, apply its tech to make the lives of every citizen that much better, a great and vast fortune will boost our entire economy. And the Founders? They want to give that wealth to you, not hoard it for elites like the Party People. Maker Money is what we're calling the guaranteed bonds for this amazing initiative. Now everyone gets the chance to invest in the future.

"You see, we want to ensure any discussion of emigration is done in a fiscally conservative manner, not by taxing you to death. So this is our promise to you: If you vote to give the Founders Party control of the *Ursula* and its bounty, you're not just voting for New Roanoke, you're voting to give *yourself* a fortune."

There was a tap on Nalini's shoulder, and she turned to see Ahmed. He was holding a sample of a Maker Money bond in his hand, offering it to her. Closer, Nalini saw it was just silver paper with the words "Maker Money" printed on it. She'd seen more authentic-looking currency in board games. Ahmed gave her a non-committal shrug.

"See? I told you, no tricks," Ahmed said, not even looking at her. "Just solutions. Simple, proven solutions."

"Bonds? We're trying to get everyone out of here, and they're talking about selling bonds? What in God's name does that bullshit even solve?" she asked him.

"Panic. Fear of income instability. Bonds would pay for expatriation initiatives down the line, eventually. Every civic goal doesn't have to be the next big thing since the invention of fire, Nalini," he whispered back, and she was hit with a wave of relief that she'd chosen to leave him.

Onstage, Bob was staring right into the camera with a Maker Money bond by his face. "The Provider didn't just give us this great land. He also gave us the intelligence and ingenuity to thrive on it. When the Founders Party wins the referendum, everyone will be taken care of. This is the future, people. A solid way to invest in our success, and reap all the benefits down the line. With the Founders in charge, you'll all get the chance to own tomorrow."

The hosts executed their clap function, enthusiastically banging their hands together. Bob beamed till they stopped, then added, "Safety and security in this time of uncertainty, ensured by the Founders Party!"

"Yeah, see, the thing is? He's lying," Chase told Nalini.

They were in the handicap stall of the third-floor ladies' room. "I hate to say it—I mean, he's been real good to me—but it ain't right. I made a promise to the Admiral and, out of respect to Lloyd Talbot's memory, I'm keeping it. Founders folks ran internal polls; Bob knows they can't win if they don't get on the other side of the escape issue. But the guy told me, right to my face: They have no intention of doing a damn thing besides what they already planned—taking the tech and stripping that ship for parts. His plan is, and I quote, so don't shoot the messenger, 'Kick the can.' "

" 'Kick the can'? What can?"

"That's what he said, 'Kick the can down the road.' You let the Admiral know I said so."

"Lordy. Even for Bob, that's an impressive level of cynicism. Did you get it on your watch?"

"On what?"

"On your watch, on your arm. You have the same one the Admiral has, right? It records audio and video. Unless you shut it off, it's on." Nalini pointed at it; then she witnessed the look of realization flash across Chase's face as if she'd struck him.

"Like even in the bedroom?" Chase asked, looking off, his face draining; Nalini pretended she didn't hear that. "Sure, I was wearing it—they said to—but we were alone on Harry's hospital floor. If I give you a recording, Bob's gonna know it was me. I'm not trying to get caught up in this politics stuff. I just thought the Admiral should know."

"Chase, you just said they're lying about letting people leave— *you* told *me* that. That's too big for being chickenshit. There're ways around you being caught. We can plant a recording device there for them to find later, put a little audio recorder on the TV stand or something, so they'll think that's where it came from."

"Yeah, no thanks. I'm not picking sides. I'm what they call 'non-partisan.' I'm, you know, like Switzerland in this, okay?" Chase started heading for the bathroom's exit door, still looking Nalini's way as he tried to end the conversation. She grabbed his arm.

"That's not how this works, Eubanks. There's no middle ground between right and wrong. You're not Switzerland; nobody is Switzerland. Claiming you're 'nonpartisan' is just a way to be self-righteous and complicit at the same time."

Chase described the audio file he forwarded to Nalini as "a discussion between me and Bob," but she found it to be more of a classic Bob monologue. And though she detested Bob Seaford's grating, nasal voice, and the sounds he made through his smug grin, Nalini enjoyed the recording immensely. Particularly:

"Our guys say, once we strip it down, we can milk new gizmos out of that *Ursula* junk for decades. *Decades,* man. And we'll get a cut of that—a real cut, not some shiny coupon bullshit. I mean, sure, I'm sure eventually someone will build a few ships to leave, in case of emergency. But that's not our problem—we'll be long dead by the time they ever get around to actually trying to blow town. If ever. All we need to do is help them kick the can down the road and we're basically set for life."

Also when Bob said:

"The tech on that ship's decades ahead of anything these yokels have. Imagine taking every innovation of the last forty years, going back in time, and cashing in. I mean, these townies barely have a functional internet. There's no social media—how amazing would this place be with that here? There's a fortune to be made in hundred-g phones alone. And those old rich blue-bloods, they need someone to sell it to the public. So we get that cut. You and me, we can be like Nikola Tesla, Steve Jobs, and Joel Embiid all rolled into one. That ship is our cash cow. Shit, it's a whole damn herd of cattle."

And Nalini's personal favorite:

"Polls say the majority of likely voters want an emergency evac plan, so, fine, we give them a plan. Costs nothing to promise something, and it'll cost us nothing in a few years, when they get used to its always being a few years away. We could even come up with some kind of PR blitz about what a shit-hole Earth is. Tell them about the constant wars, and the eco-famines, or what happened to the polar ice, or the hurricanes. The nukes, too—it's not like we'll even have to lie. We do it right, nobody'll be thinking about a few randos getting their heads squashed. Okay, yeah, the data says the phenomenon's getting worse—but the public's already trained to ignore that stuff. I'm sure the next generation will figure it all out. Somehow. Who knows? But trust me, these people don't care about specifics. They just follow whoever makes them feel good about themselves. And that's what I do best, which is why I'm headed to the Governor's mansion and taking your handsome-captain self with me."

There were more juicy quotes on the recording, arguably even better ones for the cause, and the Party of the People planned to release them to the public in good time. But these were the quotes Dwayne, Ethel, and Nalini agreed on for now.

They sat in the Party of the People headquarters; the former radio-station lobby's couches were the most comfortable in the building. Wires hung from the ceiling, wallpaper in the process of peeling off the walls all around. Nalini felt that the building might fold in on itself at any moment, that it was held together by idealism and calcified hope. But it was the best place to dictate the quotes and have them printed up at poster size, the text laid over the same absurd Founders Party propaganda they were using to promote their referendum position. Within hours, the posters were already being spread across the city by elated PoP volunteers.

And yet, to Nalini, it still didn't seem enough to counter the tribal instinct ingrained in the social structure. Paper lacked the reach of television and the power of the evidence itself. Anyone could write those words on posters. They could paste their flyers on every blank wall in the city and it would still be less effective than playing the actual clips for thirty seconds on air.

"The world needs to hear this. And not just the choir on the PoP feed."

"I agree." Dwayne shrugged.

"Then why aren't we playing it for everyone?"

"Come on, lady. You know why: I agreed to stop all pirate broadcasts until the election. That was our part of the deal." Dwayne spoke with the full force of a person who'd like to respond to a repeated question a final time. "We air that thing, they're going to use it as an excuse to storm in here and throw us all in jail."

"Well, can you get the RBC to air it themselves?" Admiral Ethel wanted to know.

"Yeah, I doubt they're suddenly interested in branching off into actual journalism."

"What about getting it to *Steve Sterling at Midday*?" she asked. In her brief time in New Roanoke, she'd become quite the fan, too. In hiding, Admiral Ethel had watched more television than in her entire life. "He seems to present himself well as an independent journalist."

"Wait. I know someone even better," Nalini told them.


"Maker Money is icing on the cake, but it doesn't really matter, we don't need to actually build a fleet. It's not like anyone's going anywhere. I mean, come on—do you know what a population drop like that would do to the stock market? We just got to tell them we're building some backup lifeboats. And we will. A few ships, eventually, for party members and donors, just in case. All the public really needs is the message. It's like when you get on a plane and they do all that 'in case of an accident' life-preserver bullshit—totally useless in a crash. But it makes the punters feel better."

When the recording stopped, Nalini swiped it back to play Bob talking again, and again, until Ahmed reached out to stop her. He had his shiny Maker Money sitting on his desk; it provided no cushion when Ahmed suddenly slammed his head on it.

"We're never going to escape this place," Ahmed said into the polished wood.

"No, we're getting out of here. On the *Ursula*. If the PoP wins the election, Admiral Ethel's going to deliver them exodus schematics. After that, they can take care of themselves. And it's our time to go."

"Take me with you," Ahmed said, solid and straightforward, as if this was a negotiation. "You have to. I want to see my family again, in this life. I refuse to die in a place without a proper ocean. And yet they have lobster. What a world."

"The exit meeting's tomorrow at lunch. Emilio's Family Style."

"Eating in at Emilio's? Have you experienced their dining room? Nobody orders in there."

"Exactly. So we'll have privacy. Ahmed, listen to me: Bob cannot know about this until it's time. He'd narc us out in a second. Just get this recording to Steve Sterling. No way we can win this otherwise."

"*Steve Sterling at Midday* is an excellent choice—he's a real professional. I told you he was worth watching, and you said to me—"

"Are you serious? Just get it to him to play it on air. You do that, and when we get to Earth I'll push you in the ocean myself."

# CHAPTER 22

Ada always kept the TV on, a leftover latchkey-kid habit that Chase barely paid attention to. He was napping on the couch just eight feet in front of the ancient, boxy thing as it blared, but he paid it no mind until he heard ". . . in an explosive audio recording obtained by the *Steve Sterling at Midday* family. The leaked recording is allegedly of the Founders Outreach Ambassador, newcomer Bob Seaford, discussing the Founders Party's internal rationale for—" Chase turned it off immediately. "Let's go for tapas!" he yelled, because that was the first thing he could think to cover it up.

But Ada was already leaning on the couch's arm beside him, and she picked up the remote as fast as he put it down. The sound of Bob talking popped into their living room. As Ada raised the volume bars, Chase's gut dropped. Bob's voice played, and then Chase's, all while the text of their conversation slid across the screen.

"That's you," Ada said, turning to him. "That's—"

"Yeah." Wasn't any use fighting the obvious—that just made it worse. Start with a confession to the smaller crimes, and save energy for the prosecution stage of the real stuff. "Wow, baby," he said. "Wow. Just . . . wow. I don't even know what to say." The sincere look of shock on Chase's face was, at the moment, his greatest defense. But it was a weak one.

"You don't have anything to do with this, right?" Ada was getting all worked up—that never ended in a place he enjoyed visiting.

Chase let the tremble into his voice to attest to his innocence, but it was really because he was scared of what Ada might do to him. "Hibiscus, I didn't know nothing about this," which was technically true, on account of he *did* know *something* about it—Chase swore he'd never lie to Ada, and took pride in keeping that promise.

"Did you record this? Did you give this to them?" That's what she cared about. She wanted to know if he'd snitched Bob out. *What did you do, Chase?* is what Ada was asking, even before she put that exact question to him.

"Okay, what had happened was, we were outside Harry's hospital room, right? The way I figure, they must have had it bugged—Harry's room." Again, technically true; being honest was important. The PoP folks had put a listening device in there. It's just that they did it after the conversation in question, as a cover story.

"The debate is just two days away. Buckle up," the host Steve Sterling told them from the screen. Ada buckled up her mouth and immediately stopped talking to her ex-husband.

They went out for tapas.

They'd always meant to go for tapas back in Albuquerque, but never had, so Chase thought this might actually cheer her up, or was at least his best chance at that. On the walk to the restaurant, Ada was still silent. Finally, Chase got more frustrated than scared and asked, "Come on, baby, what's wrong?" even though he knew the answer.

Ada, her hand limp in his, responded, "It's nothing," which he knew meant he was royally screwed. The key word in her sentence was "it." When she said "it," Ada signaled that there was indeed something and that she was laying the groundwork to discuss it.

"It's nothing we have to talk about right now," she added.

"Okay, honey!" Chase responded immediately with all the cheer he could muster. But it didn't work, and she kept going.

The restaurant was real nice—had a valet, which Chase appreciated even though they'd walked. Ceiling like a church and live guitar music—guy was good, too, but you could barely hear him over the sound of a hundred people eating and clanking silverware on plates and talking at once. And, holy shit, the smell. Like when you come home starved and your mom's already got dinner ready. They were a little underdressed, but as soon as they walked in, the host recognized him from *Good Morning Friends!* and, next thing he knew, they were getting a seat at the special balcony table, overlooking the Horseshoe River. Chase started getting nervous that this was one of those super-fancy places he'd always heard about, without prices on their menus—but, no, they had numbers, big numbers, and with the checking account Bob had hooked up for him through the Founders Bank, Chase could afford them.

Looking around, he was so impressed and busy marveling at the place that he almost forgot Ada wasn't speaking to him. But after the bread came—hot bread—she started talking. "I just don't think you understand how fortunate we are right now, Chase. I don't."

"I'm a lucky man, I know that. I got you back in my life. I lost an Ada, and I gained a Hibiscus."

"What you got is the chance of a lifetime, Chase. What would we be doing back home right now? What would we be doing, first Saturday of the month?"

Chase didn't even have to think about it. "Bingo!" He laughed.

"That's right. Bingo. Every first Saturday of the month. Fucking bingo."

From the way she said it, Chase was a little offended. Personally offended, but also for the innocent, carefree, and surprisingly affordable world of bingo. "You love playing bingo," he reminded her. They always got lit with the retiree crowd; it was a ball.

"Yeah, but I don't want it to be the highlight of my social calendar every year till the day I die."

"Fine, fine. If we go back, no more bingo. No biggie."

"And even if we go back, who's to say we won't just be plucked back here again? You ever think of that, Chase?"

"I don't know, seems like a pretty random selection of folks here, right? Like a one-in-a-million chance of getting abducted once, let alone twice. I'll take them odds."

"But why bother? Chase, look around you. We ever get tapas at home? No, costs too much. We ever live in a penthouse? You literally landed into the best situation of your whole damn life. Me, too—I'm making art for a living. Founders did that."

"Yeah, but they're a little wacky. I mean, come on, let's just admit it. They believe in some crazy stuff, no disrespect."

"Well, you can't say their worldview isn't working for us. Shit, I could barely manage my old studio apartment here, before you came. But now, with Bob opening the door for you with the Founders? It changes everything."

"Baby, I barely know that slick sonofabitch. That's what's great about Harry, you always know what he wants—he just yells it at you. But Bob? I got no idea what the hell he really wants from me."

"Who cares what he wants? It's about what he's offering. *The good life.* Look around you, Chase. You really want to give all this up and fly away? We're living the dream—hell, I wouldn't even have dreamed a life this great, I'm not going to lie. That's only possible here, not back in the goddamn desert. Don't you get that?"

"You're right, you're right, you're right." Sometimes, when Chase wanted to end a conversation, he'd say things three times in a row. That always shut Ada up, because she hated when he did it and gave him the silent treatment.

Having murdered the mood, the two sat there silently, both staring off at different parts of the restaurant's dining room. Watching all the couples who were better at dinner chat than them.

Every bit of small talk Chase could think of, they'd already worn out. You couldn't talk about the weather when it was always perfect. Chase couldn't think of anything in the world, this one or the other one, that was a safe topic. Then he remembered the one question she never got around to answering.

"Baby?" Ada was looking off, didn't hear him. The room was too loud. Or she was ignoring him. So he tried again, louder. "Baby?"

"What?" When she turned around, Chase saw on her face how mad she was at him. "Speak up."

"What the hell are the invisible things?" Chase damn near yelled to her.

Ada went quiet. And the entire dining room got quiet with her.


She wouldn't let him talk the whole walk home. But the moment they got back to the penthouse, Ada took him by the hand and guided him to the bedroom, whispering in his ear, "Let's just do this. Let's just get it over with."

Chase thought he was about to get lucky, and found the "get it over with" part both confusing and a little hurtful. So he didn't expect it when Ada led him to her walk-in closet, but that's where they went.

A windowless room larger than the first studio they'd shared in Nob Hill. Instinctively, he reached for the wall switch as they entered, but Ada's hand pulled his away and into the center of the room before letting him go. She motioned for Chase to take a seat directly on the carpeted floor.

"Ada, what the hell?" he said, and he knew it was serious when she didn't bother correcting him for messing her name up.

"Just wait," she told him, and started hunting through cabinets until the final one was slammed back shut.

They were in complete darkness for a moment; then Ada clicked a flashlight and sat down next to him. In her other hand, a whiteboard.

"What are you—" Chase began, but Ada stopped him with the board, handing it over to him with a marker. Taking her lead, Chase wrote out his question instead.

*What is going on with you?* Chase scribbled, and handed it back to her.

*You want to know about the "I" things, this is how we talk about them.* Ada handed it back again.

Chase's first response was to roll his eyes, but when that failed to garner a verbal response, he wrote, *Fine, baby. Again, then. What are the invisible things?*

Ada took the pad and wrote. Wrote a lot. Erased it all with the sleeve of her cardigan. Stared at the blank surface. Then put, *A hallucination where people claim to have seen things that aren't there. Or felt them.*

*That makes no kind of sense,* he quickly handed back.

Ada took the board and wrote in one determined push, *What people say when they feel or see stuff move, but nobody's there.* And barely before Chase could finish reading, Ada added, *Goes back centuries.*

*So—urban legend or something?* Chase wrote to her.

*Both,* Ada returned. Then, *That is the official Church of the Collected position. We don't speak of it publicly. Nobody does.*

*Why? Why won't anyone talk about it?*

Ada took a long pause again. Chase tried to make out her face in the gloom, but couldn't without the direct light. *Real taboo,* she finally wrote. *Just starts shit for no reason. Not done in public. Everyone's got a different opinion, so it's too easy to start a fight, get canceled. Everyone's tired of thinking about it. Not real.*

"If it's not real, then why are we writing this invisible-thing convo out in the closet, in the dark?" Chase whispered this as quietly as he could so Ada could still hear it, but she jumped, grabbed the board back from him, and started writing her response out.

*Because sometimes when you talk about them out loud bad things happen. And sometimes when you get too excited, or pissed off. Or start talking about getting out of here.* And then Ada erased that as fast as he could read it. *That's just what some people say,* she added. *I don't want to have nothing to do with it. It's not real, anyway.*

Chase took the flashlight from Ada's hand. Just to hold it to her face. Just to see her. There was no smile there. No humor. No anger, even. What he saw wasn't just Ada being nervous. It was definitely fear.

Chase thought about it before he wrote, *Does it do stuff like crush people's heads?*

After shining the light to the board, Chase aimed it back up to Ada's face. She was just staring at him.

He kept the light on her. She kept staring at him.

Finally, Chase wrote, *Lady, you're freaking me out.*

Ada wrote back, *GOOD!*


He had a lot to think about. Ada wasn't awake after Chase finally turned off the TV and came to bed that night, and he was happy about that. He didn't want to hear—or, to be real, talk—about anything anymore that day. He figured they'd just get some rest and wake up, reset to factory settings.

Every night he went to sleep next to her, and every time it hit him that he'd actually and finally found her. It was just too wild a fact to keep clear in his head during waking hours. And things were going pretty damn good between them—at least in comparison to some of their other romantic eras. That might not last; Chase knew it could always go south. But this time, it really could be different: Living in New Roanoke meant Ada could never run away from him again without a word. There was nowhere for her to hide. She couldn't steal his heart and hide it again without at least an explanation.

But when Chase woke in the middle of that night and reached blindly for Ada across the mattress, to feel her warmth like it was a propane heater for his soul, he found only a pillow. And the long-endured sense of dread he'd felt during her absence flooded back at once.

Then Chase saw her. She was there. Above him.

"Be. Very. Still." Ada's eyes were wide, her chest bouncing from labored breathing. About four feet above the bed. Floating there. In the air.

Frozen, Chase stared. For those seconds, Chase watched her, and around her, and watched anywhere he could, for something to explain how she was floating. In the air. Wanting to help her. Looking for what was holding her, because something had to be holding her there.

But no. There was nothing to detangle her from. The best Chase could do for her at this moment was to look directly into Ada's eyes and whisper, "Breathe."

Seconds later, when Ada suddenly fell down, Chase caught her. And Ada hugged him harder than she ever had before. But neither one said a word about it that night. Or later, in the morning. Or the next day, or ever.

# CHAPTER 23

An hour before the debate at the RBC, Nalini arrived to see an already packed studio audience, seated and waiting. Every chair filled with an obvious Founders Party loyalist before the Party of the People attendees were even let in the building.

Squatting on a stool backstage, Vice Deputy Chairman Brett Cole ate a muffin. Nalini'd never seen this man look so relaxed. Pointing toward the audience, she asked, "What the hell is that about?"

"What?" Brett seemed genuinely surprised, wiping his mouth with a napkin as his eyes darted around the auditorium. "What is it? What do you see?"

"A full house. I see a full house, Brett, before my people could get one seat. I see an audience—one we specifically agreed was going to be split evenly along bipartisan lines—rigged. What the hell is going on?"

"*Rigged?* That's not—that's not a rigged audience." Brett made his distinctive snort, one she'd heard from him several times before. It was part guffaw, part croak of disbelief. "That's an assemblage of nonpartisan, highly respected RBC employees. Nothing to worry about. RBC is an independent news source."

"After all we went through, you're going to pretend RBC isn't a propaganda network?"

"How can you say that? What about *Steve Sterling at Midday*?" Brett asked, mildly confused.

The debate host, Steve Sterling, started off by asking the two representatives about their favorite pets, and that was silly, and vacuous, and perfect, because it was tense in that room. Not one person in there hadn't heard audio of Bob Seaford selling out the country, and for months they'd been told Dwayne Causwell was a monster bent on destruction. So "favorite pets" was a good warm-up. Dwayne reminisced about the miniature potbelly pig he'd adopted in third grade, sliding in smoothly that this was what inspired him to become a lifelong vegan, strategically humanizing himself in a way that Nalini could not have been prouder of. When he wanted to, Dwayne could be charming, and now people beyond PoP sympathizers would get to see that. Dwayne even got a chuckle out of the audience of "nonpartisan, highly respected RBC employees" when he revealed his pig's name at the end: Porky McPorkenstein.

"Yeah, I had a cat, and it was cute—but let's just cut to it, shall we?" was how Bob chose to respond. "Our nation deserves more than small talk."

Next to Nalini in the booth, Brett said, "Buckle up!," and smiled.

"Before we begin, I think we need to address the bigger issue here. By now, many of you have heard a certain recording. One of yours truly, saying some truly awful things. And it's despicable. But it's about this, the reason why we're here. The fundamental issue at hand. If the Party People are already willing to use the technology of the *Ursula 50* to alter audio to assassinate my character, how can we allow them to control the awe-inspiring bounty of technological advancements that should be the inheritance of us all?"

The seated nonpartisan, highly respected RBC employees clapped enthusiastically.

Nalini kept watching, and it just got worse from there. Dwayne went from talking about his pet pig to immediately rocking between defensiveness and outrage. "This audio-doctoring accusation is a despicable lie! Yes, sure, it was edited, but not for content, just to . . ."

*Oh, Dwayne, my Dwayne,* Nalini kept thinking. It was just all off. The more Dwayne became indignant, the more little Bob attacked. Steve Sterling, in what seemed a good-faith attempt to be fair, would ask a basic question, and Dwayne would answer sincerely and pragmatically. But then Bob would ignore that question and instead answer a different one he selected from inside his reptile brain. Softballs Bob placed on a tee and then knocked out of the park, over the head of an opponent who seemed to think they were playing tennis.

Everything was off. The vibe in the room was off. Dwayne looked off. The stage lighting was off: It shot up from the base of the podium and gave Dwayne that haunted shadow that kids with flashlights use to tell ghost stories. It looked bad onstage, and it looked even worse on the screens in the production booth. The video tint color was toned to make Bob's sallow flesh look like it had a Miami tan. The same filter made Dwayne, with his beautiful russet skin, look like a black hole with eyes.

Even Steve Sterling looked lost; he kept trying to pull Bob back to the initial questions with each follow-up, to no avail. Bob did what he used to do on the ship: dominated. He dominated with his patented deniable sadism in front of the TV audience of Founders Party officials to show them that he could dominate their enemies for them as well. He used his oratorical flourish to send a message to everyone on the planet that you should either agree with him or endure the social discomfort of contradicting him.

As Nalini leaked hope, the men both talked about logistics for building cryoships, the dignity of the common New Roanokan, and the importance of voting in the referendum. Safety, danger, the sanctity of democracy and human life—all that good stuff. Bob was being Bob—shamelessly stealing PoP positions and denying known facts in an attempt to exhaust not just his opponent, but everyone. Nalini simply wanted it to be over.

Dwayne Causwell wanted more than that.

When Steve Sterling told both men they could make their final arguments, Nalini expected Dwayne just to say what they'd planned for him to say—recite what he'd practiced and end this disaster. Then they could leave with the hope that everyone could see Bob's obvious disingenuous, ambition-fueled obsequiousness for what it was. And maybe they could stop at Dairy Queen on the ride home.

"This guy next to me is totally a malignant narcissist, representing a leadership much the same," Dwayne said out loud, to the entire New Roanokan viewing audience. The room inhaled. Dwayne stepped out from behind his podium and into the silence, and walked directly over to Bob. He didn't stop until he was two feet from Seaford's podium.

Nalini thought, *Dwaaaaayne, please don't whup this little man's ass.* And the little man himself seemed to have the same concern. The entire viewing audience saw Bob Seaford flinch when Dwayne reached out and took the other's microphone. Then Dwayne laughed at him. Looked right at Bob and wagged his finger in the man's face. Kept doing it, while smiling. The more Dwayne did it, the more Bob's face got both sallow and red, like a Rainier cherry.

Dwayne put his hand down, looked to the cameras, and said, "Let me tell y'all something, folks. I came in on the same Collecting Bob did. And we were on the same cryoship for months before that—one just like the subject of this debate. I lived with him. I trained with him. I broke bread with this man. And I can tell you:

Bob's full of shit. Bob's just doing this because he thinks it's the most advantageous move for *Bob*. And this will sound corny, but it's true: I just want what's best for all of New Roanoke. Not just the one, not just the few. Not just the powerful or connected."

The studio audience was quiet. There were no cheers. But there was nary a boo or a cough, either. Nalini leaned forward to see them sitting down out there. They were frozen. And that was the best she could hope for.

Dwayne knew he had the room. "Let me tell you what you need. *What you need* is the ability to get off this cue ball if you want to. To make that possible, what you need is free and open sharing of the bounty the *Ursula 50* has brought, not more suffering from those who'd profit from a gift meant for all of us. You need leadership that tells you the truth, not the type of leadership that tells you not to listen to what's been recorded coming out their own damn mouths.

"So let's just speak truth now. Let's stop censoring ourselves and say it out loud. Together. That's half the problem: We shut ourselves up even before anyone else can. And the truth is, *all y'all were kidnapped*."

That got the room talking; even some seated right in front of Dwayne tried to yell him down. But only a few, and Dwayne brother-boomed right over them. "That's right, I said it. You were *kidnapped*. Or you're the descendants of the kidnapped—and, trust me, I know a little something about that ancestral phenomenon. Taken against your will to this place by God knows what. I mean, I'd like to believe it's actually a wise, benevolent Protector who has 'Collected' us, like the Founders say. But let's get real. It's long past time."

Dwayne went silent for a moment. Even Bob didn't break in. Nalini didn't move, either. She knew what Dwayne was going to do. It was like watching a man covered in petrol, preparing to strike a match.

"There are *invisible things* out here!" Dwayne Causwell yelled as loud as he could manage, and Nalini imagined she saw the glass of the studio bend from the vacuum of the collective gasps. "There are actual *invisible things* that will slap the shit out of you and toss you around like a pit bull does a squirrel! And most of y'all won't do a damn thing about it. Won't even acknowledge it. Won't even whisper it out loud! Because you're too damn scared! Think about it: Isn't it convenient that you're never supposed to discuss something you need a strategy to deal with? Something—we're told—that gets mad if—"

Dwayne said some other stuff after that. Nalini could see his lips moving as he went off, hearing muffled words through the studio's glass. But his mic was cut by someone determined to interrupt the spell Dwayne was casting. He was about done, anyway, literally dropping the mic to emphasize his conclusion. As it rolled off the stage, Dwayne returned to his seat.

"Mr. Seaford? Your response?" Steve Sterling asked—the professionalism of this man was inspiring.

"Ladies and gentlemen . . . ," Bob began, then stopped and took a somber breath of air before continuing. "I'm so sorry. I'm so sorry you had to witness the display that we've just seen. I don't think I have to tell you how worrying this is for me, as Dwayne's former colleague, regardless of party politics." Pointing over at his opponent, Bob added, "Dwayne, I love you, man. Get better."

One person laughed. Possibly the audience member actually thought that was funny, but more likely she was just overcome by nervous energy, Nalini figured.

"There is a reason we don't talk about that . . . stuff. And it's not because of superstition. Or ignorance. Or even fear. No. I'll tell you why.

"It's because of *tradition*. That's right. By following the old ways of this exemplary community, we pay respect to those who sacrificed so that we could inherit this utopia. *That is not a lot to ask, for all we're given*. And besides—and let me be clear about this—there is no such thing as invisible things." Bob smiled assuredly at the audience, and assured they were. The assemblage of nonpartisan, highly respected RBC employees rose for a standing ovation.

It was amid this torrent of applause that Nalini noticed Bob Seaford was floating off the ground.

Nalini saw the gap under his feet. How his shoes started dangling around a little. Both, at the same time. How that meant they weren't carrying body weight on a surface, as was their wont. Because Bob was going up in the air, Nalini saw. So slowly. Like a semi-deflated birthday balloon moving back through time.

Even as she witnessed this, Nalini still clung to the notion that it was a trick of angle or light. Others were still on their feet and clapping, as if everything was normal, so maybe it was. But, slowly, lighter claps. Fewer cheers. Most didn't seem to notice. Or chose not to. Until Bob was suddenly yanked up a dozen feet in the air in less than a second. Then it got real quiet, real quick.

Once Bob Seaford was around twenty feet off the ground, arms and legs out like a starfish, everyone knew.

Halfway between the floor and the orchestral auditorium's ceiling, Bob looked as surprised as anyone as he started leaning to his side. Ninety degrees over. Continuing to turn clockwise, like the hands of a clock itself. Upside down, then back again. Then again. Accelerating. Until that little man was whirling. Spinning like a pinwheel on its axis.

And the whole time, the little man was screaming. Loud.

But it wasn't just senseless sounds, Nalini slowly realized. It was words. It was the same words, it sounded like to her. One prayer, again and again. When Bob's whirl finally started to slow, Nalini could make out what he was saying.

"*THERE ARE NO SUCH THINGS AS INVISIBLE THINGS.*"

Again and again, his speech slowing down as his body did.

*"THERE ARE NO SUCH THINGS AS INVISIBLE THINGS."*

In that moment, Nalini saw a shared expression on the faces of the studio audience, one she'd never witnessed before that day. They glowed, intoxicated by the act of publicly proving their faith to be stronger than what they all saw with their own eyes. Nalini had no term to capture their response. But her own was horror.

And then, as Bob stopped turning, his body stilled. Staying up there but upright again, between gasps of air, he yelled with what seemed the entirety of his flesh and will.

"A true patriot of New Roanoke knows what is real! A true patriot of New Roanoke does not speak of the *unreal*! A true patriot of New Roanoke has faith that there's no such thing as things that don't exist! A true patriot isn't—" Bob began, then fell two dozen feet to the floor.

Bob Seaford's landing was a meat thud.

Everyone was frozen at the sound of it. Even those watching at home. Nalini closed her eyes, because there was nothing else of use she could do. Even Dwayne was motionless at first, and he was the first person to get to the body.

Nalini was crying, and the sober portion of the reptile section of her brain hated herself for that, but the rest of her knew that even Bob didn't deserve what had just happened.

Then, to her surprise, with Dwayne's help, the corpse stood up.

Because it was still a body with life inside; it was Bob Seaford. Left leg not bending the right way at all, a welt already inflating on his head big enough to be seen from where Nalini stood, thirty yards away.

Bob Seaford raised a fist in the air, to the camera and everyone beyond.

"There's no such things as those things. But there *are* true patriots," Bob declared. *"And I am a true patriot!"*

The assemblage of nonpartisan, highly respected RBC employees went absolutely wild.

"Only thing better here than on Earth is the oat-milk ice cream." Dwayne's shoes were off, his dress shirt unbuttoned, a gallon of tin-roof in one hand and a single spoon in the other. "For real. The flavor and texture are the greatest I have had in my life." He ate it right out of the carton as he leaned on his desk. Big scoops that swelled off his spoon and most likely froze his throat going down.

"Dwayne, that was—I don't even know how to process that. . . . You think that display will put Bob over the top?" Admiral Ethel wanted to know. He rolled his eyes and dipped his spoon once more.

"Honestly? Honestly, I think people who want to keep things the way they are just got a hero. And after that, I don't know. I like to think that the folks who aren't high on their own delusions saw exactly what they needed to see, to remind them of what's at stake here. And that there's hope. What's the other choice?"

Nalini tried to put some cheer into her voice. Some optimism. Inject it like cream into a doughnut. "Well, tomorrow we just have to get our people out to the polls."

"Not 'just' get them out—we got to protect their right to be heard. Those Founders devils are going to lie and cheat and do anything they can to take the victory, and right now they're not losing a lick of sleep over it. Let's just hope they respect the outcome if they lose."

"They don't have a choice: It's a democracy. Free and fair democratic elections, the 'New Roanokan Way' and all that."

"They believe in democracy—they just don't believe anyone who can't afford to rig an election should be able to win one."

"What the hell could do that?" Admiral Ethel asked. Neither

Dwayne nor Nalini had doubts about what the Admiral was refer-
ring to. She'd been on the edge of their conversation, observing, as
was her habit, but it was clear she wasn't going to let the discussion
end before tackling the subject.

After an exhausted shrug, Dwayne added, "You know how the
old-timers say if everyone tries to see it at once it can actually be
seen?" Dwayne chuckled bitterly. "Well, the whole damn town was
just watching, and I didn't see a damn thing. So I think we can
scratch that theory off the list."

"Really? We don't know that. It was a broadcast, not a literal
crowd. And I'd argue that the majority of those actually in the room
were specifically trying their hardest to ignore it. Gleefully, even,"
Nalini felt compelled to point out.

"Fine, but my point: There's no rules. Not for this invisible thing.
Can't be, because there I was, talking about it, calling it out, naming
it for everyone to see and—"

"And it appeared," the Admiral injected.

"Yes, it did. So maybe there's something to the legends, *but it went
after Bob*. Not me, Bob. All these urban myths? 'Don't talk about it,
act like it's not happening, don't get worked up.' What are they good
for? They're useless."

"Not useless." Despite preferring to avoid Dwayne's souring
mood, Nalini couldn't help but marvel aloud. "You're describing a
solid social-control mechanism. It provides the illusion of personal
agency in a situation in which the community's actually powerless."

When the Admiral spoke, it was directly to Dwayne, as if Nalini
had said nothing. "If that's what it did just because people were talking about leaving, what's it going to do when we actually do?" Admiral Ethel asked, as if he had that answer.

# CHAPTER 24

For the Party of the People, the question was not whether they had more potential referendum votes than the Founders, because they knew they did. In fact, this was one of the only things both parties agreed on. The PoP base consisted of three key demographics: people who weren't rich, people who weren't fanatics, and people who didn't think nationalism was a personality trait. All of which meant the Party of the People had a significant majority. So, though all they had to go by was likely-voter data, which was an inexact measure Nalini trusted as much as newspaper astrology, things did look good. Every poll commissioned had the PoP up at least nine points. The question was whether or not that lead was big enough to compensate for the fact that the Founders had a three-century head start, and had created an electoral system weighted to ensure that their descendants' votes weighed more. And on top of this, the Founders also had a long and impressive record of just straight-the-fuck-up cheating.

The first election-day news to hit the PoP office was that most of New Roanoke was now covered in flyers, dispersed in the dark the night before. The good thing was that these notices urged everyone to get out to vote for the Party of the People! The bad part was that they recommended that the best day to vote was the day after the election was over. Even to Nalini the circulars looked convincing, forcing her to check again to make sure she herself hadn't gotten the dates confused.

"This is standard. A volley to serve" was how Dwayne described it. The PoP was ready, prepared by similar "pranks" pulled in past New Roanokan elections. PoP block captains were already assigned, and actively spreading the evergreen reminder that the Founders Party was trying to fix the vote, hoping that the insult of this attempt would galvanize more people than it disenfranchised.

The next news wave came with the sunrise: Block captains returned to say that some polling places in the area still hadn't received ballots, so were directing voters to new locations. These new locations, it turned out, were largely abandoned. Preapproved ballot sites relocated overnight by governmental decree, without warning. If there was a notice of a change, it was simply a sign on a door stating: *Closed.*

In response, the PoP's volunteer transport fleet was summoned to begin shuttling voters to other locations. Loudspeakers on the vans announced the changes in venue to passersby. When the voters showed up to those new-new locations and found their names removed from the rolls, or dismissed because of clerical variations in their files, or turned away because of slight signature deviations, the pro bono PoP lawyers were given the signal to flood the courthouse. There, they argued to exhausted judges that the polls should be opened as required by law.

Nalini, amid the chaos, paused to shove a nutrition bar down her throat and note how familiar it felt to witness firsthand the surreal nature of blatant injustice. No one around her was surprised by all this, either. Not the old-school, hard-core PoP folks who now crowded its offices. Not the Founders volunteers or low-level politicos she encountered at the sites, who looked at the chaos and smiled warmly. They'd all seemingly accepted that this was the way of things, that this was what an election looked like. That ubiquitous anti-democratic barriers were just another feature in the glory that was democracy. That it was normal that the underdog didn't just have to get the most votes: They had to go beyond that and get enough votes to overcome the immune response of the status quo. In addition to all the standard emotional responses to this madness, it made Nalini a little homesick as well.

The only type of victory that counted was one so convincing that denying it became absurd. The acceptance of this unsaid assumption—never once discussed explicitly by any person Nalini had ever heard—was the establishment's greatest strategical advantage. And it was as invisible as anything else in this place.

The selected members of the crews of the SS *Delany* and SS *Ursula 50* sat in the dilapidated dining room of Emilio's Family Style Italian Restaurant, all so focused that no one bothered complaining about the place's peeling wallpaper, the stain-speckled tablecloths, or the overpowering ketchup smell.

Those who worked on the election were weary, and they'd worked hard to get that way. The referendum vote was set to close in two hours, and even for Dwayne there was nothing left to do but await the verdict. Amid the election chaos, no one would notice any of the crew slipping away, making it the perfect time to gather for an exit briefing.

The decision to invite Chase was the Admiral's, and even she made it reluctantly, and only because she'd made a promise to Harry to do her utmost to get him off this moon again. Chase, for his part, read the hostility in the room from the non-Bobists and made the correct decision to order food and hide behind his plate.

"Ladies and gentlemen, it's our time to end this portion of our journey, and finally head home, *tonight*" was how Admiral Ethel Dodson started the meeting, offering an answer to the question everyone in the room wanted to know. As they took that in, Dwayne joined the Admiral at the head of the table.

"I've taken steps to ensure we have friends working the *Ursula*'s security detail." Dwayne cast this info into the air, a secret unveiled. "They should be able to get us in whenever we're ready."

The mention of guards piqued Nalini's anxiety. "Can you trust those guys? How do you know they're not Founders loyalists? These are people who chose to become guards, right? My guess would be that this impulse toward policing betrays a worldview that precludes free thinking."

"They became guards because they were broke and didn't know better. That's just a thing young men with few options do to sustain themselves. You should know that," Dwayne told her. Nalini did know that, but there was a vast difference between believing a theory and betting your life on one.

"Two A.M. No later. While they're still focused on counting ballots," Admiral Ethel added. "And, Dwayne, I want you to relay this to whomever you trust to make the most of it." Reaching into her pocket, Admiral Ethel pulled out what appeared to be a thick stylus, then threw it the few feet to him.

"A fountain pen? Nice retro piece," he said, staring at it, trying to make sense of the gesture.

"It is. But it also contains the entirety of humanity's digital footprint. Everything: the complete digital library. Everything online. Books, movies, video, the entirety of our shared educational and technological legacy. If human society collapsed tomorrow, this would be our backup folder. Before we leave, make sure it goes to whoever can use it to help all the people here being left behind. Then get back before two so you're not stuck here with them."

"I'm sorry," Chase Eubanks began, in a tone that contradicted his apology. "What are you guys doing? This wasn't the plan, was it?" Annoyed—that's how he sounded to Nalini. The other former *Delany* crew members, who only knew him from the newscasts, now noticed him sitting in the back for the first time. They voiced their displeasure in a sudden rustling sound. "I mean, you guys made a deal with the Founders, right? Wouldn't it be better to at least wait until after the results are announced to decide to skip town?"

"The vote is only about who gets the tech *and* controls the state's use of it," Ahmed joined in. "That is between them. But I want to go home. To hell with this place. Let's just go." He was the only known former Bob in attendance, and that was allowed only because Nalini'd vouched for him.

Chase put his fork down, lifting his hands in disbelief. "People, come on. I mean, is running away in the night really the smart move? Admiral, you said it yourself: This emigration is going to take time; the people who want to escape are still going to wait here for a minute, no matter what. This trip was just for feeling it all out. A first stage in a—how did Lloyd Talbot put it?—'a diplomatic out-reach mission.'"

"Didn't you say this Lloyd Talbot fellow doesn't have a head any-more?" Nalini asked him.

The Admiral ignored her. "We are not sacrificing ethics: If the Founders win, we'll make sure the PoP hands over a copy of the exo-dus plan. If not, Dwayne has arranged for the remaining PoP board members to take control of the project and its funding. But, as for the *Ursula 50,* that's *my* ship, my command—and I'm taking it home. And, frankly, from what I've seen of the leadership here, I don't trust them to honor our contract."

Chase got up and walked right to her. "But, Admiral, hear me out: You do this sneak-out thing and you're blowing a golden opportunity for this to go down smooth and diplomatic, like. I bet the Founders would want to throw you a big send-off. Let me talk to my RBC connections."

In a tone that was the rolling eyes of sound, Nalini said, "Brilliant proposal, Chase. And by RBC connections, I assume you mean Bob?"

"Sure, he'd help. He's a little off, but he ain't that bad. Then you could do your skedaddle right. With no bad blood."

"The blood was poisoned when they decided it was okay to seize my ship. We came to observe, provide an escape for both crews, and deliver the blueprint for a long-term evacuation. And that's what we've done. So we're leaving. End of story."

With that, the Admiral started to gather her things, signaling the rest of them to start preparing to go as well. All except Chase, who stood his ground among them. "Wait, you just going to leave Bob, too? What about the other crew members, the ones Bob hangs with? They aren't here. You not going to tell them you're running, either?"

"We're telling the rest of the *Delany* crew tonight, when it's too late for any nonsense," Dwayne assured Chase, without bothering to look over at him.

"What about Harry?" Chase asked, and finally got the Admiral to pause.

"Sweet Lord," the Admiral nearly wailed. "You're supposed to get Harry, Chase. Come on. That's the only reason you're here, remember?" It was the first evidence Nalini had seen that the older woman had a temper.

"Fine, my job. But you said you'd bring Ada, too. That was the deal."

"If she wants to come with you," Admiral Ethel told him, but she didn't get the satisfaction of seeing his response, because immediately the restaurant's front doors burst open and a whole lot of cops poured in.

Later, Nalini was surprised that she hadn't seen it coming. Or at least noticed all the police cars outside the windows when the cops surrounded Emilio's while, inside, clueless, the attendees were acting as if the battle was already won. Uncomprehending at first, Nalini simply thought the restaurant was finally getting the customers they so desperately needed. She was not even looking in the direction of the attackers when her head was slammed down to the checkered tablecloth.

From behind her, Nalini heard Admiral Ethel yelling, "Unhand me immediately," but even though Nalini was being yanked herself, the reality of the situation didn't connect fully until she was turned around and saw Dwayne's face pressed to the linoleum by a uniformed knee, while two other officers held his torso and limp legs as if he were struggling.

It was then that Nalini noticed all the RBC-TV cameras pouring into the dining room. Clunky, obsolete metal boxes the size of tubas. Slung over the sagging shoulders of the reporters gathered around. Each one's lens sharing with the New Roanokan viewing audience what Nalini could see with her own eyes. Aiming at her, at Dwayne, but largely ignoring Admiral Ethel, who was sectioned off from the rest of them with a fence of standing black uniforms and effectively erased from the public narrative.

All the *Delany* and *Ursula 50* crew members in attendance were in cuffs and in the police van in less than a minute. Everyone except for Chase, she realized, then judged and damned him in absentia.

# CHAPTER 25

Nalini couldn't see the protesters from the cramped cell she shared with the Collected crews of the *Delany* and *Ursula,* but she heard them. Chanting on and off for hours, louder every new round. "Time to go!" was the main one, but others, like "Free Causwell! Free the cause!," were popular, too. And then there was Nalini's personal favorite, "Ain't no party like a Party People party cuz a Party People party don't stop!" The words bled together a bit, but once they got the rhythm down, it gained clarity. The sounds were coming from every direction around the New Roanoke Police Department's Thirty-second Precinct. Nalini couldn't see them, but could hear them and smell them, too. Their cell reeked of burnt wood and rubber from whatever the protesters were burning down. Dwayne couldn't see any of what was going on outside, either, but he was smiling, tapping his foot to the sound of chants.

"They're going nuts out there," Nalini told him.

Dwayne nodded. "You can't get people to fight a problem they won't even acknowledge. This is just part of the process."

"Sounds like they're screaming bloody murder." If any of the others could dispute Ahmed's assessment, they didn't bother.

"That's the sound of them starting to acknowledge reality," Dwayne said, unaware that Ahmed, never a fan of his more sanctimonious modes, was grimacing behind him.

The cell had just one bench, and it was covered in illegible carvings and a hint of urine. Ahmed motioned for her to take it, but Nalini chose to squat on the slightly less smelly floor, and he took the bench instead. It was then that Nalini realized that, aside from nods and single words, he wasn't talking to her.

"What are you thinking about?" It sounded slightly absurd outside of her mouth. Casual kitchen-counter conversation, except in a jail cell with what sounded like a riot happening in their honor outside.

"I'm considering that you have possibly ruined my life. Not to be histrionic, but facts are facts. I had an executive position at a prominent corporation. I had the solid job security that comes with employment at a monopoly. But you came back into my life, and now I'm locked in a jail cell."

Nalini thought about it, thought about all the things she could say, or ways she could defend herself. But she just went with a resigned "Yeah, can't argue with you on that one," then got up to stand over by Dwayne, so Ahmed had the space he needed to be furious.

"I doubt they'll keep us captive long. Too much pressure to let us go. I mean, do you hear them out there?"

"Yes, I do, Dwayne. How can one not notice the sound of a bloodthirsty mob?" Ahmed said to his back. "I don't care if they let us leave instantly—I'm not going anywhere until the streets are clear once more. I did not fly four hundred forty-four million miles from Earth just to be killed in a garden-variety fascist-versus-anti-fascist riot. The police are doing us a favor by keeping us locked up. At this point, it's safer in this cage."

Dwayne paused, spun around. Nalini saw that the man's face had ignited with emotion.

"What if this whole moon is the same as this cell right now?" The wonder in his tone was so thick that Nalini would have thought he was being sarcastic if she didn't see on his face that he was serious.

"Overcrowded and odious?" It sounded like a joke, but that was the only connection Nalini could think of.

"*Protecting us.* Maybe we are all a sample of one nation's human life, collected and placed to the side for safekeeping, in case the original is damaged or destroyed. In case we finally destroy ourselves back on Earth. In a universe likely filled with long-dead civilizations, that actually makes sense, right? Whatever's behind this could do anything they want to us, but they just chose to make a copy of our reality, and maintain it."

"Why bother?" Admiral Ethel said from across the cell, sincerely asking the question. Nalini wasn't even aware she was listening. "We're just lowly fauna compared to whatever could pull this off. It's pretty arrogant to think the universe cares if we go the way of the dodo."

"Admiral Ethel, if you could go back in time and rescue a dozen dodoes before they went extinct, wouldn't you? If just for the sake of science?"

Even though he wasn't being spoken to directly, it appeared that the sound of Dwayne's voice was such an irritant for Ahmed that he took the man's every statement as a direct challenge. "We get it, Dwayne. It's a zoo, fine. Bars and all. You've basically been saying the same thing since we got here."

"That's not what he's saying." Nalini couldn't keep herself from

pointing at Dwayne as if she'd guessed the magic word. "Not a zoo.
*An ark.*"

"An ark!" Ahmed yelled in a clownish voice back at them.

"It's plausible. Best hypothesis I've heard so far." Admiral Ethel's
calm voice a contrast to Ahmed's increasingly loud one.

"How wonderful! That changes everything! I'm locked in a jail
on an *ark,* then. That's so much better." The grin on Ahmed's face
was wide and manic and matched the look in his eyes. "When I was
locked in a jail in a zoo, that was horrible, but now that I'm stuck in
jail on an ark, I feel so much freer."

The metallic buzz announced the guard at the door before the
uniformed man pushed it open. With a sense of hope and faith that
Nalini didn't know he had the capacity for, Ahmed sprang up, grabbing his coat off the bench to take it with him. When only her and
Dwayne's names were called, she didn't have the emotional energy
to look back and see the fear on Ahmed's face as the bars closed behind them.


Bob looked like somebody had whupped his ass and left him just
alive enough to tell the tale. He had a cast on his leg as thick as a
duvet, and a crutch under his arm held by a smaller cast on his other
hand. His bloated black eye looked as serious as a paper cut in comparison to the rest of him. Nalini's empathy for the tore-up little
man in front of her outweighed her desire for the destruction of the
symbolic construct of Bob she reviled—to her own pleasant surprise.

"There you two are. Well, glad you're okay. I was getting worried
for a minute there," Bob said, and Nalini doubted that very much,
until she realized his concern was not for them but for what he was
looking at: the crowd outside the window.

Nalini figured it was a considerable one; sparse gatherings don't roar like that. But she still wasn't prepared. Armored officers stood in a line behind impromptu fencing to keep the mass of protesters at bay. It was a symbolic performance rather than a practical measure: There was no way they would be able to hold all that back.

Catching her looking at the scene as well, Bob said, "Yeah," shrugging before offering, "Given the temperature out there, I think we should let bygones be bygones."

"You just had us locked up," Dwayne told him, as if to remind Bob of the script.

"I didn't lock you up; the cops did. I reported I heard you were meeting up to discuss skipping town, that's it. My civic duty, no more, no less. Stop being a drama queen." To Bob's credit, he seemed to realize he'd used the wrong euphemism with Dwayne, a particularly careless mistake given his own current state and his distance to the back of Dwayne's hand. "They're all out in the streets. Not just your Party People, either—everybody. It's like this all the way to the cryoship. We got a violent mob out there to deal with right now. Why focus on the past?"

"Because we're literally still in jail, asshole," Nalini told him. This time, it was Dwayne's turn to reach out to calm *her,* putting a hand on her shoulder as if she threatened to shoot up like an errant rocket.

"Your bosses have a real situation on their hands. Maybe they should have thought about this before trying to steal the election." There was no gloating in Dwayne's tone. It was still *I told you so,* but not in a way Dwayne seemed to be taking pleasure in.

"Fair enough, but they been calling for you."

"So that's what this is about. He wants you to go shut them up," she told him. "That's why they sent Bob."

Bob ignored her, talking straight to Dwayne as if she'd vanished from the room. "Say I get you all out of here—that's still not like it'll solve everything. If you take off in that cryoship, you're going to leave a bloodbath behind. Especially you, Dwayne. This is on you."

"Bob, please contain your propensity for bullshit. I didn't create the problems, I just gave them a voice."

"Well, now they won't shut up. I'm just calling it like it is, and you're the one who's always saying how much you care. You either go out and talk to these people, or come up with another way this doesn't end bad. For everyone. The others can go, do whatever they're going to do—fly back, whatever. If they can manage it, fine. But you've got to stay here and help clamp this down."

"I come with you, they all go free? No games? And you'll tell the cops to let them get to their own damn ship, unharmed?"

Bob nodded, but Nalini was sure all three of them doubted his commitment to that agreement.

When Bob left to get the release paperwork rolling for the others, Dwayne turned to Nalini to say, "I'll take care of the crowd. You just get everybody out and on board as fast as possible. There's not going to be another chance."

"You can't be serious. You're not going to stay behind."

"When it's time to go, just go. Whether I make it there or not."

"This is all about them chanting your name, isn't it?"

"Totally. *Busted.*"

"What am I supposed to tell the *Admiral*?" Nalini asked, as if a matter of etiquette was enough to stop him.

"Tell her I'm going to try and talk some sense into the good guys—and stall the bad ones. Tell her I'm going to do whatever I can to make sure you guys can actually get off the ground."

# CHAPTER 26

"We won!" Ada yelled through the house the second she heard Chase's keys in the door.

He found her in the bedroom repeating this: "We won!"

Chase, who really didn't feel like a winner at the moment, had no idea what she was talking about. She was so excited she was speaking at twice her usual speed. "Honey, you're not going to believe this. That Nalini lady? She called this morning, while you were sleeping. Said there was a meet-up with the rest of the crew for—"

"I know, I snitched on them." Chase said it as an exaggeration, to make fun of all the guilt he was feeling, but when he heard it out loud, it sounded like what it was: true. "It was the exit meeting; they were talking about how we're about to go. I told Bob about it—they said not to, but it just wasn't right. He and his should have a chance to choose staying or going, too."

"Is that even a real choice?"

"Well, damn, Ada, I guess it is, because it looks like he chose to call the cops." Chase pointed to them on the TV, the cops.

"Well, pouting won't help now. Election's over. Are you listening?" Ada said into Chase's hands, which covered his face. "They just announced. Founders Party won the People's Faith Referendum! I can't believe it. I mean, I can, but—damn!—that's you, babe, you helped do that. This is going to be huge!"

"Doesn't make a damn bit of sense. Polls don't close till six. Turn the volume up." Ada did, and immediately Chase could hear the mood of the laughing anchors: relief.

Ada headed into the kitchen, and Chase kept watching the bedroom screen until he heard a pop like a BB gun. When he followed her, he saw Ada at the small marble island of a kitchen counter, pouring a bottle of champagne into crystal flutes. "This is the good stuff. Been in the fridge since we moved in."

It didn't matter how loud the TV got, it still didn't make sense to him. "Why in God's name are they saying it's over?"

" 'Voter irregularities,' you said so yourself. The Party People were trying to cheat. They had a secret meeting, and were gonna steal the ship and everything—that's what they're saying. Caught them conspiring treason."

"Cheese and crackers, Ada. *I was there*. That's not how it went down. The Admiral wasn't talking about nothing but flying home on her own damn ship."

"Jesus, Chase. Why are you bugging? They're already out on bail. Look. Look, see?" In the front of the lifeless concrete façade of a municipal building, the Dwayne guy. Gripping another megaphone like it was his iron lung.

"See? It's not like they got sent to Siberia or something. This calls for a celebration. We're on the winning team."

"Oh, man, this ain't good. Not cool. Baby, get what you can carry. We have to get ready to go. Like, right now."

"What are you talking about?"

"They're leaving. We got to get packed—now. I gotta pick up Harry from the hospital, then I'll swing back and—"

"I thought we were going to talk about this."

"I know, babe. We just did. It's been nice, but party over, out of time."

There was a luggage set on the top shelves of their walk-in closet. Pulling it down, Chase noticed they were the same bags Ada had always had, generic and black and only differentiated from all other luggage by the lime-green zippers.

"What do you want to take?" he yelled out to the bedroom, faced with a room full of new clothes of which he was utterly unprepared to assess value.

"I'm not going." Ada said it, and Chase knew from the way she said it that, sure, she really didn't want to. That was understandable: It was a lot to digest, and a long ride, and Ada didn't even like flying on airplanes, so a spaceship was a big ask.

"Chase. Stop."

"We don't got time to stop."

"Stop! Put it back." Ada stood in the closet doorway, arms folded. "I'm serious, Chase. Put it back. I ain't going nowhere. You're acting crazy."

"I'm crazy? I came to free you."

Ada didn't acknowledge any of this. Made no move to unfold her arms.

"I'm free here. And you're a *captain* here. Captain Chase Eubanks, official. You really want to go back to just being a tuxedo taxi hack?"

Chase stopped packing, dropped the clothes that were in his hands, and waited for something inside him to tell him why she was wrong.

There was an empty ambulance parked in front of the hospital's ER, its doors hanging open for no one. The main entrance to the facility was nearly vacant as well—one receptionist and an old lady smoking out front as she muttered to herself, but absent the usual visitors and the pulse of medical personnel. As he'd fought his way through the protesters to make it out of downtown, it occurred to Chase that most of the city was on the streets. Yet, still, he didn't expect the hospital to appear damn near vacant. Chase saw a scattering of people in the halls as he headed up the stairs, nurses who blurred past, clearly overwhelmed by the needs of those patients left behind.

"Oh, look, it's Chaz. Finally deciding to show up. I take back all the things I was thinking: You did show up, albeit very late." Harry was in bed, the television blaring before he lifted the remote and froze whatever he was watching.

"Sorry, sir, it's been crazy. I would have come out sooner, but there's so much been going on. But I made it. And you're looking good, Harry. Very healthy. So I don't know how much time we got—Admiral Ethel and them, they're talking about leaving now. Like, ASAP. So we should probably—"

"Calm down. Sit, sit," Harry said, pointing at the one lounger. And then, when Chase didn't, Harry added, "We have time."

"Sir, again, I don't know when—"

"We have time because I'm not going anywhere." So Chase instinctively complied.

"Harry, not being disrespectful—obviously, I'll do whatever you want. But you brought me to help get you here and back. You sure your meds aren't talking for you?"

"There's nothing wrong with my judgment. I've got three parasitic alimonies at home, two pending class-action lawsuits at the job—FYI, turns out creating a war zone is a horrible business plan. But none of them will get any money, because I *really* owe the IRS. So I gave my money to the government, *on my terms*—for this trip. I'm officially a failed businessman, Chaz." The old man glanced past Chase to the TV on the far wall, lifted the remote again, and turned it to the live RBC feed. "Will you look at that? All packed in the park. It's like they're going to a party out there."

The RBC broadcast showed a newscaster reporting from the roof of one of the skyscrapers that loomed over Grand Circle Square. Beyond and below the correspondent, a sea of humans took up every bit of the lawn. The only break in the crowd was the *Ursula 50,* which sat in wait.

"I bet, if you asked them what they expect to accomplish by protesting, no two answers would be the same. They're just mad."

Looking back at his boss, it occurred to Chase that Harry either already knew Chase didn't want to leave New Roanoke, or didn't bother thinking about the fact that if they took their time Chase would miss his chance to leave.

"Well, it's a really nice place. Lot nicer than Albuquerque, in my opinion. Makes sense. I'm staying, too. Ada really likes it here."

"This place is horrible. It's just like home; the only difference is, here I'm even more broke. There's not even any aliens to be seen, not even that novelty. It's *exactly* like home, for the most part. Just as bad. You see that debate?"

"I was there."

"I bet you were. No such thing as no such thing, and all that. Weird. And no one wants to talk about it. I've been stuck on that since—nothing else to do but collect bedsores. And I was thinking, if there *was* something like that, what purpose would it serve?"

"I don't think it's worth talking about."

"Well, look at you. Mr. I Don't Think It's Worth Talking About. Going native, huh? Tough shit, I want to talk about it. So—it doesn't happen often, just enough to get people to be wary. Doesn't like to be discussed. Wants everyone to act calm and like it's not there."

Chase nodded, and felt brave for doing so.

"It's a security system, of some kind. That's my expert opinion. A lifeguard. Keeps the place running safe and sound."

"Sir, I'm not trying to change the subject—I mean, I am, but not in a bad way. Are you sure about staying? This is it, your last chance. If we don't go now, it's over."

"Chase, are you listening to me? That thing maintains the status quo. They're out of their goddamn minds getting back on that ship. Just because it let the *Ursula* inside this bubble, that doesn't mean it's about to let it out."

Released from the holding cells and processed to freedom, the crews of the *Ursula 50* and *Delany* didn't walk toward the SS *Ursula 50* as much as they were flushed in its direction. From the courthouse steps, through the streets flowing with shoulder-to-shoulder protesters, to Grand Circle Square. And when they turned a corner and the expansive vision of the park opened up before them, it seemed as if the entire population of New Roanoke was out there as well, yelling at one another.

Chants of "Time to go!" clashing with rebuttal cries of "Everything's fine!" occurring at the same time. Garbled into vocal rumbling; nobody would have understood anybody if everyone didn't already know the slogans. Discontent funneled through the voices of tens of thousands upon hundreds of thousands. Maybe even millions, Nalini thought, staring out at them. Flesh packed tight all the way to the ship itself. So close together that when the crew members reached Dwayne's guards at the cryoship's perimeter and were discreetly ushered underneath the *Ursula*'s towering frame, they were shielded from sight by the wall of legs that closely surrounded it. The sound of the hull's service port opening beneath the ship was covered by a roar of overlapping chants of contradicting messages, goals, and passions.

# CHAPTER 27

Looking out from the podium at the endless sea of protesters, Vice Deputy Chairman Brett Cole noted how many unhappy people there were in the world.

"Proud citizens of New Roanoke! I—we—appreciate your passion, your participation in democracy. But the election is over, and this is an unlawful assembly! For the safety of all, please disperse!" Brett heard his own words boom from the sound system, then echo back when they hit the skyscrapers at the end of the park. Brett said other things, too—more elaborate and diplomatic things—to the assembled masses, but they all failed to produce his intended effect. It was to the point where Brett wondered if they could even hear him, if there might be some technical difficulty that kept them from deciphering his peaceful words. Even thanking the officers surrounding the ship and stage in their riot gear, for their service to this great nation, seemed to spark emotions in the crowd beyond.

There were too many of them. If Brett fell from the stage, he was sure they could carry him above their heads for miles, passing him along without anyone's having to take a step. But that was a fantasy: If given the chance, they'd likely rip him into bite-sized pieces instead.

Feeling a poking on his shoulder, Brett turned to see it was not a finger, but the rubber tip of a crutch. "Let me try," Bob Seaford said to him. Or mouthed it—it was impossible to hear any individual voice without nearly lip-to-ear contact. Relieved to be relieved from duty, Brett stepped to the side and motioned for Bob to take it away. The man looked like he'd been chewed by a dog the size of a mountain, but Brett hoped that his weathered appearance might demand respect, or at least sympathy, from the protesters.

"People of New Roanoke! True citizens of this, the greatest city in the universe! And by that I mean not just the people who are here, those who have chosen to confront the malcontents in person, but also those viewing at home. The patriots who don't have to scream in the streets, because they are extraordinarily *comfortable*. Comfort is underrated. A comfortable citizen is an appreciative one. It means they're happy with the way things are—not taking our blessings for granted. And in being content—in staying home and doing nothing—they are displaying the greatest protest of all. The protest against being an ingrate. And by doing so, they are doing their part as true New Roanokan patriots to maintain order. We salute you!"

Bob didn't care about the boos. Or if he did, Brett saw no sign of it. Nor did Bob care about the scattered debris that once again came flying toward the stage.

"Every shoe coming at me, every piece of hurled trash, is just another challenge to our resolve. And we will meet all challengers!"

*He's like a fire,* Brett marveled, watching Bob weave his head to avoid projectiles, but never back down. A fire you either warmed to or were burned by. "Today, the Founders Party won a referendum vote. But it was clearly a win for *all* the true New Roanokans, proving our government works. Because, friends, when the Founders Party wins, all the people of New Roanoke are victorious!"

When the boos got louder, a modest-sized group of guys just below the stage started yelling, "Founders! Founders! Founders!" Bob picked up the microphone off the dais, put it to his mouth, then began awkwardly hopping forward on his crutches until he was close enough to hold the mic down toward them to catch the chants. "That's right!" he added. "Founders!"

But, off mic, "Time to go! Time to go!" still drowned all other sounds out. If it was a voice vote, the nays would have it. And somehow it grew louder, to the degree that Brett began to panic that the sound technician might not be able to keep muting the dissent in the live audio feed.

Then the boos subsided. To his surprise, Brett could hear a change in tone out there, could even make out some cheers, but he had no idea why until he looked back up at the jumbotron.

"Ladies and gentlemen," Bob shouted, to call attention back to himself. "Ladies and gentlemen, please welcome Party People Chairman Dwayne Causwell!" Bob waited until the applause had subsided to continue, and it took a while. "Who I'm particularly proud to introduce, despite our differences. Here to help us move toward our bright, bipartisan future as a republic!"

Brett turned to get a look at Bob's face, assuming this was one of the man's adorable pranks for which he was so famous at party HQ. But, no, rising from the back of the squad car, there he was. Tying his locks behind his head as he walked up to the stage, unhindered.

Bob made a show of shaking the man's hand, and the crowd muted out of confusion. The guys in the front row started chanting, "Traitor! Traitor!," but Bob smiled at them and shook his head, and they went silent again.

Grabbing the brown man by the shoulder, Bob said into the microphone: "Dwayne, I'm so glad you're here. I'm so glad you sought an alliance with the Founders vision. Can we get a big hand for him, everybody? Because I've been thinking: You know what we have in common?"

"Please don't say, 'We're not so different, you and I,'" Dwayne said into the mic. Bob ignored that.

"We both love this place. We both—in our way—want to build this place up, not tear it down. And that's why I've asked you to say a few words to the crowd."

"And that's why I've agreed." Dwayne took the microphone from him, and real applause came this time.

"Hey, y'all. Things are getting a little heated, right? A little dangerous. So, before somebody gets hurt, I just wanted to share some words. Look, I know you're feeling divided right now." Half the crowd cheered, half the crowd didn't. "But guess what? We're not really divided: We're all together, stuck on the same rock, just floating through space. We're all dealing with the same problems. We're one species, with one future. It doesn't matter if we like each other or not; we still have to share that future. And, yeah, that sucks sometimes, but that's how life works.

"That said, we still have a choice. The SS *Ursula 50* was sent to make first contact and rescue the crew of the *Delany*, and take them home—including me. But I'm not ready to go yet. I'm going to stay, and together we're going to work to help whoever wants to leave out of here. We have the plans to build more ships like this one. So nobody needs to steal this ship. What we need to do is get in gear, start acknowledging reality, and face our problems, together."

Bob shoved his shoulder in toward the microphone again. "Thank you, Dwayne. Everyone, big hand for Mr. Causwell. No sore loser here. And look for ongoing discussion on the role the *Ursula* will play in our lives, and how its crew will contribute—" Bob had more to say, and wasn't expecting Dwayne to yank the mic back from him.

"On behalf of the crew, I can tell you that they appreciate your hospitality, and grace. I can also confirm that they have already boarded, and are inside the *Ursula*. So I suggest everyone disperse immediately to a safe range, because they're out of here." Brett, unaware of this development, turned his head to the ship as if he might see Nalini in its window.

Leaning in, Bob's lips flicked Brett's ear. "No worries. The one good thing about this crew is that there's no way they take off with a thousand lives in the blast radius."

"Emotions are high—hell, mine included. But right now, we got to let our guests go." Dwayne had much more to say, and might have said more if given the chance. But that's when the sound system started playing music, and the police officers in riot gear came right at him.

From inside the *Ursula*, Nalini watched the monitor in horror as police officers appeared onstage and were on Dwayne before even the RBC-TV cameras could look away. Unable to do anything but shake her arms in frustration, Nalini watched as they held Dwayne's wrists behind him once more, refusing to let him go, let him get away, let him clear the area so the *Ursula* could blow its rocket boosters and escape to freedom.

"Release him!" Admiral Ethel demanded. Nalini could hear her voice loud beside her, and even louder as it boomed out of the *Ursula*'s exterior speakers to the entire assembled crowd. "All of you, leave the area before I engage the launch. This is not a bluff."

"When considering your safety, please take into consideration that we can't stand this planet!" Nalini yelled over her, but it was unclear if that made it through the speakers as well.

"You won't do that," Bob's amplified voice came back through the monitor. "Hold on, I need you to talk to someone."

"Guys?" It was Chase Eubanks on the microphone now. He was

onstage as well, appearing on the monitor in that absurd military garb. "Admiral Ethel?" he called to her and the sea of protesters. "I think, you know, maybe we should just chill a minute. Calm things down. The people aren't leaving—not the park, and most of them not ever, is my guess. You take off right now, somebody's going to get hurt. Somebody's likely to get burnt up. Hell, lots of people, innocent people. You're not a war criminal, you're honorable. I know you're bluffing. That ship's not going anywhere today. So let's all just chill-lax, okay?"

"What is that idiot doing?" Admiral Ethel asked, before hitting the intercom to ask the idiot directly. "Chase, what are you doing? Where's Harry?"

"Harry's good to stay," Chase broadcast back. "I went and asked him, I did. But he's not trying to go. He's the one seeing things clearly, is my guess. I'm good to stay here, too—it's a sweet locale. They're going to hook me and mine up. I know they'd do you right, too, if we can talk this through."

Nalini offered her expert analysis as an applied sociologist: "This is what we refer to as 'an attempt to sell us out.' "

"To hell with that guy, then," Admiral Ethel said. And then she lit the engines afire.

Outside, as soon as the ship began to rumble, people started running.

The Founders fans in the front of the stage were first, pushing out into the rest of the crowd, knocking over whoever didn't make way for them. And as they went, they triggered a wave of others running and panicking as they tried to avoid being roasted by the *Ursula*'s fire. The crowd's edge receded like Bob's hairline.

But those watching live at home didn't get to see that part. Because the cameras were still trained on the stage, now abandoned by fleeing technicians. But they did see Bob. They saw Bob think about staying put. Try to smile for the remaining cameras, lifting his arms in a theatrical shrug for anyone left watching. And they did see the moment when Bob abandoned that strategy and began expeditiously hobbling his way out of there.

Chase was the last one standing on the stage. He was struggling to stay upright, but he didn't look like he was going anywhere. Dwayne was still there, too, on his knees, the cops who'd just assaulted him having already abandoned him in pursuit of their own safety.

The Admiral hit her comms button again. "I'm done talking, Mr. Eubanks. Please evacuate out of the blast range or accept the consequences."

"Well, Admiral, here's the thing," he said into the mic. "I ain't going nowhere." Chase looked directly into the ship's cam to say this. "Because I know you, ma'am. You're good people. I know you're not a murderer."

"I am officially ending diplomatic negotiations," Admiral Ethel Dodson announced. Turning the volume up high enough so that everyone outside could hear, Admiral Ethel started reciting the takeoff sequence into the microphone. Nalini was aware of multiple studies indicating that hearing the "Ten, nine, eight . . ." countdown triggered a Pavlovian response in the brains of even the most stubborn. It was this that finally sent Chase running, as much as the roar of the SS *Ursula 50* coming to life.

"Dwayne, where the hell are you?" Nalini asked under her breath, though she knew the simple answer: not here, down there.

Admiral Ethel put her hands on the launch controls, and she and Nalini caught eyes.

"You can't hit the blast. Not with all those people so close," Nalini said, and they both knew it was one person she was specifically thinking of. The Admiral said nothing, just looked at her. There wasn't a thing that could be said out loud that wasn't already being shared between them. "We can't leave him. Please," Nalini added, pleaded.

As Nalini watched, the Admiral stared back at her, then back at the monitor, then at the controls, before closing her eyes and growing still in concentration. When she opened her eyes again and reached for the console, Nalini breathed again: She heard the sound of the engines spinning down once more, the launch sequence aborted.

But it didn't matter. With the slightest of lurches, they started floating up in the air anyway.


Silently, smoothly. Up into the sky, the *Ursula* lifted. Higher and steadily more so. Levitating above the crowd, twenty stories up. Propelled via a force unknown to humanity.

Before Nalini or any other member of the crew could think of words to make sense of this, the ship slowed, then ceased all movement.

The SS *Ursula 50* sat in the air. Caught firmly in the grip of whatever invisible force wanted to keep it there.

It took a minute for anyone remaining on the ground to realize what was happening. Above them, it looked as if the cryoship got smaller and smaller and then stayed the same size. Caught by nothing detectable to the human eye.

The nervous murmuring of the crowd grew. The most daring residents of New Roanoke even pointed upward.

"Holy shit" was the most Chase Eubanks had to say about the moment, and then he kept running.

Dwayne, still on his knees and looking down, saw the abandoned microphone on the stage floor beside him. Still on. Still attached to its cord.

"The invisible things," he said into it.

It came through his lips as a whisper. But, enhanced by the microphone, it roared.

Standing up, Dwayne stared to the heavens.

"*The invisible things!*" This time, Dwayne said it louder. Because it was all he could think to do.

Preoccupied with the vision above, he didn't notice the crowd regrouping. Slowly walking back toward the stage. But he did hear what they were saying. That they were saying it, too.

"The invisible things." How the words traveled. "The invisible things." They started yelling it. "The invisible things!"

The syllables skipped across the human sea, coming without rhythm, overlapping as they got even louder. The sounds crumbled over and against one another, vocalizing chaos, until everyone had joined in and they were naturally synched and saying it together. "The invisible things. The invisible things."

Some of those left on Grand Circle Square fled in panic, though far fewer than anyone there would have wagered. But the majority kept saying it, as they stared upward. "The invisible things." Chanting it as they stared at the ship caught in the sky. Repeating it at whatever held the SS *Ursula 50* there.

And then the thing wasn't invisible anymore.


They could see it. What held the ship above.

And they all saw it; because they all looked together.

And what they saw was horrendous.

What they saw was abhorrent.

It was even worse than that, this visible thing. It was even worse than they could have imagined. It was worse than anything any human was capable of imagining.

On board the *Ursula,* the crew could see it, too. Nalini could see it right out the window. She saw it and thought, *Yep, that's what I was afraid of.* So vast. So colossal. *Titanic* was the closest etymological fit Nalini could think of, and that word was still too small. They, humanity, were mere microbes before this monstrosity. Both in scale and in comprehension.

Admiral Ethel saw it as well. Its image was on the surface of every single cam. From the Admiral's view, she could even discern where the thing was holding them. And she could see how tenuous its repugnant grip was, how it struggled to contain them as she engaged the boosters. The strain as it met its limitations. How it seemed to flinch from the gaze of so many eyes on the ground.

In front of the entire population of New Roanoke, the SS *Ursula 50* broke free from its grasp.

In front of the entire population of New Roanoke, the crew of the SS *Ursula 50* flew away.

Because whatever it was they finally saw couldn't stop them. Because it wasn't endless. It was an abomination, but it was a discernible one.

Seeing it clearly, the citizens of New Roanoke could all take the measure of its surface, its finite mess and mass. Where it started, and where it ended. Not unknowable, but something that could be categorized. Something that could be faced. Already, they were looking at it.

# ABOUT THE AUTHOR

MAT JOHNSON is the Philip H. Knight Chair of Humanities at the University of Oregon. His publications include the novels *Loving Day* and *Pym,* the nonfiction novella *The Great Negro Plot,* and the graphic novel *Incognegro.* Johnson is a recipient of the American Book Award, the United States Artists James Baldwin Fellowship, the Hurston/Wright Legacy Award, and the John Dos Passos Prize for Literature.

matjohnson.info
Twitter: @mat_johnson

# ABOUT THE TYPE

This book is set in Spectrum, a typeface designed in the 1940s and the last from the distinguished Dutch type designer Jan van Krimpen (1892–1958). Spectrum is a polished and reserved font.